A FUNERAL IN EDEN

Paul McGuire

"The many excellences of plot, character, atmosphere, setting, wit, and detection are exceeded only by McGuire's brilliant use of dialogue that tells much about the characters and their relationships, sets the tone of the story, and gives the reader a great deal of exposition in an enjoyable manner."
—*20th Century Crime & Mystery Writers*

"Mr. Paul McGuire has given his excellent story a background original, well described, and picturesque." —*Manchester Guardian*

[The] scenery is delightful, writing good, sleuth clever, and criminal elusive."
—*Saturday Review of Literature*

"The characterization is excellent and the puzzle intelligent." —*Times* [London] *Literary Supplement*

Also available in Perennial Library
by Paul McGuire:

ENTER THREE WITCHES

A FUNERAL IN EDEN

Paul McGuire

PERENNIAL LIBRARY
Harper & Row, Publishers
New York, Cambridge, Philadelphia, San Francisco
London, Mexico City, São Paulo, Singapore, Sydney

A hardcover edition of this book was published by William Morrow & Company, Inc. It is here reprinted by arrangement.

 For information address William Morrow & Company, Inc., 105 Madison Avenue, New York, N.Y. 10016. Published simultaneously in Canada by Fitzhenry & Whiteside Limited, Toronto.

First PERENNIAL LIBRARY edition published 1985.

Library of Congress Cataloging in Publication Data

McGuire, Paul, 1903–
A funeral in Eden.

Reprint. Originally published: New York : W. Morrow, 1938.
I. Title.
PR9619.3.M324F8 1985 823 84-48178
ISBN 0-06-080739-3

---

85 86 87 88 89 10 9 8 7 6 5 4 3 2 1

The characters of this book are entirely the products of the author's imagination. The names are mostly borrowed from distant waterways, some of them dirty waterways, at that.

Contents

A FUNERAL IN EDEN

I

THE FORTUNATE ISLE

THE ISLAND of Kaitai rises six thousand feet from a purple sea. Approached from the northeast, as it usually is, it presents a sharp cone resembling, from a dozen miles to sea, a witch's hat. From the southwest, however, twin peaks appear, with a considerable valley between them. It is densely wooded, but its dark greens are slashed with the white crescents of its beaches, and high amongst the rocks are silver threads of falling waters. Amongst its woods, too, plantations of tea and coffee and sugar vary the tones, and in the low, coral-rimmed lands to the south there are coconut groves.

Kaitai, by a combination of historic accidents, is ruled by an independent Sultan. It was long uncharted and it still lies remote from the great routes of trade. Even the Spanish ships and the Portuguese, which scoured those seas in search of souls and silver, missed Kaitai: and though it was rumoured down the Great Archipelago, though ocean-ranging proas and sampans, dhows and outriggers and junks sometimes sighted it and at long intervals watered there, it remained lost to the consciousness of the world until the middle years of imperial Victoria. Even then it was neglected. Not a statesman in Europe had so much as heard of it: and those wandering seamen of the white races who might have told them had mostly been ceremonially eaten on the long beaches. But that was before Mr. Buchanan settled in.

Kaitai remains, as tropic islands go, a singularly fortunate place. Its people are plump and they shine. They have all that suffices for their needs and a good deal more at the cost of very little exertion to themselves. They net fish, when they are inclined to a little sport, in the coral lagoons; they have roast pork from the mountains; their fruits are luscious and their native potatoes are floury; their teeth are excellent and their digestions are superb. It is true that they suffer somewhat from yaws, but all mankind must bear the rod; and without yaws, they would have lacked Dr. Alicia Murray.

On the 28th of August last, Dr. Alicia Murray sat at tea with the Sultan.

"My dear George," she was saying, "it is all very well for you to talk, but yaws is not a pleasant disease, and you ought to do something more about it."

"Yes, I know, Alicia. Do you ever realize how much of your conversation is larded with words like ought and should and must?"

"*Dolce far niente* does not suit my temperament," she said brusquely.

"I know it! Don't I know it! You remind me of Buchanan the First. That is his portrait, by a native artist. I admit that you are rather less craggy . . ."

"Thank you," said Alicia.

"But you do loom over Kaitai like an emigrant Scottish brae. I wonder if the Lord understood what He was about when He loosed John Knox on Scotland. If, of course, the Lord had any discretion in the matter."

"We were speaking of yaws."

"Yes, I know."

"Please do not keep on saying, 'Yes, I know.'"

"My dear Alicia, I went to Balliol. And in any case, I was as to the manner born. One sighs and one says, *O tempora O mores* and lud, lud, too true. A cigarette?"

"No, I shall have some more tea. More tea? You smoke. Listen, George, we need a properly equipped clinic. And I need an assistant. I have written to Marjorie Pratt. She is at the Institute of Tropical Diseases in Papeete. She should know enough by now to be useful."

"Is she attractive?"

"No, she is not."

"Well, that's a point. I shall not be diverted from my sovereign task. But, Alicia, you know that you have quite a nice clinic, as it is. And Ptai and Naqa and Herbert seem to me almost violently anxious to help."

"I accept the violently."

"Ptai, you'll admit, does his dispensing with almost alchemical enthusiasm and variety."

"And with much the same results. He will poison somebody yet."

"I feel reasonably certain that he has poisoned a number of people already. He has a great reputation amongst his friends. And then there are Naqa and Herbert. I watched them inoculating a batch of their friends the other day with Anti-Tetanus Serum. They showed almost a divine enthusiasm for the mystery."

"So that's where the A.T.S. went, is it?" said Alicia bitterly. "You might have told me before, George. They all lied handsomely. I'll say that for them. They do lie handsomely."

"I think I meant to tell you. But does it matter very much? No one ever gets tetanus on Kaitai, anyhow. And we can buy some more. You should take life calmly, Alicia. You fret over little things."

"One day you are going to have trouble on this island, George," she said.

"'Man is born to trouble as the sparks fly upward.' The text is behind you. Buchanan the First imported it from London, and then he sent it back to have a gilt frame put around it. I have always suspected that the text is misquoted, but I have never dared to challenge Buchanan the First, even though he is gone triumphantly to gloom in Heaven these forty years."

"One could get on with a great deal of very useful work here, if one had the equipment and another person with a proper scientific training."

"Yet people say that the tropics are enervating."

"One can do one's job anywhere if one wants to do it," said Alicia crisply.

"Please don't think I mistake your enthusiasm. On the contrary, I admire it, tremendously. I have it in mind to award you the Order of the Covenant of Kaitai in the Birthday Honors. Second Class. I'm afraid you can't have the First Class unless you have an Order to swap for it. We reserve it for our dealings with Sovereign Rulers and Heads of States."

"George, will you please talk sensibly for a few minutes? There is a tremendous amount we could do here . . ."

"Yes, yes, I know. But I don't know about Marjorie Pratt. As it is, your Department is the most expensive in the whole administration. Even the Police Department costs less, but then, happily, Thompson has his pension from the Yard. But suppose Thompson pestered me every few days for a Fingerprints Section or a Bureau of Anthropometrics or even for a Flying Squad. I should immediately do without a Chief Commissioner."

"Yes, but Thompson and your Police Department are a silly joke."

"He's very entertaining. He has known all the really great murderers of his time."

"He's an old windbag."

"Alicia, as of one Senior Servant from another, that is unladylike. And in any case, I like windbags. Thompson helps to while away the lonely years on Kaitai. He showed me the other day how to split a ten-shilling note. And I never really knew what a jimmy was until Thompson arrived. It crippled my reading. But now I can go to my authors with confidence."

"I suppose Thompson was at the Yard once." Alicia sniffed with an accent of philosophic doubt.

"Alicia, this begins to sound like inter-departmental jealousy!" The Sultan raised his hands.

She blushed. "Don't be an ass. But all your . . . your refugee population here tells such whacking tales."

"Oh, not Thompson. He is the soul of discretion. He even wears flannel underpants in the tropics. But Thompson is a very good sort, Alicia. He just couldn't get on with melons that's all."

"Melons?"

"When he took his pension he retired to the country to grow melons. But melons would not grow for him. He came away to find a new life."

"I shall have a cigarette now, please. Thank you. Doesn't the sea look magnificent? It is a great beast, the sea, sleek and filled with power. This would be an exquisite place, George, if we only had a properly equipped clinic."

"Yes, I know. It is a natural scientific preserve. You can study responses here under almost laboratory conditions. Or you could if you were properly equipped and staffed."

"It is you who have said it."

"Laboratory conditions. So many human guinea-pigs. Mind you, I sympathize. I realize, only too well, how I must irritate you . . ."

"Enrage is the word," said Alicia.

"But at the same time, I have my own viewpoint. I am a ruler. Government is my art. And the art of government is concerned with men as men, not with men as guinea-pigs. However reluctantly, I am compelled to take the wider view. And I am compelled to admit, Alicia Murray, that my people as a whole detest your practices."

"Nonsense! They love them."

"They may love you, Alicia. We have always had a weakness for exceptionally beautiful women in Kaitai. Our own, useful as they are, seldom satisfy our higher feelings. But we do dislike being filed and catalogued and pricked and weighed."

"We do not. Whenever I put in an appearance at any of the villages now, the whole population demands to be inoculated. And the consumption of pink pills is absolutely outrageous. They love being doctored. Look at Naqa and Herbert and the A.T.S."

"You refute me out of my own mouth. Yes, I must admit that Naqa and Herbert and Ptai are doing very well from their medical practice. Ptai has just taken a fourth wife, I hear, while Herbert has more illegitimate children than any man in the island less than a Sultan should aspire to. . . . However, if you won't accept that argument, I shall think of another. Presently. Would you like a whisky?"

"No, thanks. As it is, I'm wasting the whole afternoon apparently."

"Oh, no, I hope not. You are sowing the seeds of future progress in my mind. What you too often forget, Alicia, is that governments move slowly. Governments consider pros and cons. Especially cons. And I, for my part, dislike paternalism in government. As one regards the world today . . ."

"If you are going to quote the leader from your latest *News-Chronicle,* I am going home. If I can't work, I can at least sleep."

"On top of that large tea? Well, well. I was going to suggest that we sit until the cool of the evening and then go for a swim. Or we might drop in at the Club. Or at Miss Roper's. Has she got her colors right yet, for that study of the fan-fish? I have never known anyone with such a passion for painting fish."

"When I saw her this morning she was working on the mountain. She asked me whether I had any Prussian Blue. One of her girls had taken hers for lipstick, apparently."

"Our women have always liked to blue their lips. They used to tattoo them, but my great-uncle stopped that. I've often wondered that we haven't developed a great-uncle cult on the island. A sort of devil-worship, you know. But then our people are profoundly sceptical. Except about modern medicine. We're very like you Europeans, on the whole, except that we are still civilized enough to live in sensible houses and in open air and country, on the beaches and the mountains and in the woods.

We don't slum, and we haven't heard of Manchester and Limehouse and County Council Housing Schemes. But we'd probably progress, too, if the opportunity were given us. That is why great-uncle and father and I have all tried to insulate the island. And that is why I am really rather suspicious of your Marjorie Pratt and your clinic and even, my dear Alicia, of you. You may prove the thin edge of the wedge."

"All I am concerned for," said Alicia, hotly, "is the health of these people."

"Yes, I know, I know, but their health on the whole is very much better than the health of people in Poplar. We don't suffer from malnutrition in Kaitai, at least. And there are worse things in Glasgow than the yaws. However, I still see your point."

"You've kept all the rot of modern life out of the island. Most of it, anyhow. Now you have a chance to use the benefits of applied science without suffering from its mischiefs. You can have modern medicine without industrialism, anaesthetics without poison-gas, radio without machine-guns . . ."

"My dear Alicia, but can you just pick and choose like that? Can you always have just those things you want, exactly, without the things you don't want? Life isn't so simple."

"I don't suppose you'll refuse an anaesthetic if I need to lop off your leg."

"Of course I won't, my dear young woman. I'm all for anaesthetics. But I am not for a general regimentation of the healthy population. Sickness is very annoying, and so, no doubt, is death, but I don't see why we should make ourselves miserable all the time we are well in case we should get ill.

After all, a man is not, normally, ill for more than a few weeks or months of his years. We think far too much about it all, nowadays. At least, you do in Europe, and I'm afraid that you have infected me with your morbidity."

"My poor George, what is more important than sound health?"

"I agree that it is important. But you are all so busy exaggerating its importance. Our people here still, for the most part, live out their days with a decent indifference to their livers and kidneys and innards at large, and then, when the time comes, quietly curl up and die. What Europeans try desperately to forget is that sooner or later they have to die, too. Your passion for health really is morbid. You are mistaking values." He paused. "In point of fact, you are afraid."

"You're talking like a medieval mystic."

"Well, I've known worse talk than theirs." He waved his hand. "I'm not discounting your work, Alicia. I'm all for you and it. Damn it all, I pay for you and it. I have you and your clinic instead of an annual trip to Paris, and the dear Lord knows, I am afraid, how I miss the *Folies Bergères*. And the *Château Neuf du Pape*. I give you credit. Morally, I mean. But, at the same time, I do not think that your values are the only values or even the best values."

Alicia shrugged her shoulders. "As your Director of Health, they are the values which concern me."

"I think I shall promote you to be a Minister. Your forte is general policy, isn't it? However, let us stop arguing. I shall probably succumb sooner or later to your Marjorie Pratt."

"Not if I stop arguing," said Alicia. "George, do you realize that it takes me more time to get what I want out of you than it does to keep my records?"

"But if it did not take time to get things out of me, I should never see you. Do you realize that you only come to tea when you want something?"

"I wasn't made for coming to tea, I'm afraid."

"On the contrary, I think you were positively designed to come to tea. You go with cream and strawberry jam, somehow. And they go handsomely with you."

She blushed. "I do wish that you would not comment on my appetite every time I come here."

"But then it's so healthy."

"You know perfectly well, George, that I only eat a lot here because you are the one person on the island who imports strawberry jam."

"If I order a case for you, will you ever come to tea again, while it lasts?"

"I'm not without gratitude."

"Then you shall have strawberry jam."

"And Marjorie?"

"Marjorie, perhaps. Have you a photograph of Marjorie?"

Alicia sighed. "We shall leave Marjorie for the moment. Is that *The Tatler* over there?"

"It is. If I lend it to you, promise it won't come back with strawberry jam or anatomical specimens wedged between the leaves. Nicholas always likes to see society magazines. He says that he can watch his friends growing old. He clips the pictures out and sticks them in an album. Very fascinating. As you turn over the leaves, you can see the Earl of Ballyjames Duff getting balder and balder and balder and Lady Constance Grundy getting plumper and plumper and plumper. It is just like a slow-motion picture. The Opening of the Daisy, or something like that."

"Nicholas can read *The Tatler* at the Club. There is always a copy there."

"But the Committee objects to him cutting out the pictures."

"You and your Club!" Alicia laughed. "I wonder if there is really such a ridiculous community on earth as the population of this island. I am quite certain that there is no community which represents such a packful of lies."

"Oh, but . . ! My dear Alicia, Nicholas was a Cambridge man."

"Do you believe anything Nicholas says?"

"Why, of course. There is no particular point in not believing him, and I always like to think that the truth can be picturesque."

"Do you really believe that he is in *The Dictionary of National Biography?*"

"Why not?"

"Have you ever looked for him in the *D.N.B.?*"

"Of course not. I shouldn't think of intruding."

"I have. He certainly is not there as Nicholas Swan."

"But he never suggested that he was. Whoever he is there as is dead. You have to be dead. Swan is his resurrection. His name is not Swan in his former life."

She laughed again. "All your refugees seem to have former lives. Except Miss Roper and I. We manage with one life apiece. We are the only unresurrected people on the island."

"I beg your pardon, but I am in my own original person. And there are several thousands of my subjects on the island, all persons, unless you prefer them as guinea-pigs. And, anyhow, I sometimes wonder whether Miss Roper is as simple as she seems. Some of her water-colors are very involved and subtle."

"It is curious how this little handful of people has drifted here to Kaitai."

"I assure you that sometimes I find them more than a handful. Especially when Nicholas and Mitchell get into arguments about the cricket averages in 1894."

Alicia flicked her cigarette. "All refugees, all of them. Fleeing from their pasts. Doesn't that ever disturb you, George? There is dynamite in this island."

"Dynamite? We lack the tinder to set it off."

"But one day a spark may blow in from the outer world, the world we have all left."

"A spark. We put our feet on sparks in Kaitai, Alicia." He laughed. "That sounded rather primitive, didn't it? But I care for my own."

"Do you ever realize what a strange place this is? How strange your life is?"

"Oh, often. There are moments when I feel like a film at the Polytechnic." He leaned against the sill and looked down at her. "You know, that is a strange word you use. Refugees. I use it myself, to myself. But I don't think I've spoken it of these poor devils before. How do you mean it?"

"I take it that most of them are refugees from the police."

"No. Not only the police, anyhow. Refugees from life. Life can be even more disturbing than the police, Alicia. Life can haunt you and hunt you, it can sit closer on your coat-tails than any chief inspector. Another cigarette?"

"Thank you. You do not believe that life haunts old Nicholas Swan? When I see him sitting naked in the sun he always reminds me of an exceptionally graceless old faun, rather decrepit but still leery."

"He takes shape from the quality of his own imagination.

No, Nicholas surrendered this life with good ease. He told me the other day that London was never the same after the wrecking began in Leicester Square."

"What was he in his former life, really?"

The Sultan smiled. "When he is finally dead, I shall tell you where they have already raised a tablet to his memory. A monument to his genius, he calls it. He has promised to leave me a note about it."

"But how did he die?"

"He was drowned, so he says. The body was never recovered. He regrets that a good deal. He would have liked a State funeral. He sometimes wonders whether it would have been the Abbey or St. Paul's. Once or twice, I have thought him inclined to come to life so that he could be buried to his satisfaction. But it would presumably embarrass his relatives, and he feels, perhaps, that it might compromise his reputation. Though that, he assures me, is with the gods and eternally beyond doubt or burden of mortality. Others abide our knowledge, he is free. Or so he says."

She laughed. "He is a very lovely liar. Do you think he was a poet?"

"His limericks are awful, and he detests poetry. So one may take it as probable."

"What poets have been drowned? There was Shelley, of course. Who else? None I remember."

"Alicia, stop. You mustn't break these fragile webs with your crude clutch at truth."

"I try, but I haven't your affectionate tolerance for liars."

"What are liars and what is truth? What is truth? As another administrator said before me, although he was only of an inferior grade. Alicia, if I did not believe lies, I should never hear the truth. It is only when my subjects are bored with deceiving me, that they slip in a fact or two."

"Nicholas Swan. And little Cooper."

"Cooper. He's a London clerk," said the Sultan.

"He was a London clerk. He and Bernard seem to me the only ones who don't lie. But then, Bernard never says anything. I'm very fond of Bernard. But I wonder why he never says anything."

"I wonder that, too," said the Sultan. He frowned. "Bernard is the only one of the batch who really worries me. The others all have their legends, and even if the legends vary, one can piece together a background. But Bernard has no legend."

"He reminds me of the Man Without a Country."

"That taciturnity of his. No, taciturn is not the word. It's too grim. Reticence? Reserve? Whatever it is, it is so damned absolute. One can't guess at what is beyond."

"It is the latent energy in him which provokes me," said Alicia. "He is like a dormant volcano."

"His energies are needed to preserve that calm, that face he turns to the world. I always think that his calm is like the calm at the centre of a cyclone. But where has his cyclone wreaked its force?" He shifted his position and suddenly grinned. "We must both have been thinking quite a lot about Bernard. We're charged with metaphors. How often do you see him?"

"I meet him at odd times about the island. In the villages. He listens a lot to the people. They seem to talk to him, too."

"He only comes to the Club often enough to avoid offence. I go out to his hut, sometimes. We play chess. I've given up the direct attempt to make him talk. Now I try the oblique."

"You know, George, you are not such a fool as you look, are

you?" There was a faint note of surprise in her voice: as if she had surprised herself. "One is inclined to forget that."

He chuckled. "It is almost a testimonial isn't it?"

"I did not mean to be rude. I'm sorry. But you know what I mean. You sit about, looking . . ."

"Fat and lazy. Like Louis XV."

"Well, if you will have it that way, fat and lazy. But you are keeping an eye . . ."

"A little, narrow, cunning eye."

"On things. And people. What do you know about Bernard?"

"He is a gentleman."

"I know that," she said impatiently.

"There are not many left in the world. Perhaps that is why he has fled it. But the world has left the marks of its irons."

She looked up quickly. "Yes," she said. "Yes."

"He was a Frenchman, of course. Poor Bernard."

"Why do you say that?"

"I was thinking of France. And of his France." He shrugged his shoulders.

"What else do you know?"

"If I knew anything more, I shouldn't speak it."

"Of course. I'm blundering like an oaf." She stood up. "What a lovely evening."

"You are beginning to notice evenings. And trees. And the color of ocean. And even people. We may humanize you yet, Dr. Murray."

Her face changed. "I don't want to be human."

"You don't dare to be human."

"Dare or care. Really, this is ridiculous. One's job is one's life, if one is worth anything. It is my job to observe, to classify."

"To be a machine in a laboratory. None of the great scientists, my dear Alicia, were machines in laboratories. It is only the drudges of science, the ushers . . ."

"Then I shall be a drudge and an usher." She flushed. "You cannot draw me out as you draw the others, George, however oblique your method. No, I'm sorry again. That was a rotten thing to say. I am being appallingly *gauche,* aren't I?"

"Well, I was impertinent, perhaps. But you do resist the common things of life, don't you? You put down fear, tenderness, all your affections. . . ."

"No," she said sharply. "No." She stared at him. "I have always been afraid of this tropical ease, this beachcombing existence which even you lead, George."

"So the evenings and the trees and the ocean are not really working on you yet." He sighed. "And still you propose that we have your Marjorie Pratt, to begin with all over again. Another woman like you and we shall all be civilized in no time. We shall be drinking pasteurized milk and parading in the Park for physical exercises. And we shall be inspected, oh dear, how we shall be inspected. What is worse, we shall probably need inspection. And what is worse still, we shall probably like it. I'm very much afraid that you are civilization, Alicia Murray. At last. Even Buchanan the First was only Presbyterianism."

"Let us go down to the Club," she said. "You are getting sentimental. I haven't been down for a fortnight, and it is only decent to drop in sometimes, I suppose."

"Then I had better take *The New Yorker.* I promised that I would. I tried to disguise the fact that I was getting it. But

Nicholas always turns over my papers when he comes here. He reads my letters. I'd like to keep *The New Yorker* to myself. It and *The Times Literary Supplement* are the papers I do really enjoy. I have some new novels here. Shall I send them over? Or will they make you homesick?"

"Please. I haven't read a novel for weeks. And sometimes the smell of Piccadilly is in one's nostrils. One remembers the violet evenings and the reek of gasoline and the yellow lights . . . and the buses. My heart yearns sometimes for a London bus."

"Well, this is a touch of humanity! Yes, and even I. There are times when I could bear to see the great red buses jammed at Oxford Circus. Why are buses so human?"

"Because they're used. They have life in them. Sometimes, I hate the empty lands, the lifeless places." She turned to the window. "Perhaps I am getting homesick. Home." She grimaced. "And the whole field of tropical medicine hardly skirted."

"Home. I wonder if Buchanan the First ever dreamed of his heathered uplands. Though, now I come to think of it, he came out of the Clyde. But a Scot can always be moved to thoughts of the Highlands. Consider the kilt."

"Didn't Buchanan the First put his Guards into kilts?"

"He did. And top hats. They fought as Highlanders, and they went to kirk as presbyters. But in point of fact, they fought no wars, and I am sorry to say that now they do not go to kirk. When I come to think of it, there isn't a kirk any more. They took it for firewood. My people have always had theological difficulties with hell. They haven't travelled abroad. I have, of course, and hell seems to me a logical necessity. But here in Kaitai, the argument is not so obvious."

"George, you are something of a refugee yourself."

"I am glad that my life does not command me to the world beyond. I like the things which you lack in your world: order, tolerance, grace, peace."

"'We put our feet on sparks in Kaitai.' You meant that, didn't you!"

"Yes." He turned to the window too. "Blast! There's a lugger in the bay."

She looked over his shoulder. "I can't see it."

"Against the sun. Under that long cloud. About ten points north of west. The flagstaff is west."

"I think I can see. It's still a long way out."

"About six miles. I dislike visitors. One never knows what they may start."

"A spark from the outside world," she said.

"You do play on a theme, don't you? Well, it's several months since we had an incursion. And then it was only Wan-fu, who doesn't excite us very much."

"He succeeded in selling a set of embroidered scanties to Miss Roper. This may be Wan-fu again."

"Wan-fu's floating emporium, my dear Alicia, is schooner-rigged. That is a ketch out there, and I do not recognize it." He turned from the window and whistled.

A native came grinning through the doorway.

"Benjamin, get the telescope, will you?"

"I very much regret to say, sir, that it is at Mr. Swan's."

"What the deuce is it doing at Mr. Swan's?"

"He said that he is getting too old to walk down to the beach where the girls bathe, sir."

The Sultan hissed, and Benjamin's grin expanded. "Shall I go to him and require it back, sir?"

"No, bring me my field-glasses. Here, what do you make of that craft in the bay? You've eyes like a hawk."

Benjamin nodded. "We have observed it from the balcony, and Rata is of the opinion, sir, that she is a pearling craft. She has reminded him of a Torres Strait lugger."

"But, confound it, we're thousands of miles from Torres Strait."

"Rata insists that it reminds him of a Thursday Island vessel." Benjamin smiled tolerantly.

The Sultan grunted. "I am going to the Club. Fetch my glasses. And take those books over to Dr. Murray's."

As they went down the path, Alicia asked, "How did Benjamin learn to speak like that?"

"Several of the older men did. Buchanan the First imported several shiploads of *The Edinburgh Review*. He made a golf-course, too. He thought that as the natives were all predestined to hell-fire, they might be allowed a little sombre pleasure here above. He taught several of them to read the *Edinburgh* so that they could read it to him. The villagers picked it up too. One used to hear them, in the good old days, chanting articles from the Edinburgh, about their evening fires. Book reviews and so on."

"What is Inspector Thompson doing?" demanded Alicia, halting in her stride. "Oh, taking photographs."

Inspector Thompson lifted his topee. Alicia always thought that any headgear but a bowler looked, on Thompson, out of nature.

"Good afternoon," he said in his stately voice. He must once have been very good at *Now, now, what's all this about?* He set his camera on its tripod.

"What are you taking?" asked the Sultan. He looked back. "Not the palace?"

"It is rather a compromise between a conventicle and a coast-guard station, I always think," said Dr. Murray. "With additional demerits of its own."

"Buchanan the First brought out a shipload of Scottish stone to build it," said the Sultan. "His only gesture to sentiment. The house was meant to look at its best in a Highland mist. Unhappily, we do not get Highland mists on Kaitai. Who's at the club, Thompson?"

"Swan and Mitchell, when I passed. Tempers running high too, as usual." Thompson frowned.

"Oh, what is it now?" asked the Sultan.

"Whether Jessop ever hit three sixes in succession at the Oval."

"And did he?"

"I don't know, sir. Swan refuses to accept Wisden. He wants a complete file of *The Times*."

"Nicholas is getting distinctly tiresome." The Sultan looked at Alicia.

"Yes," she said. "Come on. We may as well go through with it."

As they went up over the sandhill, the Sultan paused for a minute to look across the sea. Alicia took his arm. They stared across the waste together.

"He's making in," said the Sultan. The lugger now was a sharp triangle on the horizon. Behind it was a puff of cloud, of dark cloud.

A small cloud, no bigger than a man's hand, thought the Sultan. He wondered what ship it was that came in that omen.

2

FROM THE WORLD OUTSIDE

CAPTAIN HAWKESBURY sat with his feet on the verandah railings and his chair tipped back and back until it rested against the thin wall.

"Well, that's how it was," he said. "And to cut a long story short, we fought for twenty hours, up and down the deck and all over the ship. I pitched him into the sea. He crawled up the anchor chain. . ."

"It was fortunate that you were anchored," said little Mr. Cooper.

"Yes. He tripped me and I crashed down the companion, right on my head. I got up, sprinted down the alley, and came at him from the after-cabin while he was still looking down the for'ard companion. Well, at last, when there was blood and skin and hair all over the decks . . ."

"How very unpleasant," said Mr. Cooper.

"And I had three ribs cracked, and his jaw was out and both his thumbs, he said, with difficulty, mind you, because of his jaw, 'Well, Hawk,' he said, 'let's call it a day. No woman's worth it, not even the Queen of Gonga.' 'All right, Bully,' says I, 'but in future, you keep to your half of the Pacific and I'll keep to mine. There's plenty of room for us both.' "

"Dear, dear," said Mr. Cooper. "Just like Pope Alexander VI. You remember, he divided the New World between the Spaniards and the Portuguese."

"That's as it may be," said Captain Hawkesbury. "Well, Bully went off back to his own boat . . . Good afternoon, ma'am. Good afternoon." He rose to his feet and the club-house verandah shook beneath him.

"Hullo, Captain. Hullo, Mr. Cooper. Has the Captain been telling you more of his adventures?"

Mr. Cooper blinked over his round spectacles. "He has just been recounting a very remarkable story, a very remarkable story indeed, Dr. Murray. How many hours was it you fought all over the ship, Captain?"

"Twenty," said the Captain brusquely.

"That must have been a tremendous fight," said the Sultan, "I remember you telling me about it."

"Will you sit down, ma'am?"

"Thank you. But that's your chair."

"Take mine, please do," said little Mr. Cooper.

Captain Hawkesbury leaned through the clubhouse window and picked two chairs out at one dip.

He was a man in his middle fifties, with stiff black hair, grizzled now above his ears. His chest swelled beneath his singlet until one questioned how the singlet could contain him, his biceps rolled like the trunks of knotted trees. His face was dark, his eye was sombre, his arms were tattooed. His voice was not gentle, though it might blow in the warm South.

"There's a lugger in the bay, Hawkesbury," said the Sultan.

"What's that?" Nicholas Swan thrust his head through the window. "What's that?"

"A lugger," said the Sultan patiently. "In the bay. A lugger in the bay."

"Do you know whose it is?" said Hawkesbury, and his voice dropped away.

"No. My boys say that it looks like a Torres or a Timor boat."

Swan swung himself through the window. Then he leaned back. "They're coming to arrest you at last, Mitchell," he cried in a shrill little voice rather like a parrot's. He was not unlike a parrot altogether, except that he was a trifle larger than the largest macaw. His head was almost entirely bald, his nose was curved and pinched, his lips were the same dried brown as the brown of his face. When he spoke, his teeth showed yellow: they were apparently all his own.

"I'd welcome it," ground out Mitchell, within. "This island's getting tedious."

"Well, why do you always argue with your betters?" snarled Mr. Swan.

"I don't," said Mitchell.

"Is the boat well into the bay?" Mr. Cooper looked over his glasses at the Sultan.

"Four or five miles off still."

"The trouble with this island," said Hawkesbury, "is that too much happens here."

Alicia Murray watched them all curiously. None of them seemed to welcome an arrival. Mr. Cooper had tugged at his blue tie, and now his neat collar was crooked. Hawkesbury was see-sawing violently in his chair, until it cracked. Mr. Swan clambered up on to the railing, clawing at the post as he did so. Eventually he balanced himself, and then stared out to sea.

"You can't see the entrance from here," growled Hawkesbury.

"It couldn't, of course, be your own boat," said Mr. Cooper.

"No." The Sultan shook his head. "The mail steamer is only at Durabaya today. My people won't start back until tomorrow afternoon at the earliest, even if they are sober by then."

They all disliked the notion of a stranger, thought Alicia. It was understandable, perhaps. They had escaped the world, and here the world promised to intrude upon them. Their lives on Kaitai had an order, of sorts: they had worked out their relationships, one with another, and even though Swan and Mitchell or Swan and Hawkesbury had their silly arguments, flaring sometimes into quarrels, the community survived. A great deal was due, of course, to the Sultan's tact. He managed them all very well. She wondered, sometimes, how he could be bothered: but, odd as they were, he found them company, one could suppose, in this remote place. He was a remarkable man in his way, when one thought of it: so remarkable that one seldom thought of it. He ruled the island without, apparently, any exertion whatsoever: and the peace was kept, even in the furthest villages. The people had a sense of humor, and he played upon it: his sessions of justice, as he called them, outside his funny little palace, under the big palm, usually ended in roars of laughter. The island conducted its affairs with equanimity and tolerance: as between gentlemen, he often said. Of course, life may be easy and tolerant where there is economic abundance: but it was not only economic abundance here. There was a tradition of good behavior, of the decent thing. Violence, of word or act, was *de trop*. The angry man was an object of the islanders' wit.

They laughed him out of court. At the worst, they sent him to Coventry. Perhaps, after all, it is not plumbing and multiple stores and power politics which represent a civilized attitude.

"One can only hope," said Nicholas Swan, "that, if this is a visitor, he understands contract."

"How did the Darts Tournament finish?" asked Alicia. "I meant to come over for the Final."

"Miss Roper won it," said Mr. Cooper, "and I must say that she throws a very pretty dart. When I was a boy, I used to go occasionally to the Prospect of Wapping. There was an elderly lady there—she kept a stocking stall in the Borough Market, I remember—who had not been defeated at darts for some incredible period of time. Was it twenty-five years? But, of course, she played regularly every evening." He tugged at his tie again. "Can you see anything of this vessel, Swan? I wonder who it can be."

"He can't see anything from there," grunted Hawkesbury.

Hawkesbury, thought Alicia, might have posed for a pirate. A red bandana about his forehead would transport him, out of hand, to the Spanish Main. His eyebrows beetled, his hands were hairy, he swaggered like a champion rooster when he walked. If his stories even distantly approached the truth, his life had not belied his looks. He talked of distant harbors, of lost cities in the deserts, of the pearl fisheries, of Constantinople and Beirut, Singapore, San Francisco, Sydney, Mauritius, the Seychelles, of lonely ports in Alaska and the wind-swept pampas of Patagonia. He had bashed his men on every waterside from Rio to Batavia: he had thundered in Nome, he had been storm over the Andes. And Mr. Cooper, at least, believed it all.

Alicia suspected that Mr. Cooper was writing a book. He would listen for hours and hours and hours to Captain Hawkesbury. In some ways, Mr. Cooper was the oddest of their company, just because he was not really odd at all. But he was a man of the pavements, of the 8:30 from Surbiton, of holidays at Hastings and Bexhill, not a man of tropic islands and empty seas. One could see him trotting along with his brief-case and his evening paper and his neat black hat; even here, one almost instinctively looked for his tightly furled umbrella.

What was Mr. Cooper doing on Kaitai? She remembered a night, under the moon, on this verandah, when he had talked to her of London, of a welsh rarebit and of a half-pint at the Coventry Street Corner House, of the April tulips in the Park. He had been a clerk, he said, a chief clerk in a lawyer's office. He and his wife had been married at St. Mark's on Dulwich Hill. They had lived in a little semi-detached villa. His salary had risen by ten pounds annually. He had borrowed his reading from the libraries, and on Friday evenings he had always had his three glasses of sherry at the Cheddar in Chancery Lane. "It was something of a ritual with a little group of my friends," he had said wistfully.

The libraries were at the bottom of his excursion, no doubt. He had always taken home books about the sea, about ships, about the brilliant, stinking seaports of the East, about the islands. He had collected maps. On Saturday afternoons he had wandered amongst the bookshops along Charing-Cross Road. He had bought accounts of old voyages and colored charts.

"My great-grandfather was a seaman," he had said. "He

used to be a purser on the mail-packets out of Falmouth. No doubt, it was in the blood. I sometimes irritated my dear wife. She would never so much as take a passage across the Channel, though I once tried very hard, when we were newly married, to persuade her on a day excursion to Dieppe. I was never actually at sea myself, unless you would admit a shilling ride on the briny at Margate, until I came east."

"Why did you come east?" Alicia had asked.

"My poor wife died. She took a heavy cold in February, two years ago. She was always neglectful of herself. One of those people who will never admit that they get influenza, and then usually die of it. She refused to go to bed, until at last I called the doctor in. By then, it was already pneumonia." He had stared out over the sea. "After her death, I was lost. I continued to go to my work, as an automaton might. It didn't occur to me that there was anything else I might do. I even stayed on in the house, but I had trouble with housekeepers. And then, one evening, I was sitting in a teashop, having a poached egg, I remember, and reading a book, a book about trepanging and collecting birds' nests for the Chinese market, when it suddenly occurred to me that I might very easily go and see these strange places of which I had read so much. My wife and I had both been of saving dispositions. We had had, to our grief, no children. My nearest relative was a second cousin in Wigan. Why should I tie myself to my drab, lonely life any longer?"

He had looked at Alicia appealingly, as if he sought justification in her eyes. She had nodded.

"It might seem that I was escaping from my responsibilities. But I had no responsibilities. That night, I walked up and down Cockspur Street, looking at the models of the ships in the windows. The next morning, I took half an hour off, and I went into Cook's, and collected a large quantity of literature. But it was not for three months that I gave notice at the office. We are largely creatures of habit. When I did at last leave, the firm presented me with a grandfather clock. Not very useful in the tropics, but touching."

So he had come into new latitudes, and he had drifted from place to place until at last he had fetched up here in Kaitai. Of all the legends she had heard on the island, this was the one that Alicia was most inclined to believe. Mr. Cooper fitted his rôle. Even here, he dressed with punctilious neatness. He always wore a collar and a tie, his drill suits were carefully pressed, his white shoes were always white. When he bathed in the lagoon, he went to the beach in a sober dressing-gown. He always looked eagerly for *The Times*. But he had no letters, except an occasional remittance from a bank in the Indies. The second cousin in Wigan did not correspond.

Alicia shrugged her shoulders. She was thinking too much, of late, about other people's affairs. After all, it was very sensible of Mr. Cooper to live on Kaitai. He was out of the fogs, he was comfortable, he was content: and one could live at ease on Kaitai for a few pounds a year.

Miss Roper came walking briskly down the path. Her topee was on the back of her thin hair, her fly-veil was thrust back, she was swinging her shooting-stick. She always carried her shooting-stick. She liked, so she said, to sit down when she pleased; and of course the rocks on Kaitai are inclined to be jagged.

"What is this vessel in the offing?" she demanded, while she was still forty yards up the path. She was given to long-distance conversation. When she visited Alicia at the clinic,

Alicia knew of her coming before she burst through the covers; when she departed, her conversation continued to sound down the woodland aisles. One heard her voice, at times, remotely from the mountains. She talked to the villages across the valleys. She was one of those English spinsters whom one meets in the most unexpected places: in Arab tents, in rest-houses on the Irawady (though it is doubtful whether they ever need to rest), on Jugoslavian mountains, in the heart of China. They usually wear toques like Queen Alexandra's, and do their hair in curls. They wear tight coats and sensible skirts and they are obviously well-corseted. They carry rather worn black handbags, bulging a little: and they comment on the un-Englishness of foreigners with point, vigor, and no restraint whatsoever. They are frequently the daughters of Anglican deans or of colonels dead in Tunbridge Wells. They invariably carry the Book of Common Prayer, though they sometimes also tend towards theosophy. Usually, they paint in water-color.

The Sultan rose, smiling. "Good evening," he said.

"How do you do?" She eyed them all. "What are you doing perched up there, Nicholas, like a ridiculous monkey?"

"My dear Dorothy," he said, "your manners are abominable. I am surveying the scene."

"Then come down. The scene ought to be more than sufficiently familiar to you now, after thirty years. I have been watching this vessel from the sandhill, George. It is going to anchor off the point, apparently."

"Is he as close in as that? He must have an auxiliary then." The Sultan looked up to where a flag hung lifeless at its staff. "Perhaps I had better go down and take a look."

"One can only hope," said Miss Roper, "that, if we are to have a visitor, he will be a gentleman."

"Think I'll go and take a look myself," said Hawkesbury, who was never at ease with Miss Roper.

"Mitchell," she leaned in through the clubhouse window. "Give me a dry sherry, will you? Alicia, a sherry?"

"Thank you, yes, I think I shall."

"I do wish we could get decent crackers on this island. It is one of the real disabilities of the tropics that one can never get decent crackers. I opened a box only yesterday, and the mould was in them this morning."

"How did you get on for your Prussian Blue?"

"I had to mix. And now my ultramarine has gone. Really, these native girls are positively appalling. I would have boys, except that they have so little respect for a lady's bedroom and, may I add, a lady's bathroom. When one considers, George, that the first Buchanan was a man of strictly Presbyterian principles, the moral tone of the island . . . well! Who can possibly be arriving in this boat? At this time of the year, too."

"It is a very good time of the year to arrive," said the Sultan. "It isn't raining."

"All sorts of curious people seem to go drifting about the seas now in small boats," said Miss Roper. "I remember when I was at Rabaul, a young man and his wife . . . at least, they said that they were man and wife . . . arrived there in a small cabin-cruiser. They said that they were sailing round the world." She sniffed.

"Why are you so profoundly sceptical of everybody's motives, Dorothy?" said Swan with considerable irritation. "If they arrived at Rabaul in a small boat, it seems to me very probable that they were sailing round the world."

Two glasses of sherry appeared at the window. "Thank

you, Mitchell," said Miss Roper. She regarded Swan sharply. "Are you in one of your moods, Nicholas?"

"He always is in one of his moods lately," said Mitchell through the window. "He's beginning to break up."

Swan turned on the window, snarling: "I don't know what the penalty for murder is on this island, but it is more than likely that I shall incur it before I die."

"He didn't like being beaten at shove-ha'penny," said Mitchell, within.

"I do wish you two would talk to one another with at least common civility, in company," said Miss Roper.

Alicia laughed. "What is the penalty for murder on Kaitai, George?"

The Sultan, who had made only one or two tentative efforts to rise from his chair, frowned. "I don't know. I haven't had occasion to consider it in my time. I'll have to look it up." He shifted in his chair, uncomfortably. "What made you say that, Alicia?"

"It *was* an unpleasant thought, wasn't it?" She shook herself. It was idiotic, but for a moment there had seemed some portent in her silly question. And she hated superstitions. George had felt it too.

"We decline—the Sultans, I mean—to be bothered with criminal offences. The village headsmen do our dirty work. Matrimonial causes and civil actions give us our troubles. If A borrows B's net without B's consent and C steals A's catch and exchanges it for D's wife, to whom does the fourth fish belong, and why? We have a philosophic bent on Kaitai. We always want to know why. The people like me to give a decision which they can argue about in the long evenings. It helps pass the time."

Mr. Cooper stood up. "I think I shall follow Hawkesbury down to the beach," he said.

The Sultan finally heaved himself from his chair. "I'd better come too. I only hope it isn't somebody who wants to sell me something."

Miss Roper watched them go. "George always reminds me of an Oxford don. He is so at ease in his world. While little Cooper reminds me of a white rabbit I once had, when I was a small girl. It is inconceivable to me now why I should ever have cared to own a white rabbit, but I did. I was very grieved when it died, in childbirth."

"Well, I shouldn't think Cooper is likely to go off in that way," said Nicholas, and he cackled. "Unless habits have changed since I left Europe."

"When did you leave Europe?" asked Alicia.

"Never you mind now, Alicia." He cocked his head. "You people are always trying to discover who I am."

"It doesn't matter to us in the least who you are," said Miss Roper. "Or were. If I were asked to guess, however, I should say that you were a defrocked clergyman. And that the Bishop knew what he was about when he defrocked you."

Mitchell roared from inside. "That's about it, by gum!"

Swan's thin lips quivered. There was venom in the little old man, Alicia thought. But Miss Roper had been distinctly rude. "That is going just a little too far, Dorothy," he said.

2.

Hawkesbury and Cooper came trudging back.

"He's dropped his hook," said Hawkesbury. "And he's coming off in his dinghy."

"Pulling himself," said Mr Cooper. "He only appears to have a couple of boys on his lugger."

"Anyone recognize the boat or him?" asked Mitchell from the gloom.

"No. George is waiting for him down at the steps." Hawkesbury sank into a chair. "Where's Swan?"

"Taken a huff and gone off," said Miss Roper.

"Well, that's good. Wonder who this bloke can be."

"I do wish you would all stop wondering who he can be," said Miss Roper sharply. "We shall know soon enough."

Alicia looked at her with some surprise. Miss Roper was being tart this evening. Her tongue was frequently sharp, but it did not always flick at people in this fashion. Yet even she herself felt a little on edge. When one lived in a small, closed community like this, was a stranger always unsettling? In primitive societies, even a man from a neighboring village is a foreigner. But theirs was hardly a primitive society. They all had belonged to larger worlds. One would expect them to welcome a new-comer. But they never did. It was always like this, when a strange craft appeared. Although, in her time on the island, only three or four strange craft ever had appeared. The only communications with the world outside normally were the Sultan's cutter and his small schooner, which carried off the island's few exports, its small cargoes of copra and coffee and sugar-cane and cloves, dried fish and *bêche-de-mer,* and brought back its imports, *The Times, The Sketch, The Tatler,* gorgonzola, strawberry jam, razor-blades, bottled beer, detective stories, phonograph records, golf balls, curaçao, pickled walnuts, tooth-paste, and football jerseys (to which the natives were much addicted). At odd intervals, an itinerant pedlar of the seas, Wan-fu or one of his kind, appeared: and there had been a British sloop, a year back. But the Sultans had always discouraged sloops.

However it was, when a stranger appeared on the horizons, this little population began to fidget. Hawkesbury had been the last arrival. It had taken them a month to settle down again, and it was really two months before he was fully accepted in local society. Hawkesbury, Cooper, herself, Miss Roper; and before them, Bernard and Mitchell, Thompson and Swan. Swan had been here for years and years. He was the oldest inhabitant. He had been here when the Sultan went away to school, looking even then, so George said, like a libidinous parrot. He was the only white on the island who remembered Buchanan the First, and Buchanan had been dead nearly a generation. It was curious: perhaps Swan's strange hints were true, after all.

"Do you really think that Nicholas is a dead poet?" she asked Miss Roper.

"I should very much doubt it. I have only known one authentic poet in my life, and he lived at Tooting, and had eight children. His wife was an appalling woman. She used to sing hymns in the kitchen. And accuse him of making love to the housemaid. He was a very decent little man on the whole."

"Oh, but all poets aren't like that," said Alicia.

"No, I suppose not. There was Lord Byron, of course. But they have been trading on his reputation ever since. You know, I do wish I could get the colors of that mountain right. They constantly vary. It must be so much more satisfactory to paint still-lifes. Onions and delphiniums and flasks of chianti and things of that sort. Though a mountain is still-life, when you come to think of it. I'd go back to fish, but

I've grown a little tired of painting fish. They're inclined to get high before one has the thing as one wants it, exactly."

The Sultan came up the path, and a tall man walked beside him. He walked heavily, as though he had not yet found his land legs. He wore shirt and trousers, with a coat over his arm and an old white hat on the back of his head. He was youngish, fair, broad-shouldered. His voice was loud.

They stepped on to the verandah.

"This is Mr. Goulburn. Miss Roper, Dr. Murray, Captain Hawkesbury, Mr. Cooper."

"How do you do?" said Mr. Goulburn, and, "Well, this is very pleasant." He took Alicia's hand. "How do you do?"

His stomach was too ponderous, but he was a formidable young man. Alicia disliked him at once. His manner was expansive, but his little blue eyes were like chips of ice in the brown, flushed face.

"Drink?" said the Sultan.

"Well, sir, what can you manage?"

"Gin and Angostura?"

"This is civilization again."

"Sherry, Miss Roper? And you, Alicia? Whisky, Hawkesbury? Cooper?"

"A ginger-ale," said Mr. Cooper.

"I'll have a gin," said Mitchell from within.

"That's Mitchell, my manager, with the sepulchural voice. Ædile, factotum and seneschal."

"I work," said Mitchell.

"Sorry to hear it. I hoped that nobody worked on Kaitai."

"Nobody does, really," said the Sultan. "Goulburn? I read a book by someone called Goulburn lately."

"Sorry to hear that too."

"*European Backstairs,*" said Miss Roper. "I thought it excessively impertinent. Did you write it?"

"Have I got to plead?"

"What are you doing out here?" Miss Roper reached for her knitting, Mr. Cooper suddenly laughed, and Hawkesbury settled back in his chair and put up his feet in his familiar fashion.

"Floating round, in both senses. I'm sick of newspapers, wars, dictators, revolutions, Lefts and Rights and Browns and Blacks and Greens and Purples and Reds. The lies you hear and the lies you tell. So I thought I'd rusticate."

"The middle of the ocean is a curious place for rustication," said Alicia.

"It's off the telephone, anyhow. And out of the news, mostly. If you go back to the old home town in Dakota, it's making its story by blowing off into the Dust Bowl, mother and roses and all. If you go to Priors Pricklethorpe, the local Council is about to pull down the village inn where Queen Elizabeth tippled, and the place is full of Letters to the *The Times,* trying to get written. So I came east."

"Not all the way in that lugger," said Miss Roper.

"No, madam. I acquired this boat way up the coast. The gentleman who owned it was in jail, and he had no prospect of getting out unless he could raise six hundred dollars or the equivalent in Dutch. He'd been punching a good many Netherlander policemen, when in his liquor. He said he was an Australian, and that he used to have a troupe of boxing kangaroos, and maybe he knew. But he had taken on too many policemen, and they set the bail high. Well, anyhow, as he had nothing but his boat and his pants, and no one would lend him anything on his pants, apart from the indecency of the thing, it had to be his boat. He threw in his crew for the cash, but they're not worth it."

"What have you in mind, particularly?" asked the Sultan.

"Nothing particularly. I want a holiday, an honest-to-God holiday, and I don't care if it never ends. I've been pushing in and out of places on and off the Equator for weeks. Most of the time I fish. I've always wanted to settle down to steady fishing where there are some fish. When I get tired of the diet, I open a can of pork and beans."

"How did you come to Kaitai?" said the Sultan.

"Heard about it up and down the islands. You've a romantic reputation, you know. Fellow in Titauru said that Kaitai was a better story than Pitcairn. Well, that put me off for a while. I've seen too many busted romances, and I was having a holiday from better stories. Then I got to Durabaya, and they started talking in the Club one night about this place. So, here I am, such as I am."

"We decline, emphatically, to be put into a book," said the Sultan.

"Maybe you're wise. Anyhow, I'm not working at the moment. You'd be Buchanan the Third, I take it."

"I'm Buchanan the Third," said the Sultan.

"That's what got me in Durabaya. The Emperor Buchanan, they call you."

"Oh, do they!" said the Sultan.

"Sounds a bit more Christian than the Sultan, anyhow. You went to Oxford and got a cricket blue . . ."

"Hockey," said the Sultan, "to be precise."

"And you're a grandson of Buchanan the First?"

"Not even that. I am his grand-nephew."

"How'd it all happen?"

The Sultan grimaced. "If you have had the usual distorted version in Durabaya, I suppose there is nothing else for it but to tell the pedestrian truth. My great-uncle was a solemn man . . ."

"A missionary, wasn't he?"

"Not in any ordinary sense of the word. He was a steam-tug captain on the Clyde, and his hair was very red. I mention that his hair was red, because it had a good deal to do with his subsequent triumphs on Kaitai. He would have triumphed in any case, even if he had been bald as an egg, because my great-uncle was a triumphing sort of man. I am glad that I never knew him."

"But they told me in Durabaya that he was a very religious man."

"So he was. He was a remarkably religious man, though I wonder that the Lord could bear with him. He used to go up and down the Clyde in his tug-boat, and what with the opportunities for reflection during foggy weather and his experiences of humanity as it was represented by dockers, steamer captains, company agents, ferrymen, fireman, and his own deck-hands, he became firmly convinced that the world was entirely lost and given over to the power of Satan. Doubtless it is. As his view of his fellow-men grew darker and darker, he drew more and more comfort, as others have done before him, from the extreme discomfort of his doctrine. He believed that he had a new revelation. Calvin had been wrong, Knox had been wrong, all the most grim prognostications of the ultimate population of hell had been wrong. They had all been too optimistic, if optimistic is the word. Too conservative. To Buchanan it was revealed that but one man in each generation should be saved. He proved it out of Genesis. The case of Lot. Fortunately, in Buchanan's generation, the choice had fallen on Buchanan."

"Well, he must have been relieved," said Goulburn.

"Yet he was a kind enough man in his fashion, whatever has been said of him since. It grieved him to go on living and working and eating and occasionally drinking with a race of the damned. There was also the example of Lot. Sodom and Gomorrah should be shaken off, before they fell about one's ears, though I should like to have seen Sodom or Gomorrah fall about my great-uncle's ears. He was a hard man when he was roused."

"I've never heard the story before, not quite like this," said Alicia.

"I don't think I've ever told it before, quite like this," said the Sultan. "An oft-told tale grows a trifle tedious, don't you think? However, my great-uncle pondered on Lot a good deal. The cases were not entirely parallel. Lot, if the Scriptures were to be believed, had possessed a wife and family. My great-uncle was not versed in the Higher Criticism, though he thought it very odd of Lot. But there was the clear statement. So he actually contemplated matrimony. What was good enough for Lot was good enough for him. She was a publican's widow in Lanark. But, for good or ill, before he had settled on his proper approach, she up and married a second engineer in a Cunard ship, and that was that. When great-uncle shook off Sodom and Gomorrah, he shook them off on his own feet, but his own feet alone."

"Perhaps it was just as well for the lady," said Miss Roper. "She might have been turned into a pillar of salt."

"He probably consoled himself with the thought. Anyhow, he came to the East."

"There could have been little point in that, surely," said Alicia. "They were damned in the East as well as in the West, weren't they?"

"Yes, but he didn't mind it so much when they were only poor damned niggers. His first years in the East are a bit obscure. My father was very reserved about them, so he probably knew something. Father was very strong for my Great-Uncle Buchanan. After all, the old boy had set us up in the Sultan business."

"I don't understand that," said Goulburn, "you're not Mohammedans, are you?"

"No, we're not, but there aren't a great many titles to select from. Buchanan the First was a loyal subject of Queen Victoria, in sentiment, at least, and he would not usurp any of the titles proper to her House. King and Emperor were ruled out. And he had a strong distaste for rajahs and nabobs. And probably he didn't know any others. But while he gave the British Crown his personal allegiance, he was not disposed to compromise his island. Queen Victoria was all very well, but he had seen too many Englishmen he disliked in this part of the world."

"How did he actually come to Kaitai?" asked Alicia.

"In a canoe. It must have been a large canoe, because he brought a boxful of Bibles to prove his credentials if necessary, a large quantity of oatmeal, and calico dresses for the female population. The calico won the women, but his red hair won the men. They said that he was a man on fire, and I imagine that his temperament was sufficiently volcanic to confirm their first impressions. The red hair business may seem to you a trifle far-fetched, but there have been other instances. No doubt, Sir James Frazer has something to say about it. Anyhow, my great-uncle was the first man, the first white man, to land on the island alone and survive the cooking-pot. Not that the savages were especially savage. They have always been a sensitive people, and when they ate a man they probably felt genuinely sorry that they could not have their cake and eat it, so to speak. But white men were, for them, charged with desirable virtues, and it was notorious that the only way to acquire his virtues from a fellow was to eat him. One digested his good qualities."

"They have entirely given up the practice, I hope," said Mr. Cooper.

"Oh, entirely. My great-uncle's hair alarmed them. Yet he was obviously a man of tremendous virtue. To eat or not to eat. They began to feel the first movements of doubt. Their faith began to waver."

"I suppose," said Miss Roper, "that this story serves as well as any other."

"When one is talking to a journalist," said the Sultan, "one can get away with anything. Still, if you are not satisfied, I shall tell it another way."

"One way is enough," said Goulburn.

"However, to cut a long story short, as our friend Hawkesbury here says, my great-uncle established himself in the seats of power. He even got himself recognized, *de facto* and *de jure,* by the British Government. It was just as the time when the great scramble was on. All the south and east were resounding to European military bands, and landing-parties were busy from morning until night, running up ensigns. The Hohenzollerns had begun to shape an empire from our imperial leavings. They sent a gunboat to Kaitai. Great-uncle heard of it. When it arrived, there was a British cruiser in the bay."

"We don't want to fight but by Jingo if we do," sang Nicholas Swan, poking his head up from under the verandah. "There were men in those days."

"Mr. Swan was one of them himself," said the Sultan. "Anyhow, the thing was a mess. The Dutch said they'd discovered the island, the Portuguese said they had landed missionaries here in the seventeenth century—you can believe that my great-uncle was not having anything to do with Romish missionaries, even if they had been eaten long since—the Spaniards swore that they had sighted it two decades earlier. Her Majesty's Ministers proposed a typically Britannic compromise. They proposed that the island should become a British possession."

"We were a great people," said Mr. Swan.

"The argument went on for fifteen years until everybody grew tired of it except Buchanan. Then he negotiated a very adequate treaty with the British Government, and here we are. Sometimes I wish that my great-uncle had retired to Saffron Waldron and bought a public-house." He sighed.

"Public houses are not what they were," said Nicholas Swan, "since the Licensing Acts."

"How did you come into it all, Buchanan?" asked Goulburn.

"I succeeded my father. Buchanan the First, after his disappointment, never married. But as he got on in years, the disposition of his property troubled him. So he wrote home to my grandfather in Paisley and asked whether he had any sons to spare. My grandfather replied that he had been blessed, since the last heard from Buchanan the First, with six more sons, making fourteen in all."

"As I remarked," said Nicholas Swan, "they were men in those days."

"Buchanan the First wrote back asking for the thirteenth son, thus challenging the devil in his private citadel. The thirteenth was my father. At least, he was subsequently my father. Buchanan the First took a look at him and then sent him back to marry a wife. So are empires and dynasties founded."

"But weren't you all damned in his eyes, too?" asked Alicia.

"The old man softened towards the end. He withdrew my father and my mother and their progeny, which is me, and my progeny, which seems unlikely, from his universal holocaust. Even to our remotest generation. Having gone so far, he finally settled that we were the Lost Tribes, born again. He had a very interesting mind."

Mr. Goulburn laughed.

Buchanan turned slightly. "My father was not of his way of thought. Buchanan the First embarrassed him, I think. But he did take his inheritance seriously, and so, odd as it may sound, do I, Mr. Goulburn. What has been given to me, I keep. Where I am served, I serve. I rather like to make that clear to young gentlemen from the outer world as soon as they arrive. Now, perhaps you would all care to come to dinner with me. My boys will have put on an extra pig or two."

Nicholas Swan suddenly poked up again from under the verandah. "I'll come," he said. "I want to talk to this young man about his book. It is the most superficial nonsense I have ever read."

"There is one thing, anyhow, about Kaitai," said Goulburn. "You all appear to say what you think."

3.

Alicia did not go to dinner. She sat on the verandah and watched the dark drop down, quenching the red flare in the west as one might quench a candle.

To her, sitting in the shadow, a man came slowly.

"Bernard!" she said. "You startled me."

He did not come up on to the verandah. He stood on the path below, his head near her feet.

"Who is that man?" he said softly.

"He says that his name is Goulburn. Do you remember a book we all read a few months ago? *European Backstairs*. Inside information for the plain man."

"I remember it. I did not read more than a chapter or two. It was obviously a bad book. I have little patience with glib young journalists who imagine that they have stripped the soul of Europe in a round of interviews."

"He says that he is the Goulburn who wrote it. He happens to be lying."

Bernard lifted his face. It was curiously white in the gloom, like a white mask. One could barely distinguish the features. "Are you sure of that?"

"Certain. I saw a photograph of Goulburn in one of the American papers which came by the last mail. This man probably would not expect us to see many papers, recent papers, even if he knew that the photograph has appeared."

"How can you be sure? Photographs do not always give an accurate likeness."

"The real Goulburn is bald, almost, with a thin, sharp, sensitive face. This man looks like a slightly decayed weight-lifter."

"What does he want here? Why does he lie?"

"I suppose that people lie, Bernard, when they cannot afford to tell the truth. There are, of course, artists who lie for the sake of lying. It is an inexpensive pleasure."

"Not always," he said. "Not always."

"Probably he hasn't a reputable character to offer. So he borrows another."

"Have you spoken to George Buchanan?"

"George knows. George knows a great deal more than we suspect, when it suits him."

"What do you mean by that, Alicia?" He looked up, quickly, again.

"Only that I noticed his mouth twitch when this man said he was Goulburn."

"What will George do?"

"Let him play out his game until George sees what it is, I imagine."

"Yes. Yes, that is like George. Have they gone to dinner?"

"Yes. George invited us all. I didn't feel like it."

"Why not?"

"Well, I had eaten a large tea, for one thing. And I do not like Mr. Goulburn, or whatever his name may be."

"Has Miss Roper gone?"

"Yes, she has gone too."

His hands were resting on the planks of the verandah. He dropped his chin on to his hands. He was a tall man, Alicia thought. One did not always notice it, because he was well proportioned. She could not see them, but she remembered his hands, hardened and calloused with the labor of years. What had been his history? One saw less of him than of any of the others. He lived his own life on the mountain. Sometimes, he came and sat with Miss Roper as she painted on the beach; sometimes he came and stood, for a few minutes, at the door of the clinic. Perhaps once in every few weeks he would come for an evening to the Club and sit here on the top of the verandah steps and listen to the others talk. He came, obviously, because it would have been churlish not to come now and again: he made that concession to courtesy.

"You saw the boat from your mountain?" she asked. She wanted him to lift his face again. Unless one could see his face, he seemed so strangely impersonal, remote, as if his life was centered elsewhere and all his thoughts gone to it.

"Yes," he said. "I saw it from the mountain. It is my watch-tower. My watch-tower on the world."

"Do you need to guard yourself then against the world?" she said lightly.

He did not answer for almost a minute. Then, lifting his face at last: "Don't we all?" he said.

3

THE SWAMP

"YES, I know, Alicia, I know. I remembered the photograph myself. Have you mentioned it to anyone else?"

"Only to Bernard."

"He won't broadcast. It is just the three of us who know, then. I did not let that paper go to the Club. It had a very good article on cheese and one day, when I have the time and the stimulus, I shall write a book on cheese. Our cheese here is my penance. The very mention of cheese gives me an acute nostalgia for days. O my Roquefort, o my Wensleydale!"

"Well, what are you going to do about it?"

"I don't know yet. He may be just one of those amiable liars who cannot help themselves. In that case, why embarrass him?"

"He does not strike me as merely an amiable liar."

The Sultan looked up. "You said that with feeling, Alicia. Has he been making himself a nuisance?"

"I can attend to that," she said.

"Oh, quite so. Far be it from me to affront your womanly independence. If he is not an amiable liar, what kind of a liar is he? And what do you make of him, in general?"

"I think he is after something here. Or someone."

"Someone?"

"Oh, I'm just being fanciful, I suppose. The man gets on my nerves. I wish I hadn't seen that photograph."

"Still, it's an interesting fancy. Though you should be more tolerant of human weaknesses. Most of us like to seem of more importance than we are. However, I always have this bomb for him. I can explode it in due season, if we find it necessary to blow him out."

"He has been sleeping ashore the last couple of nights, hasn't he?"

"Yes. I invited him here the first night, as a matter of politeness. Then he had a couple of nights in his lugger. Then the last two with Nicholas. He and Nicholas were getting on very well together. Remarkably well, for Nicholas. Though Goulburn—I suppose we may as well allow him the name—told me today that Nicholas had chucked a lump of coral at his head after breakfast. Perhaps the ham was not well cured. Goulburn was considerably amused. I rather think he turned Nicholas up and spanked him, which I have always wanted to do. But I have been cramped by a quite unnecessary respect for my elders."

"He seems to have cultivated us all in turn. I saw him carrying Miss Roper's easel up the beach for her just now. They were in very ardent conversation."

"And he listened to Hawkesbury for hours and hours last evening. And this morning, he was helping Thompson take photographs."

"Goulburn has been riding a good deal too, hasn't he?"

"Yes. I lent him a pony. He has been away off round the

mountain. He has skirted the Swamp." The Sultan suddenly frowned.

"What's the matter, George?"

"Oh, nothing. Just a notion I had. He is not particularly tidy, you observe. He's dumped the saddle and stirrup-leathers there on the step. He was out again for a couple of hours before lunch. I wonder how long it will be before it occurs to one of my boys to pick up those things and put them away. Eight or nine weeks, at a guess. When the iron is rusted and the leather is rotten." He laughed. "You know, I'm in a cantankerous mood today. I've half a mind to call out the Army and drill it."

"Is there an Army?"

"There was in my father's time. But they must be all old soldiers by now. He had strong ideas about the value of discipline. He had been begotten and reared by a Scottish schoolmaster, you know. He continued my great-uncle's Guard. Though he substituted khaki kepis for top-hats. But the kilts had worn out before I succeeded, and I thought that the sporrans alone would hardly preserve the dignity of the regiment. So I called no parades. Alicia, Goulburn rode up to see Bernard before lunch. He is curious about Bernard. But then, I suppose he is curious about us all."

"Bernard wanted to avoid him, I think. He might have left Bernard alone."

"Our Mr. Goulburn is a very sociable man. Very sociable."

2.

She watched him coming across the little clearing. Why did she dislike the man so intensely? Was it that eternal smirk, or was it his feline, almost feminine grace? He moved heavily, but easily, with reserves of energy in that lazy roll. There was beast in him, dangerous beast perhaps. She felt her pulse, and it steadied at once. How stupid this was! But there had been a man of this sort before, once before . . . She closed that door, sharply. One did not look into that part of one's mind, that vile memory.

She stood up and turned her back and went inside. But she heard him coming up the steps.

"Hullo, lovely."

He was, she knew, leaning against the railing.

"Hullo," she said. She took a cigarette from a box on the table and turned again to face him.

"Light?" He moved forward with three quick strides into the room. The flame leaped in his hand. It was a gold lighter, she noticed.

"Thank you."

He smiled. "I'll take one myself."

She opened the box.

"Thanks. Sitting down?"

"On the verandah. It's cooler out there. The beginnings of the land breeze. You've noticed how strongly it blows?"

"Haven't I! Towards eleven, I just have to hoist the sail on my dinghy and it blows me out to the lugger in about five minutes. It's a sort of a gully wind, down those valleys."

She sat down. Perhaps they were going to talk sensibly, after all.

"You haven't been out to the lugger yet," he said. "Why don't you come out one of these nights? Why not tonight? No one would see you."

That was what she hated in the man: this constant innuendo.

"Why should it matter whether anyone saw me?"

"Oh, well, they might misconstrue things."

"Then they shan't have the opportunity."

He grinned. "You're hard, aren't you! Why, sister?"

She shrugged her shoulders.

"Do you know how good you are to look at?" he said.

"Have you only the one line of talk?"

"There is only one line," he said, "as between me and you."

"Then it bores me."

"No, it doesn't. Not it!"

"I'm sorry, but you're wrong. It does." She stared at him, tried to stare him down. "What are you doing on Kaitai, Goulburn?"

"What are you doing on Kaitai, lovely?" He laughed. "That's a question, isn't it? Looking after a lot of natives for a white buck of a scabby little Sultan, who doesn't know enough to see what's right under his nose, what I've found out in four days on the island."

"What have you found out in four days?" she said.

He laughed. "Not all I want to. I still want to know why Dr. Alicia Murray has hidden herself here for the best years of her life. And I'm going to find out, too."

She stiffened. "Does it occur to you that I may have found here the work I want to do?"

"Work! There's only one sort of work that women care about."

"You are being abominably rude. I think you had better go."

"That's been said to me before. I've learned how much it usually means."

"It is obvious to you, of course, that I am not physically capable of pitching you out."

"You could scream for help though," he said.

"You really are an unpleasant specimen, Mr. Goulburn."

"Well, run along and tell your friend George about it." He laughed again. "I guess you wouldn't run to George, whatever happened. Too proud, aren't you? Well, well. It's a funny place, this island. Everybody with something to hide."

She walked out on to the verandah. She flicked her cigarette far into the clearing.

"I think you had better go," she said, "Mr. Goulburn."

3.

"I'll have another whisky," said Goulburn. He reached for the bottle.

Buchanan paused in his pacing. "You've been drinking a good deal to-day, haven't you, Goulburn? Getting up your courage for this, eh?"

"I don't need to fortify myself." Goulburn squirted soda-water into his glass.

"Look at your hand, man. And you walked round the subject like a rat around a trap. Rats are sometimes caught in traps, of course. That has come within your experience, Goulburn?"

"Aw, stop talking and get down to items. What are you going to do about it?"

"Nothing."

"Nothing!"

"Nothing, my good Mr. Goulburn. Except to see you off to

your vessel and to wish you a very hearty and a long good-bye."

"Nothing!" Goulburn laughed raucously.

"We have done nothing about it for three generations, and I do not propose to do anything now. I'm rather fond of my island as it is, Mr. Goulburn. I do not like your manners. We should not work happily together."

"You're not the first who has objected to my manners. But after people get to know me better, they are not so out-spoken."

"That's a pity. I should have said that plain speaking was good for you. By the way, Goulburn, what is your name actually?"

Goulburn grinned. "It may surprise you," he said, "but it's Smith."

"I'm sorry," said the Sultan, "for the Smiths. They are very respectable people as a rule. Is it just Smith? It seldom is."

"Just Smith." He leaned back in his chair and looked at Buchanan. "Now, how did you get on to that?"

"You're a conceited pup, aren't you! Your sort, Smith, always comes to a sticky end. You are too certain of your own shrewdness, too regardless of other people's. Even now, as you sit there, you are thoroughly satisfied in your own mind that you are going to outwit me. Confidence is a good thing, Smith, but conceit is a mortal poison. I admit that I am a little conceited myself, but only in prophylactic doses."

"Talk," said Smith, "all talk. And it doesn't answer my question."

"You blow too much in bars. You've been a journalist, up in the Straits. Until you were fired. Then you got in with one of the local rajahs. You were his press-agent when he went to the United States and to Europe. And you cost him a good deal more than you were worth."

"I showed him the sights," said Smith, still grinning.

"And you involved him in some oil exploration show. A syndicate to try for oil in his territory. You must have made money out of that, Smith."

"It wasn't so bad while it lasted," said Smith.

"The money? Yes, I'd gathered that most of it was gone. You have been living fairly high in several continents, haven't you? But now it is time you made some more money."

"It is more than time," said Smith. "So there isn't much leisure for haggling." He sat up. "Come on, Buchanan, let's get down to things. Your little bits from *Who's Who* are all very well, but are you going to give me the paper I want."

"What paper exactly do you want?"

"Your chit will do. Simply an assurance that you'll grant the concession. I can bring my people together on the strength of that, and then we'll send out a man from Trinidad to inspect."

"What first suggested this to you, Smith?"

"Oh, it's been hinted at up and down the coast for years. The Germans were on to it before the War, so I've heard."

"As a matter of fact, my great-uncle had tests made thirty-odd years ago. I can assure you that it is quite a valuable property. But I do not propose to exploit it, Smith. I have seen what has happened to native populations in other places, and I do not propose to sacrifice the bodies and the souls of my people to make myself—or you—a millionaire."

"That," said Smith, "is the bunk."

"I said before that I did not like your manners. And I said

too that I would do one thing for you. See you to your boat and say good-bye. It's half past eleven. Don't you think you might be going?"

Smith rose. "I'll see you in the morning," he said.

"I hope not. Is that your hat?"

They walked out into the night.

"I have a torch," said the Sultan. "You seem a little unsteady. You really should not drink so much, you know, Smith. You advertise your business in too many bars, and things get about in the East. Further, you must be growing hob-nails on your liver."

"Well, it's my liver," said Smith.

They walked on towards the beach. The wind from the high peaks and valleys blew strongly to the sea. They walked past Swan's bungalow, where a light was still burning, and Hawkesbury's, Cooper's, and Miss Roper's. As they approached Miss Roper's, her light went out.

"The old lady has gone to bed," said Smith. "I wonder what she dreams about."

"You'd better be careful tonight, if you're using a sail on your dinghy. The wind's stronger than usual. Are you sufficiently sober to manage? I'll call a boy and send him off with you, if you like."

"I can do my own sailing, thank you. The trouble with you, Buchanan, is that you've got the Emperor complex. You're too bloody patronizing."

"And the trouble with you, my young friend, is that you ought to have been kicked hard and often in your youth."

"Is that so! Here, give me that blasted torch." His voice rose in a sudden burst of alcoholic rage. "I've half a mind to crack you one, Buchanan, and relieve my feelings. But get this, do you hear, get this! You needn't think you're going to shunt me off this lousy island with a flea in my ear. You're not. Not by a long chalk. You're going to give me a concession to work that asphalt lake back there in your swamp, or you're going to regret it. I may not be Plugs Goulburn, but I still know how to make a story break in every newspaper in the world. I'll spread Kaitai over the front pages. And you won't like it. . . ."

"Probably I won't," said Buchanan. "But what is your story?"

"I guess you know that as well as I do, Buchanan. And I wonder what your blasted independence would be worth if the world knew that you harbor gaol-birds and crooks. A policeman or two would be pleased to hear what I could tell them about Kaitai. If I'm not mistaken, there's a reward worth the having, too. And the story will syndicate for thousands. You can have it your own way, Buchanan. But I don't leave Kaitai walking on my uppers. I cash in. One way or the other. And I'll be seeing you. In the morning. I'll be ashore for breakfast at eleven, and you might see that the coffee's to my liking."

Buchanan stood, very still, on the edge of the hard. And he watched the light of the torch go down over the soft sand hummocks. Then, slowly, he turned and walked on.

4.

The dawn came, a pearly sea and sky, with a cool wind blowing back to the land. The sky grew to rose and yellow behind the great purple peak of Kaitai. Across the bay, moving in with tide and wind towards the further point, drifted an upturned boat. And on the beach, sprawling grotesquely on the hard sand, his arms outflung, was a dead man.

A circle of seagulls rose screaming as the fishermen came down to the beach.

4

DEAD FROM THE SEA

"WHY is it that death looks so pitiful in the sunlight?" said Mr. Cooper.

"We don't want the ladies to see this, sir?" said Thompson.

But Alicia Murray was already crossing the beach.

"Alicia is our only doctor," said Swan, with his hard, çackling laugh.

"What happened?" asked Alicia. She stared down at the sprawling thing on the sands. Her face was very white.

"You needn't look," said George gently.

"I am a doctor, you know. What happened?"

Thompson pointed to the dinghy, across the bay. Two native canoes were alongside it, and there were boys in the water. They had succeeded in straightening the dinghy, and they had lowered its sodden sail.

"He must have capsized last night," said George. "I'm going off to his lugger presently to hear what his own boys have to say. They've been signalling excitedly since they spotted the dinghy, but I've kept our people away." He raised his glasses. "They're on the deck now. Two of them. It doesn't seem to have delayed their breakfast. They've a fire up in the galley."

"What time did he go off last night?" asked Swan. "It must have been after eleven. I heard him talking to you, Buchanan, as you walked down."

"It was somewhere about half past. You heard us talking, did you? The wind was up rather more than usual. I told him to be careful, though I thought it was safe enough."

"Was he sober?" asked Alicia. "He had been drinking when he came to me before dinner. I suppose he had dinner with you, George."

"Yes. He wasn't exactly sober. But he wasn't incapable of managing the boat. Or so I thought. I should not have let him go off alone, if . . . Still, evidently he was not capable of managing the boat." He wiped his forehead. "This is a rotten business. After all, it wasn't a tricky bit of sailing. The wind was blowing steadily, it wasn't gusty or squally, and the tide was running out. It isn't as if he'd have met a cross-sea."

"Did you go right down to the boat with him?" asked Thompson.

"No, I didn't. I didn't go beyond the hard, back there."

There was a moment's silence. Then: "Didn't you?" said Thompson.

"Surely he wanted a hand to push off the boat," said Swan, and then he cackled again.

"No," said Thompson, "he could get the dinghy off all right, I've seen him. One shove and she is afloat."

"Providing the tide had not left her high and dry," said Swan. "Did your argument develop, Buchanan? Goulburn was noisy when you passed my place."

Buchanan looked at Thompson. "We were arguing a bit. Nothing important."

Thompson nodded.

"He took my torch at the edge of the sand. Said that there was no point in me going on. I stood for a minute and watched him making his way across the hummocks. Then I turned back."

"They have the dinghy in tow," said Cooper.

Buchanan raised his glasses.

It had been an unpleasant moment, but Swan was apparently unrepentant.

"*Nil nisi bonum,*" he said, "which is always one way of putting it. His judgment of Shelley was ridiculous, utterly ridiculous."

"That's odd," said Buchanan. And then: "That's damned odd. Surely they had the sense to bail her out."

"What is it?" said Alicia. "Oh, I see. The dinghy is sinking again."

"She's obviously filling," said Buchanan.

Alicia had a curious sense of unreality. They were all trying to be as matter-of-fact as they could, to talk as if the thing under the sheet had not been warm flesh, moving and speaking amongst them twelve hours ago. People always tried to be matter-of-fact: and there was always this grim sense of unreality, until grief broke through. She remembered when her father had died. But no grief would break through here. No grief. . . .

She stooped suddenly and pulled back the sheet. The hair was in strange little curls. There was sand amongst them, and a strand of seaweed. She felt the cold cheek.

His nose was sharp and pinched. The flesh was grey. How quickly we lost our humanity, how incredible it was that this cold, emptied thing could be the full meaning of us, the whole end of life. Yet this was what we all visibly came to, this and no more. Visibly. A box of worm-seed, a salvatory of crude mummy. No more than that. No more than that?

Buchanan drew the sheet over his face again.

"His eyes are gone," she said, in a voice she did not know.

"He must have been some hours in the sea, Alicia," said Buchanan gently.

She stood up, and for a moment it seemed that there was a dark ring about the sun.

"It's horrible!" cried Cooper. "Horrible. The fish . . ."

"Cooper!" Buchanan's voice was vehement. "Cooper! You and Swan go and keep the natives off the beach."

"This won't upset them," said Swan.

Buchanan turned on him. "Will you kindly do what I ask!"

The blood rose in Swan's sallow cheeks, and the little eyes were like blue flames. Then, suddenly, he relaxed. He turned away and walked up the beach. "Come on, Cooper," he said.

Thompson took a deep breath. "Just as well, sir," he said. "Cooper has been on the brink of hysteria. Nasty sight, I must say. They've turned the dinghy over again. Looks as if they're trying to get her in bottom up."

There were boys swimming about the boat.

"She must be holed," said Thompson.

"Alicia, wouldn't you rather go away?"

"No. No, I'm all right, George. Heaven knows, I shouldn't be squeamish. But those eyes . . ."

"I know. I know. Leave this to Thompson and me."

"Don't you think I should . . . look at him? I am the only doctor here, George."

"Is it necessary, my dear? Isn't it all too plain?"

She braced her shoulders. "George, after all, this is my job. What are you going to do with the body?"

"I don't know. I haven't thought. We . . ." He looked at Thompson.

"I should suggest burning it, sir."

"You had better have him carried up, first, to the clinic. To the mortuary. And you must let me examine him, George. If there are any inquiries afterwards, it will be as well . . ."

"I don't like it, Alicia. It's . . . well, it's not only his eyes."

"This is my job, George."

"No, no. Thompson . . ."

"Dr. Murray's right, sir."

"Oh, confound it, man, this isn't London. It's plain, perfectly plain, what has happened."

"A dinghy that won't float, sir?"

"What do you mean?" He swung again to the sea.

"They'll beach it just under the point there," said Thompson. "There they come now. They must be on the sand-bank. They're on their feet, anyway. They can lift it in now."

"Thompson, you stay here. I'm going to look at that dinghy. Alicia, my dear . . ."

"I shall come with you."

"I think I had better get a couple of boys and carry him up to the mortuary, sir, as Dr. Murray suggests."

But Buchanan was already running along the beach.

Alicia ran behind him. Presently he paused, and waited for her. He was sweating, she saw: but she had run a mile with him along this beach before, and had not seen him sweat.

There were a dozen boys about the dinghy. They were carrying it on their shoulders now. They were wading through the surf, they had brought it to the beach. They were gathered around it. Then one began to wave excitedly.

"Damn!" said George. "There is something wrong with that boat."

The boys saw him coming. They all turned to face him. Yet not one moved forward. As he came up, they backed away a pace or two.

"What is it?" he said harshly.

One boy stepped back to the dinghy. "The plug is not in, sir. The boat fill, and she sink."

Buchanan stooped to look. And when at last he raised his head again, Alicia thought that he suddenly seemed an old man.

"It couldn't have been pushed properly home," he said. "It must have sprung, and been washed away when the dinghy sank."

"But Goulburn would have noticed the water rising," she said.

There was a murmur from the boys.

"It must have sprung," he said. "It must have." He made an angry gesture. "Clear out. Clear out, the lot of you. I'll see to this. And keep all the others off the beach." He broke into the native dialect, and Alicia knew that he was giving them orders. She had never heard him speak so before. He spoke with such rapidity and violence that she could only take a word here and there, though she could understand her patients well enough when they spoke slowly. And the boys were afraid. Never before had she seen one of his people cower before Buchanan. But they were cowering now. They retreated, facing him; and then one broke into a run, and another, and another.

He wiped his forehead. "This business has upset me," he said, but he did not smile. "Now, let's have a look at the boat. That damned plug may be under one of the boards."

But the boys had already loosened all the boards.

"Well, it isn't here." He straightened his back and stared about at the sandy shelf. "Looks as if she foundered, not capsized, eh? You think he would have noticed the water rising? He would, unless he had gone to sleep at the tiller."

"He surely wouldn't have done that. And even if he had, the water . . ."

"Would have wakened him. It may have awakened him too late."

"But he was a very good swimmer, George."

"The sharks."

"But had the sharks been at him?"

"I don't know. No. Smaller fish." He pushed back his helmet. "This is devilish. We mustn't let our imaginations run away with us. Suppose she foundered . . . how far out is the lugger?" His eye ranged across the water. "A quarter of a mile beyond low-water mark. Suppose she foundered when he was nearly there. And that his own boys were asleep and didn't hear him if he cried out. It would have been a long swim back. But no, he would have swum to the lugger."

"If the plug was out when he put off from the beach, wouldn't the dinghy have filled before he got very far?"

"I don't know. With the wind blowing strongly off-shore, and his course was within a few points of the wind . . ."

"But he must have noticed the water rising. And he would not have had time to go to sleep."

"I wonder whether the boom could have hit him. But it's

such a light sail. Made for one man to handle as he sits at the tiller. He wasn't too drunk . . . he must have known what he was doing."

"It isn't possible that he could have pulled the plug out himself, is it?"

"Why? Why would he? Unless he wanted to commit suicide."

They stared at one another across the dinghy.

"Suicide?" whispered Alicia. "No."

"It doesn't sound like Goulburn, does it?" said George grimly.

"George, you were the last to see him. What do you think?"

"He said that he would be ashore to breakfast. And he wanted the coffee to his liking."

"Was he . . . in a quarrelsome mood?"

"Why do you ask that?"

"Because, when he left me . . ." She broke off. "Oh, it doesn't matter."

She turned to the sea. But she felt George's eyes still on her face.

"Did he . . . make himself a nuisance, Alicia?"

"Rather."

"I see."

She turned to George again. "He talked as if he had made some discovery on the island," she said. "Some unpleasant discovery."

George sat down on the gunwale of the dinghy. "Did he? What? Did he tell you?"

"No. I made it sufficiently clear that I did not want to know."

"Yet it impressed you all the same. You believed him."

"I don't know whether I did . . . do . . . or not."

"This is disturbing."

She made a gesture of compunction. "I'm sorry, George, but I thought I should tell you, now."

"Yes, but you know what a liar the man was. You don't take this seriously, do you? And in any case, it doesn't really help us if you don't know what it was."

"No. No, I suppose not."

"I had better go back to Thompson. Alicia, why don't you take breakfast with Miss Roper?"

"I haven't seen her this morning, have you? It's strange she hasn't been down to the beach."

"Very sensible of her."

They went back along the beach. The tide had begun to recede again, and there was a strip of firm sand between the hummocks and the sea.

"High tide was at half past six or so," said Alicia.

"About half past six." He caught her sense. "And it was ebbing then when he went out last night."

"Wouldn't he have had trouble, then, in getting his dinghy off the sand?"

"He came in yesterday morning when the tide was only an hour or two from low-water. And he dropped his grapnel well out. He waded ashore."

"But didn't you say that Nicholas Swan was throwing coral at him yesterday morning?" Alicia's hand flew to her mouth. "How beastly! It sounded like a joke yesterday, and now one feels that one should not have remembered it."

"Goulburn went off to the lugger after breakfast. To shave.

And I suppose he liked to keep some sort of eye on his boys."

They came up to Thompson. He had lit his pipe: and they sensed, at once, some change in his manner.

"Was the dinghy holed, sir?"

"Not exactly. But the bilge plug is missing. It looks as if she foundered."

Thompson shifted his pipe from one corner of his mouth to the other. Then he took it out and pointed with the stem. "Take a look at his shoes," he said.

Buchanan stooped and jerked back the sheet from the dead feet. They were cased in dirty, salt-stained sandshoes, and the skin was swollen and yellow about his ankles.

"What's the matter with them?" he said.

"They're on the wrong feet," said Thompson.

Buchanan lifted one foot. "The shoes, you mean. They're almost shapeless, anyhow."

"He's right, though, George." Alicia bent down. "They are on the wrong feet."

"Yes. Yes, I suppose they are." He looked up at Thompson. "What's the meaning of that?"

"Do you ever put your own shoes on the wrong way round?"

"No, no. I see."

"Someone else pulled them on. In the dark. And because they are so shapeless, did not notice that they were on the wrong feet." Alicia stood up. "Is that what you mean?"

Thompson puffed at his pipe and nodded. "What else?"

"Oh, here, I say, he surely might have done it himself. Don't overrun the course. He probably pulled his shoes off to cross the hummocks and the soft sand, and then just jerked them on again when he had pushed off the boat and got in. With a pair of canvas bags like this, he probably didn't notice himself which was left and which was right."

"I've done that myself," said Thompson. "Mine are as old as his are, but though I might wander about the bungalow without bothering to put 'em on right, I'd notice that they weren't right. Especially if I laced 'em up. And his are knotted."

"What exactly are we talking about?" said the Sultan.

They looked at one another, standing in the sunlight about the shrouded thing. Alicia bent and pulled the sheet again over the feet.

"I think you had better carry the body up to . . . perhaps it had better be the mortuary. I'm going off to talk to the boys in the lugger."

"I'll come too, if you've no objections," said Thompson.

"I'll see to the body," said Alicia. "Naqa and Herbert are amongst those boys on the sandhill. I'll send them to fetch a stretcher."

2.

The lugger rode lazily at anchor, the shadow of her green hull shimmering beside her in the placid morning sea. Beyond her, a porpoise rolled with a slow wash, and a shag dipped above the silver. The boys had fishing-lines out, and three damp singlets hung, motionless, from the ropes.

"What's the law of all this?" said Thompson.

"We've got to inform his consul at Durabaya, obviously."

"Does he satisfy himself about the cause of death and so on?"

"I am the sole legal authority on Kaitai. I shall give him all the essential information."

"Has he consular jurisdiction here?"

"Yes. The consuls at Durabaya also look after whatever interests their nationals may have in Kaitai. None of them ever bothers to come here, of course, but when they are appointed to Durabaya, I usually formally recognize their status in Kaitai as well."

"Is there any provision under your ordinances for an inquest?"

"For a judicial inquiry into the cause of death, yes. I make it at my discretion, and in convenient form."

"You are, in effect, the sovereign power."

"Yes, but at the same time, I do not want any trouble with consular authorities. We have preserved Kaitai because we have never given the Powers any excuse to intervene." They were coming up with the lugger. A yellow face and a chocolate face appeared, and two bodies clambering up from the cabin. "Swing in under the stern," said Buchanan to his boys.

Thompson leaned out to catch a rope tossed by the Chinese.

"Coming aboard," said Buchanan.

The boys fended the boats with their hands, and Buchanan hoisted himself on board. Thompson followed, with rather less agility.

The Chinese was very old and very yellow, and not unlike Nicholas Swan. But his manners were better. He bowed before Buchanan, and offered him a camp-stool.

"Your master is dead," said Buchanan.

The Chinese bowed again. "I had feared it," he said.

"What is your name?"

"John Sym Lung, sir."

"And his?" Buchanan turned to the second boy, tall and incredibly thin and obviously excited. His coloring was curious, a very dark brown, almost black, streaked with a reddish bronze.

"Charlie Lord Nelson," said the Chinese.

"What place belong you, Charlie?" asked Buchanan.

"I Darwin."

"A Port Darwin boy," said Sym Lung. "He is half Australian aboriginal, quarter Malay, and the rest, God knows."

"Where do you come from, Sym Lung?"

"The sea." The Chinese smiled. "I was born on the sea, I have lived all my life on the sea."

"But from what part of China? Are you Cantonese? Hong Kong?"

"I have never seen China, except once, when I went to Shanghai and ports on a Red Anchor ship. My father came many years ago in a junk to the islands. We are fishermen, we serve in ships, I cook with the pearlers."

"How did you come to sign in this vessel?"

"We came from the Timor with this lugger. Our owner was mad. He says that there are no more pearls in the sea, that he will fish for mermaids in the Gulf of Aden. Once, he says, he has seen a mermaid in a tank at Steamer Point, Aden. I have seen that too, but it is not a mermaid. But he says that it is. Never mind, I do not care. But now he is in jail, because at last he thinks that he is a merman and the large Dutch ladies are mermaids. It was gin." Sym Lung shook his head, not in sorrow, but with the philosophy of one who has seen many men and many seas. "Mr. Smith buys the boat. We stay with him. Why not? Where else? Now, Mr.

Smith is dead. Do you buy the boat too?" He looked anxiously at Buchanan.

"I think you will always find a boat to live in, Sym Lung. It is always a south wind when one has an easy conscience."

"I am a very excellent sea-cook."

"I don't know whom the boat belongs to now. Did Mr. Smith deal through a lawyer for it?"

"His register—register—"

"His registration?" suggested Buchanan.

"Yes. It is at Durabaya. I have looked at the papers."

"We'd better take charge of the papers, Thompson. Have you stolen anything, Sym Lung?"

"No, I have stolen nothing."

"Where are the papers?"

"There is a safe. In the after-cabin."

"Did Mr. Smith leave his keys on board?"

"No, but he left it unlocked. He was very careless man."

"When did you first realize that there had been an accident, Sym Lung?"

"An accident?"

"That Mr. Smith had been drowned."

"When I come up on deck this morning. I see the dinghy floating. At first, I thought it was an island canoe, but then I see the sail in the water too."

"You noticed nothing last night?"

"No. Not me. Charlie was sleeping on the deck. He saw the light."

"What light?" Buchanan turned to the brown man.

He grinned. "A light on the beach," he said, in an odd high note, as if he were about to break into song. He grinned extensively.

"A torch. He saw a torch flashing. It went backwards and forwards. First it came down to the dinghy, then it went back. Then there was no light for this time. Then there was a light again."

Charlie nodded.

"You couldn't see, of course, who was carrying it," said Buchanan.

Charlie shook his head.

"Well, what happened?"

"Charlie went to sleep," said Sym Lung.

Thompson grunted.

"You didn't notice when the dinghy left the beach?" asked Buchanan.

"He went to sleep," said Sym Lung firmly. Charlie shook his head.

"You heard nothing? You did not hear Mr. Smith call?"

Charlie continued to shake his head.

"There are bamboos in the island, Sym Lung," said Buchanan, "for those who bear false witness."

The Chinese bowed. "We tell no lies," he said.

"It is a way of wisdom. I rule here, Sym Lung, and I do not rule in the fashion of the men who talk and talk and talk. Nor is my jail a place where one eats and sleeps at ease, protected from a wicked world by sheltering bars. Now, show me the safe. And produce whatever things you have mistaken for your own."

"I am no thief," said Sym Lung.

They dropped into the after-cabin. It was large for the size of the lugger and its work, with two bunks along one wall, a chipped enamel basin in a bracket, a lamp swung from the roof, and a safe let into the wall behind the lower bunk. On the other wall was a shelf, with a rack of test-tubes, a retort, a little pile of dirty crucibles, various bottles.

"Gentleman had a chemical turn," said Thompson. "That looks a solid bit of safe."

"It is. That is where the pearler hid his pearls, when he had any. While he was asleep, you could only have got at it over his body. One takes precautions when one fishes for oysters, Thompson." He turned from the apparatus opposite, and tried the safe. It opened.

"He was a very careless man, as you remarked, Sym Lung."

"He was aware that I am an honorable sea-cook."

"No doubt." Buchanan lifted two long canisters from the safe. He unscrewed the top of one. And then he smiled grimly.

"What's that muck?" said Thompson.

"That muck," said Buchanan, "is from the swamp between the peaks of Kaitai. Well, well. When did Mr. Smith bring these on board, Sym Lung?"

"Yesterday morning, after breakfast."

"Did he say anything about them to you?"

"He was very pleased." Sym Lung's eyes suddenly gleamed. "What is it?" he said. "What is this stuff?"

"So it woke your curiosity, did it, you Oriental sea-cook?"

Sym Lung had lowered his lids, and veiled his eyes. "It was interesting. I merely wondered."

"I'll bet you did. Stick 'em in your pocket, will you, Thompson? Thanks. What else? A bundle of letters. A log of sorts. Personal diary. Money." He slipped a bundle of notes into his hand. "Just count, will you, Thompson. And check the numbers."

"It's a sequence. 00508 to 00558. Fifty pounds."

"These are fives."

"773 to 793. One hundred pounds. Made up in these packets by the bank, obviously."

"They must have been a grievous temptation, Sym Lung."

"The practice of banks is not unknown to me." Sym Lung folded a towel neatly and placed it on the bunk. "The numbers, no doubt, are recorded."

"A passport. A packet of visiting cards. H'm'm. He did not leave one when he called on me. And here are the ship's papers. Well, I'm damned! Sym Lung, what was the name of your previous owner? The one who mistakes Dutch fraus for mermaids."

"Mister Goulburn."

Buchanan flicked the papers with his thumb and passed them to Thompson. "So that is where he acquired his *nom de guerre*. I wonder whether this Goulburn is any relation of the author Goulburn, or whether it just amused Smith to let us jump to conclusions. Make a comprehensive note of that lot, Thompson, and I'll initial it. We can look through them ashore. Sym Lung, can you read and write?"

"I was educated at the Government Schools in Singapore, Batavia, Port Darwin, Broome and Thursday Island," said Sym Lung with dignity.

"Then read what Mr. Thompson writes and initial it, too. No, sign in full. You witness that we have removed from the ship's safe of the lugger *Timor Trix*, on the morning following the death of her master and owner, at Kaitai, the items here listed. The date is September 2." The Sultan hunted for a pencil. "We are going ashore. The lugger stays here, Sym Lung, until we have instructions from the consul at Durabaya or the executors of the deceased. And you will keep a careful record of all your withdrawals from stores."

He swung up the companion; and then he turned and looked down. The Chinese was staring up. Buchanan could almost feel the prick of a knife at his spine.

5

THIN SKULL

"I SHALL send Rata off, to represent the Administration. If Charlie Lord Nelson has anything to say which we did not hear, Rata may extract it."

"They seemed to have a straight enough story," said Thompson.

"Lord Nelson had been carefully drilled. He's afraid of the Chinese. Still, as you say, the story is straight enough. So far as it goes. But it didn't go very far."

The boat grounded, and the boys leaped out to drag it up on the beach. The Sultan stepped across the seats and jumped onto the sands.

"It was from about here that he put off."

Thompson came squelching. "The tide's been over it all since. No use poking about."

"I didn't propose to poke about. I wonder why he was wandering up and down with the torch, though."

"Perhaps he dropped something," said Thompson.

"Perhaps he did."

They walked together across the beach, their feet making hardly any impression on the firm, tide-washed sands. The

Sultan stopped and looked back at their course. Then he walked on again.

"The tide must have been a few feet higher last night than it was this morning," said the Sultan. He stopped again by a wavy line below the hummocks. Beyond it, in sand slightly softer, was another wavy line.

"Crabs have been up," said Thompson.

Buchanan looked down at the curious, striated track which a crab makes in the sand.

"Spider crabs about too," he said, "by the look of those holes. Five holes, more or less in a line. Fingers and thumb. You haven't been setting up your camera on the beach, have you, Thompson?"

"Someone sat down there, maybe."

"This is the way he came from the bungalows. That might quite easily be his track, but in this soft sand, how is one to tell?"

There were depressions in the soft, wind-blown sand above high-water mark, but they were quite unrecognizable, except that they followed a course.

"You couldn't even tell whether it was someone in shoes or with naked feet." Thompson stamped in the sand, and watched the tiny cascades and dribbles of grains until the impression he had made had lost the outline of his shoe.

"Yet it looks like two tracks there," he said. "It looks as if two people had walked up and down there, on the edge of the soft sand. That's when Lord Nelson saw the torch moving about."

"I'm afraid it is not the slightest use trying to read the riddle of these sands," said the Sultan. "If you look to right and left, you can see dozens of tracks, to and fro. The crabs are the only people who leave satisfactory prints. Odd habit, walking sideways. Yet we all do it a good deal, don't we? This must have been a big blue crab. Quite a formidable trail. But those holes are not the holes of spider crabs. You get spider crabs round on the swampy beach. They like mud, not sand. What are you thinking about Thompson?"

"A dinghy that foundered. Shoes on the wrong feet. Did someone else put them on him? And a drowned man, with a cracked head. I can't help feeling . . ." He paused, and felt for his pipe.

"That there is something wrong. Of course there is. But what? Thompson, let me make myself plain. I have to think of the general welfare and interests of the island at large. We are a small community, we whites, and we cannot afford to let suspicion and fear loose amongst us. Further, I hold the natives chiefly by prestige. By, in a sense, moral suasion. I cannot and will not have any wild talk. You understand me?"

"Yes." They walked on a hundred paces. "But what are you going to do? Leave things as they are?"

"Let's first make sure what they are. Meanwhile, we do not want a cloud of talk and rumor. Goulburn went off in his dinghy last night. Somehow, by some chance, it foundered, and he was drowned. Accidentally. That is the view you are to express in the hearing of your boys and at the Club. Especially at the Club. And that is how, to begin with I shall report it to the Consul at Durabaya."

Thompson smacked out his pipe on the palm of his hand. "I follow you, sir. Even in England, of course, police work is not altogether detached from general policy, what they call the public interest. But it isn't very pleasant to think that there may be a . . ." He stopped.

"A murderer loose on Kaitai? I don't think we'll use the word, Thompson. Yet."

They came up past the little line of bungalows. Hawkesbury was sitting in his doorway.

"Morning," he said. "This is a nasty affair. What's it all about, Buchanan?"

Buchanan stopped. "Meaning?"

"Well, it's all over the village that the plug was out of that boat."

"So it was. Plugs do come out, you know. The boat had turned turtle."

"She was over on her side, according to Swan. With the sail trailing in the water."

"Has Swan been talking to the boys?"

Hawkesbury grinned. "He's running about like an excited chimpanzee, talking to everybody. He pulled back the sheet as they were carrying the body up. Dr. Murray ticked him off proper."

"I'm very glad to hear it. Where is he?"

"Gone off after Miss Roper."

"And where is she?"

"Don't know. She went out with her paint-box first thing, so I'm told."

"Who told you? You weren't about yourself very early."

"Swan told me. She'd gone when her cook turned up this morning."

"Has Swan been questioning Miss Roper's women?"

"He's conducting a general investigation."

"Damn the fellow! Thompson, you had better find Swan. And bring him to me. What a mischief-making little scut the fellow is. Where's everyone else, Hawkesbury?"

"Mitchell is over at the Club. Cooper is in his bungalow. He's looking sick. Gave him a turn, this business. I haven't seen Bernard. He hasn't been down this morning. Swan says you'll have to hold an inquest. That right?"

"Has Swan any evidence to offer at an inquest?"

"Not that I know of."

"You didn't hear the alarms this morning, Hawkesbury?"

"Didn't know a thing about it till my boy brought me breakfast."

"You sleep soundly. Didn't you hear Goulburn go down to the dinghy last night?"

"With you. You were arguing, according to Swan. . ."

Buchanan smacked the verandah post. "You see, Thompson. One mischievous tongue and the whole island is in a ferment. Hawkesbury, did you hear us?"

"No, I didn't. I must have been asleep. You can usually hear anyone going up or down this path, unless you're asleep."

"Did you sleep soundly all night? You did not hear anyone about at all?"

"No. Once I roll up in my bunk, I sleep like a log or a lizard."

"You should be obliged to your Maker. Hawkesbury, it isn't good for morale on this island to have a horde of wagging tongues. If you hear your boys at it, stop them."

"It would seem, then, that Goulburn was drunk," said Hawkesbury.

"Is that what Swan is suggesting?"

"He says you were both drunk."

"Thompson, fetch Swan. I'll go on up to the hospital."

2.

Alicia Murray drew off her rubber gloves, and went to the sink in the corner and washed her hands. She dried them carefully and walked out on to the little porch which faced her bungalow.

"Naqa," she said. "Bring me a cup of tea. And cigarettes."

She sat in a long deck-chair, and stared down at the green scrub and the rim of sparkling sea beyond. She felt a little sick. And the job wasn't finished yet, not nearly finished. Why should she finish it, unless George said so? He, after all, was the legal authority in the island. It was his affair, not hers.

She pushed back her hair wearily. There were drops of perspiration on her forehead. It had all been harder than she had expected. She was a squeamish idiot.

It had shaken her. She held out her hand. It was not steady, even now.

She had taken an oath. Good old Hippocrates. Yet her vocation had been real to her: it had given meaning to her work and to her life. One should not let one's individual affairs obscure one's social responsibilities.

What an immeasurable length of time since the boys had come running this morning. She had been standing, waiting, on the verandah. She had watched the slow rising of the sun. It was always full day before she saw the sun over the purple mountain. Naqa had come up, running from the beach.

What was in Naqa's mind, behind those sharp, curious eyes of his? How much did he share of her life, see of it? What, indeed, did she herself know of her life? Proust had been right. Life was nothing but the memory of things past, an odd jumble of impressions, inaccurate, confused, blurring into a grey nothingness. Could she, now, account for the motives which had moved her, even yesterday? Could she be sure of the motives which might move her tomorrow? What had she really felt and known and wanted when Goulburn had sat, half drunk, wholly obscene, in her room? And their understanding was darkened. How true that was. Men were not sufficient to themselves. It was necessary to accept a code, a discipline, a pattern, a map of life: otherwise, life would always be formless, undirected, both end and means escaping one constantly.

She shrugged her shoulders. Much better to get on with one's job and to distract oneself. It was so easy to imagine that wisdom might lie in passivity, in quietism. Their understanding was darkened. God allowed for that, no doubt. One hoped so. Otherwise He must long since have destroyed us. Only His understanding and His sense of humor could have preserved us.

She rose. "George, I am glad you have come."

He stepped up on to the porch. "I think you meant that," he said.

She nodded and put out her hand. "I did."

"What were you thinking of, sitting there?" He looked to the mortuary beyond.

"Original sin."

He dropped his helmet on to a chair. "Yes," he said. "Yes. So was I, I suppose, as I came up the path. There is a serpent in Eden, death in flowers, queer twisted things in one's mind and heart. Yet there is Eden, there are flowers, one has a mind and heart. I trust so. Mine at the moment are not in view. I thought perhaps I might borrow yours."

"Mine have queer twisted things in them, too."

He looked at her white overall. "You've been working?" Then he turned to the open door behind. "In there?"

"Yes. I've been making a preliminary examination. As you said, George, he is not pretty."

"Funny that one can't reconcile this sort of job with you being a woman. Seems positively horrid to think of you messing about with a post-mortem. Actually, of course, you must have seen scores of much more unpleasant sights than I shall ever see."

"Men always assume that women have no stomach for unpleasant things. Yet, women really live much closer to raw nature, to nature red in tooth and claw, then men do. Women's nerves are made much tougher, to meet her emergencies. Women have children, women nurse the sick, women lay out the dead. It is not we who are the delicate sex, however nature decks us in her seasons."

"Oh, yes, quite so. I remember a very intelligent woman saying to me once: 'The first lesson a girl has to learn is that men are tender at spots where we are pachydermatous.' "

"It's true. Men may be better shaped to run and hunt and fish and plough and occasionally kill one another, but women are tougher, their fibre is stronger, they can endure more." She laughed. "That is why I ordered a cup of tea. Will you have one, George?"

"I have brought two cups," said Naqa beaming, "when I observed the arrival." He set down the tray with a clatter. "And the cigarettes. Matches. Sugar. A lolly bun."

"I don't think we want a lolly bun at this time of the morning," said Alicia, eyeing it with distaste.

"No? I shall return it." He picked it off the plate and put it in his pocket.

"I think perhaps that you had better eat it yourself." Alicia stooped to pour out the tea.

"Milk, tongs, slop-bowl."

"Singular efficiency this morning, Naqa," said George. "It is only right that we should have our attention drawn to it. But I'll bet there is no hot water in the jug."

"Hot water? Yes. See." Naqa lifted the lid.

"I am confounded."

"We are both astonished," said Alicia.

"And deeply appreciative," said George.

Naqa was gratified. He glowed. "I may assist perhaps with the cutting of the corpse."

"No, you may not!" said Alicia emphatically.

"Love's labor lost, Naqa," murmured George.

"Go back and get on with that list of the children in Tundi. Be careful with it. And if your uncle comes to the surgery again, with his perpetual colic, do not give him any more pink pills. They are bad for him."

Naqa retreated, somewhat damped.

"He is dying to do a dissection. I'm afraid his uncle has cancer. Even here in your Eden, George."

"Buchanan the First died of cancer, you know."

"Yes. I knew."

"The old man lay up there in agony for days. He was quite conscious, I am afraid. He lay with his teeth clenched. He did not once groan, complain even. My father sat beside him, moistening his lips now and again with a little whisky and water. Ever since, we have had a doctor on Kaitai."

"What persuaded you to accept my application?"

"The women. It has been hard to get good men doctors to come here. The last was a brute of a man. I wanted someone who would understand that these people are worth saving. There must be change, they must feel, more and more, the impact of the world. We have tried to let the change come gradually, to graft what we had to give them on to the best in their own traditions and customs. The tragedy of the colored peoples is this, that their own way of life is smashed, before they can enter ours. We have worked for time. Time to bridge, time to form the new associations, to give them the new experience. It is all we can do for them. We can no longer hope to save their own life, inviolate. It is not desirable that we should. There is much that is mean and ugly and vicious in the grass houses, Alicia. That is one reason why I wanted a woman here. She can work with, work on, their women. It is the women, the women in the grass houses, the mothers of the children, who must do our job for us."

"George," she said, "you love these people, don't you!"

"This is the thing that was given me to do. And it is worth doing. I am the one barrier between my people and the world. If I break, then the deluge. *Après moi,* you know. I told you I looked like Louis XV. I'm sure that history hasn't done the old boy justice. There is considerable virtue in a man who can sit on leaks. And Louis and I are both—well, adapted at that end."

She watched his face. He caught her eye and smiled, but she did not smile.

"You would do a great deal to—keep the world away from your people."

"I want to give them time to adjust themselves, to assimilate the new notions, to grow. You cannot plan a society. Human society is not a machine, it's an organism, or something more like an organism than a machine. It consists of living parts. You can't take it to pieces and remake it, any more than you can take a baby to pieces and remake him. And we Europeans have been damnably, damnably busy taking other people's societies to pieces, in Africa and Asia and all through Oceania, and now our own is going. But we shall not easily put them together again." He put down his cup and grinned. "And that, Alicia, is the answer to your question: why did I accept your application."

"It is the answer to more than one question."

"Well, then I have not set up my pulpit in vain."

"You have cleared my own mind, in a sense. Do you know that you often use a phrase about general policy? You talk about the need to subdue particular issues to general policies. This is your general policy, what you have just been saying."

"Pretty well. If I were asked to say what I think I am doing on Kaitai, that is roughly how I should answer. But don't ask me too often. It is rather a strain. And I feel embarrassed now."

"Well, your general policy settles my mind about a particular issue."

"Goulburn?"

"Yes, Goulburn. George, in our carefully policed society, we have been taught to give great importance to individual life."

"When, of course, we are not conscripting all the young men to go out and to lose their individual lives." He nodded. "But I see your point. I was thinking about it as I came up the hill. It was that, really, which set me off after original sin and serpents in paradise. The law must prevail. An eye for an eye, a tooth for a tooth, a life for a life. That's what you mean?"

"Yes. It need not be so *quid pro quo,* perhaps, so tooth for a toothish. But the law must prevail. The reign of law. We are inclined to admit no exceptions. But sometimes, surely, we must make exceptions."

"When general policy demands it," said Buchanan.

"Yes. Yes. George, I believe in your general policy, I believe in your judgment, your mental and moral balance. And I want you to remember that, to stick to your own convictions. It may be hard. But remember this charge you have, your people. And do not mistake yourself for a police magistrate."

"I see," said George. "Goulburn was murdered then?"

"I think he was. Now you have to make a decision. Am I to do a post-mortem and perhaps establish the fact, or am I to forget what I have seen, to give a certificate of death by drowning, to break my oath? I am willing to break it, George, if you believe that best. But then, you must burn the body."

He reached for a cigarette and tapped it on his thumb-nail. "Have you a match? I seem to have lost mine. Thank you. One for you? Alicia, why are you ready to assume that I should prefer to suppress the fact, if it is the fact?"

"First, because you were obviously distressed this morning when it looked as if the thing might not be a simple accident."

"Naturally. Weren't you?"

"Yes. But it wasn't only a matter of personal feeling with you."

"That is true enough."

"Secondly, because the situation of our little group of whites will become intolerable if we begin to believe that there is a murderer amongst us. It's already . . ."

"It's already what?" he said after a moment.

"Well, Swan is already talking."

"Echoes have reached me. He says, I gather, that Goulburn and I were both drunk when we went down to the beach last night."

"He hints at it."

"He has been up here, has he?"

"He followed up after the body." Alicia shifted in her chair. "George, he is a horrible little man. He wanted to look at it. I had to turn him away."

"I shall deal with Mr. Swan." He leaned back. "What else? I agree that if we are to live comfortably here, we must avoid silly and irresponsible talk. But it is not the same thing to suppress a murder, Alicia."

"No. But what would be the effect on the natives?"

"That is a much more serious matter."

"And what of your whole position here if the thing goes out to the world? Governments have used lesser occasions for intervention."

"I am very much aware of that." He stood up and paced the porch. "What does concern me most is this, and I tell it to you in absolute confidence. Goulburn or Smith or whatever you like to call him came here because he knew of unexploited resources in the island. And he probably had people behind him who know. They may use the occasion to break me or my resistance. We've known, ourselves, we Buchanans, about this stuff for a long time, but we have also known that it would be the end of our effort here if we permitted its exploitation. One can't reconcile this primitive fishing-farming economy with industrialism."

"Was that your quarrel with Smith?"

"Yes. He asked for a concession. I refused it."

Her face had hardened. "Then you must stop Swan's talk."

"I realize that."

"George, what are we to do then?"

"I've told you what I have told you because the decision must be in some measure your own. I had no intention of telling anyone, and I'm afraid I've done a little mild lying already. But if it is a question of you—well, compromising your professional conscience, then you have a right to know."

"Thank you."

"And now you tell me what you have to tell."

She rose. "You had better see for yourself."

She led the way into the mortuary. The thing that had been Smith was on the long slab, face down. The back of the head had been shaved. George's lips tightened. Alicia pulled on her surgical gloves and took up a forceps.

"It's a violent fracture radiating from here." She described something like a semi-circle at the back of the skull. "You can't see it clearly because of the messiness, but I think the wound was made with a weapon shaped rather like that. I haven't done the section yet, but the skull was unusually thin. The bone is splintered, here and here and here."

"Was it a very heavy blow?"

"It need not have been. The skull is thin. It is the shape of the injury that I want you to notice. From the direction of the fractures, it suggests something like a horse-shoe."

"A horse-shoe? How could it possibly have been a horse-shoe?"

"Were your ponies loose? Though the ponies could hardly have put him into his boat."

"They were stabled, anyhow. Alicia, was he dead when he went into the dinghy?"

"I don't know, but I should be able to tell, from the condition of his lungs, whether he was dead when he went into the sea."

"Whether there is water or not in them, you mean."

"Yes. But this is the point at which we must decide whether to go further or not. It is still possible to assume that he was knocked out of the dinghy by the boom, say, that the dinghy capsized and the plug was lost, that he drowned and in some way shattered his skull on something. I shall assume all that, if you wish. But the body must be coffined and burned as soon as possible. I have told Ptai to have a coffin made. I gave him the measurements."

"There are still the odd shoes," said Buchanan. "Who put them on him? Could that injury have been made by the boom?"

"No. It was made by something U-shaped."

"What about a rowlock?" he demanded. "The dinghy's rowlocks are U-shaped."

"That might be it. But how did he come to be hit on the back of his head by a rowlock? Unless somebody was using it as a weapon."

"Couldn't he have fallen against it? No, of course, not with a wound like that in account."

"The lungs will be the final test, George."

"You must go ahead. We must know, for certain. Yes, of course you must go ahead."

"I shall lock the doors. We do not want Naqa to know even what I am doing."

"When will you be finished?"

"I shall come down to you."

"Thank you."

She followed him to the door. He took up his hat and he went, across the clearing. She stood and watched him until he passed into the trees. Then she turned back.

6

SWAN

SWAN was sitting, cross-legged, like a squat idol, in the large basket-chair.

"Well?" he said.

Buchanan tossed his helmet on to a couch.

"I want to see you," he said.

"So Thompson remarked. Rudely. He was so rude, in fact, that he roused my curiosity, and I came. What do you want?"

"Did you find Miss Roper?"

"I did."

"Where was she?"

"On the mountain. Painting. Painting very badly. It's incredible that the woman even begins to take herself seriously. But when I point out that all her color is wrong . . ."

"Why did you go after Miss Roper?"

"To tell her, of course, about Goulburn. Or Smith."

"How did you know that his name was Smith and not Goulburn?"

"What could be more probable?"

"Did Goulburn tell you that his name was really Smith?"

"My good Buchanan, is this an inquisition?"

"It is. No, sit where you are, Swan. You have been talking freely enough all the morning, and now you can talk to me. First, why did you think it necessary to find Miss Roper and to tell her of Goulburn's death?"

"I did not find it necessary at all. It pleased me. And I wanted to watch her face."

"Why?"

Swan grinned. "After all, the young man appeared to be paying her some attention. Only yesterday, he carried her easel and stool along the beach. But she disappointed me. She just went on painting."

"Why have you taken it upon yourself to talk as you have been talking?"

"How have I been talking?"

"Like an irresponsible idiot."

"If I am going to be abused, I shall have another cushion, please." He settled himself on his chair. "Thank you. What were we saying?"

"It is what you were saying that concerns us now. Swan, I will not have you discussing this business at large with the natives."

"And, of course, you prefer that I do not mention that you were tight, last night."

"Do you believe that I was drunk last night?"

"Well, you must admit that you were rather violent. I may be making too much of it all, but you must remember, Buchanan, that there is so little to make anything of on Kaitai. I have lived here continuously for very near a generation, and I have learned to make the most of our mild excitements." He chuckled, grotesquely.

Buchanan breathed deeply. "How do you know that Goulburn's real name was Smith? You must have overheard us talking here."

"As a matter of fact, I did. I saw your lights up, and I thought I'd pop over for a whisky with you before I went to bed. But when I got on to your verandah, I saw Smith, through the window. We had had a tiff earlier in the day—about Shelley—so I didn't come in."

"You stayed and listened instead!"

"Oh, only for a minute or two. It ought to be a warning to you. Anyone, any of the boys, might have overheard your conversation. I naturally inferred that you were drunk, especially when I saw Smith reaching for the bottle."

"What exactly did you overhear?"

"Something about the pitch deposits or whatever they are. I've known of them for years, of course. And then you told Smith who he was and he appeared to agree. He didn't seem to be a person of any interest or consequence, so I went back to my bungalow again."

"You know, Swan, the incredible thing to me is that no one has ever wrung your neck."

"Your father felt much the same in his time. By the way, I suppose Smith or Goulburn—Smith is really more convenient, don't you think?—was drowned accidentally."

"Meaning exactly?"

"Well, the boys say that the plug was out of his dinghy."

"That is perfectly true."

"Then how? And why?"

"Swan, you have been on Kaitai for nearly thirty years, is it? And for a considerable amount of that time, you have made a nuisance of yourself. I am responsible for whatever inquiries need to be made, and I shall make them. And, for this once, you will kindly leave matters to me, and restrain your curiosity and your tongue. Is that plain enough?"

"You make yourself clear. I have still my own inclinations to consult, of course."

Buchanan stood up and walked across to his desk. He took his keys from his pocket and unlocked a drawer. From it he lifted a small steel box. He unlocked this, and he took out a folder of papers.

"Do you ever consider, Swan, that you live here rather on sufferance?"

"What do you mean, on sufferance?"

But it was evident in his face that he knew what Buchanan meant.

"How much did you tell Smith about yourself?"

"What I have said to the others. The story grows familiar by long habit. I find that I even use the same phrases, the same sentences. And always with the same restraint." He sighed. "I used to embroider a little. Now my fancy fails me I am becoming an old man, Buchanan."

Buchanan laughed. "The great merit of your story is that it's so highly improbable."

"I do not even believe it myself any more. I have always lived on Kaitai. Europe, England, London, they are all things I have read about. Or perhaps I visited them in a pre-existence. I keep in touch. You must admit that I take an intelligent interest in their affairs. But they have no significance for me. I do not really believe that they exist. There is nothing but Kaitai, the sea, the sky, and the successive generations of the Buchanan family. Which bores me more and more as it proceeds."

"Have you ever developed any twinges of conscience whatsoever?"

"None at all. I have sometimes had my regrets. On the other hand, I have lived at my ease, my unfortunate wife was handsome, possibly, in her widow's bonnet, and I am sometimes mentioned by elderly gentlemen in their memoirs. The simple fact of the matter is, my good Buchanan, that I could not possibly have gone on living with my wife. Not to mention my daughters. They were so fearfully like their mother. And that house at Brighton! God help us, Buchanan, every chimney in the house smoked. By the end of the winter, we resembled a family of salmon. And my wife used to wear three flannel petticoats."

"Your wife is dead a good many years now?"

"She has gone to her reward, whatever that may have been, nine years in February. The notice was in *The Times*. She approached the Lord, I have no doubt, with a great deal of unction. If He chanced to have forgotten, she certainly reminded him of her good deeds. All of them. I doubt whether any man was ever more happily drowned than I was, Buchanan. Do you realize that I have not written a single book-review in thirty years?"

"That has always seemed odd to me, rather. After all, writing was your job. Haven't you missed it?"

"As an ex-convict might sometimes feel a faint nostalgia for his prison-cell. Here I have all the advantages of being able to conceive books without any of the trouble of writing them down. I can assure you, Buchanan, that the world has lost some very remarkable literature by my early departure. On the other hand, I have been saved from an intolerable labors, from smoky chimneys and from flannel petticoats. Brighton! With every respect in the world, blast Brighton! The air is better in Kaitai. Though I sometimes miss the Royal Pavilion."

"It's extraordinary that you ever got away with it."

"But why? I left no debts behind me, my wife was something better than resigned to widowhood, the authors I had reviewed were only too happy to attend my memorial service. I had made provision for my family, I had slowly hoarded a sufficient capital in Bank of England notes to buy me a tiny income when I reached the East. All I had to do then was to take a holiday in Cornwall, to change my clothes in a secluded cove, to leave my old suit and go off in my new, to take passage in a Breton smack to St. Malo. I imagine that other men have done as much in their time, though I doubt whether any has done it with such good heart."

"Yes, I suppose the facts are rather less exciting than your public hints."

"But I did publish a book of verse in my youth. It was absolutely essential in those days, if one was to get on. And it was no worse than most other verse. I have found items in several anthologies."

"What has always puzzled me is the breaking of the spring, the spring of your will and ambition. Smoky chimneys did not do that, Swan."

"No, but flannel petticoats did. And everything that goes with them. You must remember that I was not an ingenuous youth. I was a man already approaching middle-age. All his life my father had been a literary hack. He had some reputation in his time, and he made a living, and even left some money behind him. And I was bred to his trade. I learned a little wisdom from it. I learned how much reputation really is worth, how it is made, what is its cost. I have never been able to make up my mind whether there is a future life or not, but I am quite convinced that there is nothing in this life worth a man's sweat."

Buchanan raised his brows.

"My dear boy, what would it all have come to? Every Saturday morning, by post, a half-dozen books to review. Every Wednesday, by post, the reviews to go in. Colds in the winter, visits from my wife's relatives in the summer. Literary luncheons at intervals. A chair in a stodgy club. Chess at the end, perhaps draughts or dominoes in the last dotage. There were only two things to say for the old England, beef and beer. And I never liked either. And I believe that one can't get even beef and beer nowadays. So far from the spring of my will and my ambition breaking, it appears to have operated with singular success. It shot me right out of an utterly tedious environment, from a flannel-petticoat world into a delightful island which is, to say the least, charmingly unpetticoated. And didn't your great-uncle Buchanan do much the same thing?"

"I don't think he was looking for an unpetticoated world."

"The Scots have always shown remarkable ingenuity in disguising their more generous motives, even from themselves. Consider their metaphysicians."

"I doubt," said Buchanan, "whether there is a more shamelessly cynical old man in the universe. And it is past the time, too, that you should make your soul."

"I have yet another version which I shall offer at the Judgment," said Nicholas.

Buchanan walked across to the open doorway. "And you really believe that there is nothing in this world worth a man's sweat?"

"The only thing which can make this life worth anything is another life. A man grubs in Liverpool or Cardiff, he gives his days in doing this or that or the other thing. Perhaps he makes money, perhaps he makes a lot of money, though very few men do. And then they stick him in a box and forget him. What has been the point of it all?"

"Work has a value in itself?"

"What value? When work was a moral discipline, maybe. But what value is there in adding up columns of another man's profits and losses? Moral disciplines are decidedly out of fashion. What remains to justify work? Getting the bare necessities of life, if we want to live. That's good. But beyond that? We work for money and for what money can buy. But what can money buy? Well, look at what it does buy. At the end of your time, your few brief silly years, what else can you think of yourself but that you have been a fool? Assuming that you can still think anything."

"Oh, I agree, in part," said Buchanan.

"Most of the poor devils have to work like dogs in a treadmill to earn their lean bone. But if one has one's bone, why not lie i' the sun? Unless, of course, we assume a God with other plans for us. In any case, He would probably prefer us to lie in the sun than to get up to all the nasty little tricks we do get up to. Like your friend Smith's, for instance. God must surely prefer me to Smith. I, at least, resigned from the racket. Smith is better dead, Buchanan, better dead."

"You are very familiar with God, obviously. But does that

allow you to assume His prerogatives? And what did He think when you ditched your wife and children?"

Swan suddenly shot his legs out from under him. "There are not many millionaires of sixty-seven who could do that trick," he said. "George, Smith is much better dead. What I have been saying has straightened my ideas about Smith. Smith promised to be a nuisance, a pestilential nuisance, to a perfectly satisfactory island and its islanders. Asphalt! What do they want with asphalt, except to make more and more miles of suburban roads? I'm very glad you took a firm line with Smith, even if you did have to pull the plug out of his boat. And now I want something to eat. I only had a pineapple for breakfast."

"Smith may be a menace dead as well as alive," said Buchanan. "If you were eavesdropping last night, you probably gathered that there were other people besides Smith interested in his excursion to Kaitai. The less said about that plug the better, Nicholas."

"Oh, I shan't give you away. I was a little over-excited this morning. Reading all these detective stories puts ideas into one's head."

"Well, you're to behave yourself. I can't have the whole island upset. And I shall have to handle the affair gingerly with the Consul at Durabaya."

"That would be Pilks. I met him a couple of years ago when I went over for a day or two in the cutter. You remember. He does physical exercises every morning on his front lawn." Mr. Swan touched his own toes with the greatest of ease. "He is determined that the tropics will not get him down."

"Yes, I know, and that is the point about Mr. Pilks. He

may easily be inspired to action, if he thinks that action is demanded."

"It's a great pity that it isn't old Kolitis, with his plump Malayan girls. Buchanan, one of these days you might burn that photograph of me which you have in your little tin box. Heaven knows how your father ever found it. And I really don't see why he needed to tell you about it."

"You provoked my father's curiosity overmuch. I suppose he made discreet inquiries. And it was very sensible of him to tell me. He knew your capacities for . . . tricks."

"Well, now that my wife is safely dead and my daughters settled in life, so to speak, I hope that you'll let my flannel-petticoated past be buried in my grave. Though I'm sometimes tempted to leave an autobiography behind me."

There was a knock at the door. Mitchell came in.

"Oh, you're here," he said.

"My good Mitchell, doesn't even the wind of death improve your manners?" Swan started for the verandah. "Have you spoken to Bernard, George? He seemed rather distressed when I met him." The little man skipped down the steps and was gone.

"I came across to see if you wanted anything done," said Mitchell. "There are these chits to sign, anyway. Copra's down again. I've just been listening to the market-reports."

"It always is. Mitchell, what about the transmitting set? Is it working?"

"If I start up the engine, it is."

"I suppose we ought to send out a message to Durabaya."

"It'll look rather odd if you don't," said Mitchell. "Any reasons against?"

"No. No, except that one doesn't want any . . . well, officiousness from Pilks."

"Well, you can always say that he was accidentally drowned, can't you?"

"What else should I say?"

Mitchell shrugged his shoulders.

"Don't you think he was accidentally drowned?"

"Dinghies have been known to capsize," said Mitchell. "And plugs do come out. It's your business, not mine."

Buchanan looked at him, and Mitchell shrugged his shoulders again. He was a heavy man, in his middle forties, with a somewhat sullen, boyish face: on the whole, a competent man of business, who looked to Kaitai's trade and kept its books and managed its stores. Actually, as Buchanan sometimes remembered, he did an astonishing amount of work.

"Why did you take this job here, Mitchell?" he asked.

Mitchell stared. And then he laughed. He very seldom laughed.

"I've been here for a fair while," he said. "Has it just occurred to you to ask me that?"

"No, it hasn't. But I don't pester people for motives which are almost certainly unusual. Unless there is occasion."

"And when there is occasion, you always have Thompson."

"Thompson came here because he wanted to come here."

"But he has useful connections. He can always put a private inquiry through for you to his old friends at the Yard, can't he?"

"Thompson is here because my treaty with the British Government provides for some office of police. Someone had to have the job. Thompson heard from the Home Office that it was going, and asked for it. His favorite reading was De Vere Stacpoole. And, confound it, Mitchell, there may be times when I need to know something about the debris washed on to these shores."

"Do I take that to myself?"

It occurred suddenly to Buchanan that Mitchell was in an ugly temper. The heavy brows lowered a little more than usual. There was an edge to his voice.

"No, don't be an ass."

"Well, what actually do you know about me?" said Mitchell.

And, as Buchanan thought of it, he realized that in fact he knew very little.

He had met Mitchell one night years ago in the British Club at Durabaya. It had been rather a violent occasion: rubber was up, it was the King's Birthday, Forbes had just taken a wife, and old McMurty had fallen over a precipice and left a thousand pounds to the local Jockey Club. Everyone was there. Someone had even brought along Kolitis. And Mitchell had been introduced as Mitchell of Sydney.

He had been in Durabaya only a few days, he told Buchanan. He was on a health trip, he said, though he hardly looked as if he needed to search for health. His white mess-jacket had been a trifle soiled, Buchanan remembered, and his black bow had been rather excessive. Odd that one noticed these silly things, but one did. Appearances count for so much in the tropics. They represent face, and one must preserve one's face. At least, all the people in these little scattered communities, these tiny European islands in a sea of black and brown and yellow, think so. Kaitai was the only one of the lot where a man could be at ease, where this sharp insistence on European superiority did not constantly prod you. Here, of course, there was no fear of the natives.

Mitchell had drunk a great deal, but he had not got drunk. He did not dance. Buchanan had thought him shy of the women. But he had played bridge and won a few pounds. He had said very little.

Next morning, Buchanan had run into him after breakfast. Mitchell was staying out at the Bristol, but they had met in the bank. And Mitchell had asked him up to lunch.

They had not had a great deal to say to one another. Mitchell was not a talkative man, and they lacked a common acquaintance. They talked chiefly about Kaitai and its items of trade. And Buchanan had the impression that this was the price of his lunch.

"How actually do you manage?" said Mitchell. "I've heard that you used to have a fellow on the island to look after your affairs, but that he'd left."

"We used to have what my father liked to call a factor. But the last man went home to Dundee a year ago, and I haven't found anyone else for the job yet."

"It's a pretty isolated spot, I reckon," said Mitchell.

"Yes, that's the problem, of course. Young men nowadays like to join one of the large firms which will move them about a bit and give them home-leave every three years and that sort of thing. Life on Kaitai is not particularly lively, especially if you are twenty-five."

"I'm forty-six," Mitchell had said, unexpectedly. "And I'm sick of cities, sick of crowds, and dirt, and politics and street-cars and men on the make and women on the make and all this damned sediment of civilization."

Buchanan had laughed. "Are you offering for the job?"

Mitchell had looked over his tankard of Dutch lager. "Why not? It'd do me as well as anything. I'm a good accountant, and I've had some experience, in Sydney, of the islands trade. How many people a year come to Kaitai? White people, I mean."

"One or two, perhaps. Now and again, a stray trader or copra agent or something of the sort." Buchanan had sat back in his chair. "Are you seriously proposing yourself, Mitchell?"

"I'm looking for a job. I won't starve if I don't get one, but I don't want to loaf about. And I'm not going back to Sydney."

"Why not? It is almost the one city in the world where I could care to live. Excepting Buda and Oxford and Paris, perhaps, and one hears pleasant things of Rio."

"The climate doesn't agree with me," said Mitchell; but it was not the climate he meant.

A woman, probably, Buchanan thought. There had been a sting just now when he spoke of women on the make. He looked like a man who might expect a lot of one woman, and sour if she failed him.

"I haven't got my accountancy certificates with me," said Mitchell. "I came away in a hurry, not knowing or caring much where I went or what I did. I'd been ill, as I think I told you last night."

That was a lie, Buchanan thought, but everyone is entitled to his own legend, within reasonable limits.

On Kaitai, his father had always accepted a man's story, unless there were evident reasons for probing further. Buchanan the First had had his legend. It had established a sound tradition. So Buchanan the Third nodded now.

"You can come across with me and try Kaitai for a few weeks, if you like. On probation."

And Mitchell had come.

"What do you actually know about me?" Mitchell repeated.

"That you're a good factor. You've managed our affairs very well. I shall probably budget for a surplus next year, if I can only keep Dr. Marjorie Pratt off the island."

"You always have this pose," said Mitchell, and his voice was very near to sneering, "of taking people as they come. As they say they come. But I don't believe that you are as indifferent as you pretend."

"My dear chap, I have the normal weaknesses of human flesh. Curiosity, amongst them. But I reduce it to a proper order. Anyhow, none of you is as interesting as you sometimes seem to think you are. I suppose, if I spent enough money and took enough trouble, I could uncover all your pasts, but to be horridly frank, it has never seemed to me worthwhile."

"I wonder!" said Mitchell.

"Nowadays, what with the newspapers and with that police mentality which infects us all, no one believes that there can be any secrets but dishonorable secrets. I refuse to accept that. We hide what is best as well as what is worst in us. Though we may open the best to the god."

Mitchell grunted. "Maybe, but what you are thinking and what I am thinking hasn't much to do with religion, I guess. Why was Goulburn bumped off? That's the question which is itching me. You, too. Unless you know already."

"Are you challenging me to investigate your past?"

Mitchell grunted again.

"The implication being that if I investigate you, I shall have to investigate everyone else." Buchanan leaned forward suddenly. "Mitchell, what do you know?"

Mitchell stood up. "A murder when I see one."

"Really!" said Buchanan. At the moment he could think of nothing else to say, which surprised him rather. But presently he added, "After all, a murder has something to do with religion, you know. The gods don't customarily approve of murder. Not the best gods."

"And the king is the voice and the arm of the god," said Mitchell. "It's up to you, Buchanan."

"Are you promoted to be Keeper of my Conscience?"

Mitchell grinned, and that was surprising too.

"I'm not prompting you. I'm merely stating a fact."

Yet why was he stating it? Did he protest too much? Shakespeare had been a remarkably shrewd observer of the human thing. He was always providing the apt reference.

Now that one thought of it, Mitchell's reference to Thompson and the Yard had been decidedly pointed. Was it meant to prick him into action?

"It's your affair, not mine," continued Mitchell. "You can leave the thing alone, if you want to, I suppose. But it won't make the island pleasant to live on."

"In what sense?"

"Everyone of us is looking cross-eyed at the others already. You won't bottle this up without risk of an explosion, Buchanan. We live too close together."

That was true enough, Buchanan already knew. In a small community, law must strike quickly and shrewdly. The more closely people are knit, the swifter a mood spreads. Hence, the essential discipline of ships, of expeditions, of tribes. Obviously, he must take a strong line. If it was to be death by accident, then he must insist from this moment on death by accident. And suppress any other version.

"Everyone knows it was murder," said Mitchell. "Dr. Murray's boy, Naqa, has just come down to the village. By now the village knows what you said to Dr. Murray and what she said to you, with dramatic additions by Naqa."

"Damn!" said the Sultan. "After all my years of Kaitai, I should remember that these people have extensile ears. And a knack of fading into the scenery."

He regarded Mitchell thoughtfully. If the news had only reached the village with Naqa, then Mitchell had acted on it and come here with remarkable dispatch. Had he been so eager to make his impression?

"You're beginning to see the point?" said Mitchell.

Buchanan laughed. "I'm beginning to think that you may be a suspicious character, after all, Mitchell. You shouldn't put notions into my head. I get along without them very well, in the ordinary way. Heaven knows, once you start it, where a notion will run."

And Mitchell looked oddly disconcerted.

7

ASSEMBLY OF THE PEOPLE

ALICIA came again out from the death-house. The sunlight was strangely yellow and the trees were strangely green to her tired eyes: the sky and the woods were like a heavy curtain.

Miss Roper sat in a chair on the verandah. She had dropped her painting things, her shooting-stick, and her basket beside her. She usually carried her lunch in the basket, and roots of flowers and ferns which she transplanted from the hills to the plot beside her bungalow. She and Bernard often hunted together for new specimens.

"Naqa told me you were working," she said, "in there. I thought I would wait."

Alicia sat down opposite her. She brushed back her hair with a tired gesture, and her fingers stretched the muscles of her eyelids.

"I'm going to have a drink," she said. "Will you have one, Dorothy?"

Miss Roper nodded.

"Whisky?"

"No, a lime, if I may."

Alicia leaned back in her chair. "Naqa," she called.

There was no response.

"I'm afraid he has gone down to the village," said Miss Roper. "At least, that is where he appeared to be going when I met him."

Alicia rose and went into the bungalow herself. Presently, she returned, with decanter and glasses and biscuits, ice and lime.

"A biscuit will probably make me sick," she said, "but I shall conscientiously eat one. Have you been out painting?"

"Yes. I went up to the mountain before dawn. I'm determined to get the color right. Some color right. I thought the solid, dark mass of blue against the flat olive-green, just before the sun strikes, might be manageable." She held up a sketch. "It's worse than the others."

Alicia thought to herself that it was much worse than the others. "You hurried it," she said.

"The light changes so quickly." Miss Roper flushed a little. "Still, all these studies are useful in their way."

Alicia nodded. It was not easy to be interested in Miss Roper's studies at the moment. "Don't overtire yourself," she said.

"Do I look tired?"

"Yes, you do rather." Miss Roper's skin was pinched and the rims of her eyes were red. "One sometimes forgets, when one is working, how strong the glare off the sea is. You should bathe your eyes after you have been painting for a long time, or you will get what the Australians call sandy blight." Alicia stirred the ice in her glass.

"You look tired yourself, my dear. You shouldn't have been asked to do . . . well, what you have been doing."

"It's my job. You know about it, then."

"Yes. Nicholas came to me up on the mountain. And I met Naqa as I came down. Alicia, was the man murdered?"

"What makes you ask that?" Alicia had paused an instant before she spoke, steadied herself.

"Naqa says that he was murdered. That is why Naqa was off in such a fever to the village. He apparently overheard you talking."

Alicia's mouth tightened a little. Then she laughed. "What's the use? Of being angry, I mean. These people are children." Her mouth tightened again. "But Nicholas isn't a child. Why did he hurry to tell you?"

"Because he is a child too, in the sense that he's a moral irresponsible. If children are morally irresponsible. All these years of comparative solitude have exaggerated the natural irresponsibility of Nicholas' character. He was as excited as a child, certainly. He had a piece of exciting news to tell. He was bursting with self-importance. He's a horrible little man, and yet grotesquely human in many ways."

"Like a gargoyle," said Alicia. "Like an animated gargoyle."

"He was so obviously eager to shock and startle me that I just set my teeth and went on painting," said Miss Roper. "Now I suppose that he will tell everyone that I was callous and indifferent. Actually, I am shocked and startled. This is a terrible thing, Alicia." She jerked at her hat. "But I was not going to indulge Nicholas's morbid sensations."

"I know," said Alicia. "Have you finished your drink, Dorothy? I must go down to George Buchanan."

She carried the tray indoors, and she found her topee. Then she came out, locking the bungalow behind her.

She crossed the compound and locked the doors of the hospital and the mortuary.

"I don't know what I shall do about Naqa and Ptai. They have both taken leave. And now I come to think of it, I haven't seen Herbert all day. They've all gone bounding off, I suppose, to discuss the affair with their friends."

"From every possible angle. They will rehearse his appearance, his qualities, his virtues, his vices, each single circumstance they can remember and all they can invent. Have you ever been to an Irish wake?"

"No. But I'd much prefer it to our habit of furtively shuffling off the dead." Her mind went back to George and to her talk with him. All the great philosophies of life, she thought, sprang from the contemplation of death. Life did not explain itself. She remembered D.B. Wyndham Lewis: "Madame Life, Lady Life, the well known strumpet and purveyor of pleasure to the nobility, gentry, and middle classes."

They walked down through the green scrub.

"I shall never succeed in painting it," said Miss Roper. "The colors are absurd. As soon as one puts them on, the effect is utterly unreal. A European, even though he sees this every day, cannot really believe in it on canvas."

They came down into the village, and walked on together to Buchanan's house. Alicia noticed Ptai and Naqa sitting in a chattering group near the stables. And there was a European assembly in George's lounge. Mitchell was there, slumped in a corner, with a drink at his hand. Hawkesbury was standing, with considerable effect, his hands clasped behind him and his hindquarters spread to what would have been a comforting heat if there had been a fire in the fireplace. Swan was cutting photographs out of an illustrated magazine. Thompson was playing patience on the long table. George came through from his study as the two women entered.

Only Bernard and Cooper were wanting to complete the group.

"How is Mr. Cooper?" asked Alicia.

"Taken to his bed," said Hawkesbury. "Says he's got a fever."

"One doesn't get fever on Kaitai," said Swan, bristling for argument.

No one challenged him. They were all watching Alicia. They all knew why she had come.

She crossed the room towards George's study. He opened the door for her and followed her in. Then he closed it, firmly.

"Well?" he said.

She nodded.

"I see. I suppose I haven't really had any doubts. But there was always the chance . . ." He sat down, and again he looked as he had looked this morning on the beach, an old man.

Alicia touched his hand. He took hers, and grinned crookedly.

"And now we're for it. I only wish I had the guts of old Buchanan the First." He squeezed her fingers and dropped them. "What about it, Alicia? Was he dead before he went into the water?"

She nodded again. "Yes. He died from the blow at the back of his skull."

Buchanan reached for his cigarettes and offered her one.

"I see. Do you mind if we have Thompson in?"

"You're going ahead then, George?"

"We have got to go through with it." He lit her cigarette and his own. "Mitchell sent out a radio to Durabaya this afternoon. You'd better prepare a written report, in full parade order."

She unbuttoned the pocket of her tunic. "Here it is."

He took it, and went to the door. "Thompson," he called.

Thompson came in.

Buchanan opened the folded sheets. "Tell him, Alicia."

Alicia turned to the ex-policeman. "Smith was dead before he went into the water, Mr. Thompson. He died from that blow on the head."

"Yes," said Thompson, and then after a moment, "Yes." He began to fill his pipe. "Lungs, of course. It must have been a heavy blow, doctor."

"It was a heavy blow and he had a thin skull."

"What d'you think it was done with?"

"I thought it might have been a rowlock from the dinghy."

He looked over the bowl of his pipe at her, and his eyes were shrewd. "That shape, wasn't it?"

"More or less. It suggested that."

"Did you measure the wound?" He turned, and clucked. Nicholas Swan had opened the door.

"Can't we all sit in on this?" he said. "Or must we wait for the special editions? Or for Mr. Thompson's memoirs."

The Sultan looked at Thompson. "Let 'em in, sir. We can always turn them out again, if we want to."

"You don't know Nicholas as well as I do." The Sultan sighed. "They had better all know the facts, now, and then perhaps there will be less temptation to invent. And if we are going into session, it may as well be in the other room, where there are enough chairs."

He walked out, and to the head of the table. He squashed his cigarette in a tray, and looked round.

"Goulburn was murdered," he said. "Dr. Murray has just completed a post-mortem. Someone on the island, perhaps a native, and if not a native one of us, is a murderer. I think you have all guessed as much. You have had time to consider the implications. And I want the assistance of every honest man and woman amongst you. Kaitai has given you a home. It has dealt with you in kindly fashion. Now it needs your loyalty. I expect each of you to answer freely and honestly any question it may be necessary to put to you. And I ask each of you to refrain from unnecessary conjecture and talk amongst yourselves, especially in the presence of the natives. Dr. Murray will tell you why she believes that this man was murdered."

Alicia told them.

"There are other circumstances," said Buchanan. "As you must all know, the dinghy foundered. Its bilge-plug had been removed. Goulburn was put into the dinghy after he had been struck, the sail was hoisted, the dinghy was shoved off the sand, the strong land-breeze carried it to sea, perhaps for a hundred yards before it foundered. Obviously, the murderer hoped that the body would be washed out and never recovered: or, if it was, that we would assume an accidental death by drowning."

"I wish the body had been washed away," said Miss Roper violently.

"It seems to me," said Swan, "that the murderer could have taken the boat out and then pulled up the plug and let her settle. He could have swum ashore himself." He stared about him. "Most of us here can swim."

"The boom was lashed," said Thompson.

Buchanan looked at him sharply. "Are you sure of that?"

"The boys who brought the dinghy in said that they had to cut the lashing free before they could get her upright," said Thompson.

Buchanan felt for another cigarette. So Thompson had been doing a little detective work on his own. And, characteristically, had said nothing until Buchanan had made his own decision clear. Thompson, of course, must have believed it murder from the beginning, but he had guarded his tongue. There was a good deal to say for the habit of discipline.

"There was the missing plug," said Buchanan, "and there were the sandshoes. They were on the wrong feet. Mr. Thompson noticed that, and I think he thought then what I think now: that it was the murderer who put them on Goulburn's feet. Probably Goulburn had taken them off to cross the soft sands."

"I think that the murderer had first put them on his own feet," said Thompson. "He carried the body down to the dinghy, and he stepped into the dead man's shoes to do it."

"Why?" said Hawkesbury.

"So that, if he left a track, we might think it was only the dead man's track."

"In a sense it was," said Mitchell from his corner.

"'This was the way that she went,'" quoted Nicholas.

Thompson spoke directly to Buchanan. "There was one footprint, more or less recognizable, just in that strip between last night's high and this morning's high, sir. It had been pressed fairly heavily, almost as heavily as my own leather shoe with my weight on top could press. And the heel was digging in. I think that someone was dragging a weight to the beach."

"I see," said Buchanan. "I see."

They could all see, thought Alicia, see a dead man being dragged like a sack down across the sands. But perhaps there was one there who could see more clearly than the rest.

"When I found that, sir," said Thompson, "I looked about more closely. And there is a sort of smear across the sands. It crosses those crab tracks you noticed. As soon as you get down to the hard sands, you lose it, of course. The sea has been over. But I've no doubt at all in my own mind that the killing was done above high-water level and the body dragged down to the beach."

Buchanan at last found his cigarette case, and his matches. "This afternoon, we reported the death to Durabaya, by radio. Unless we establish the truth, I must permit, I am afraid, an investigation from the outside world." He let it sink in. "And none of us, I believe, will welcome that."

No, none of them, thought Alicia, would welcome that.

"And so I ask each of you to help me. If it is necessary to ask you questions which are difficult to answer, I hope that you will still answer faithfully. You all know—" he smiled a little—"that I am not given to excessive curiosity. But murder makes a new situation. We are no longer, on Kaitai, our own masters. You can estimate the possible effects if this story goes out to the world's newspapers."

Swan cackled. "So we're to know the truth about one another at last. It will all be very dull, I suppose. Buchanan, is this really necessary? Confound it, man, why disturb our pleasant arrangements for the sake of a fellow like that? I am perfectly willing to assume that the murderer had a reasonable and sufficient motive, if only he will give us some assurance that the performance is not to be repeated."

"That," said Mitchell, "is a point. I've no particular grudge against the fellow, whoever he is, but how can we be sure that the performance will not be repeated?"

"It's the sort of thing that grows on you," said Hawkesbury. "I remember a bloke in the Yukon . . ." But Hawkesbury did not remember a bloke in the Yukon. He broke off, biting his lip. He was very pale, and it occurred to Alicia that Captain Hawkesbury was far from his ease.

"Please!" said Buchanan. "There is only one way out of this affair, for your sakes, for mine, and above all for the sake of Kaitai and its people. And they, I hope, have come to mean something to you."

"Who was this man Goulburn really?" said Miss Roper suddenly. "He was not Goulburn, the writer, was he?"

"No," said Buchanan. "He was a man named Smith."

"What was he after?" said Hawkesbury in a low voice.

"The asphalt deposits," said Nicholas and cackled again. "He was trying to persuade our Buchanan to turn millionaire."

Alicia, looking at the darkening window, was suddenly aware of Bernard, standing outside. She stared at him through the glass, and he seemed to stare back at her.

"What've you done about the lugger?" asked Hawkesbury. "Just left the heathen Chinee in charge?"

Thompson again spoke directly to Buchanan. "I sent one of my own boys off with your lad Rata, sir. Thought it just as well to have a pair of them on board. You never know with Chinks."

"That's right," said Hawkesbury. "I remember once . . ." and again he broke off, before Swan had interrupted him:

"Give your imagination a rest, Hawkesbury!" He sat up in his chair and kicked his heels. "Well, where does the investigation start? With the last person known to have seen the victim alive. You, Buchanan." He turned to Miss Roper. "Did you hear them going down to the beach together, last night?"

"No," said Miss Roper. "I suppose I was asleep."

Bernard came through the door.

"I've been eavesdropping," he said, "at the window."

So he knew that she had seen him, thought Alicia. How characteristic it was of Bernard to stand there, outside their circle, outside the light, listening. Perhaps, if he had not seen her look at him, he would have slipped off again into the dusk. Yet, was it characteristic of Bernard to eavesdrop? No, but it was not as if he had been really eavesdropping. He had been listening without joining in the talk. That was characteristic, that was what she had meant. Bernard always listened. And always, she realized, one strove to think the best of him. There was something in his thin, long, sensitive, tired face which made one want, always, to think the best of him. One knew that he was a man who had suffered abominable things, things abominable to him, however they would seem to other people. He was a man, as George once said, who had built himself a defense against the world. He raised his reserve like a shield. He retreated, not because he was a coward but because he could not tolerate the harshness of our casual lives.

It was curious, too, that she always sought to explain him like this. Sometimes, when he was gone, she laughed at herself. This was sheer sentimentalism. Yet, surely, no man was less an idle beachcomber than Bernard. It was he who had first suggested to her the word refugee. He was a refugee.

"Well, you've heard it all, I hope," said Buchanan wearily.

"I'd like to hear more," Bernard said, "about the asphalt deposits."

2.

It was dark when they came out.

Alicia, Bernard, Thompson, and Buchanan stood for a minute at the top of the steps.

"I went off to the lugger myself today," Thompson said. "I thought I'd like to have another look at that pair."

"What did you get out of them?" said Buchanan.

"Nothing. But I gave them hell." Thompson grunted heavily.

"And you found," said Bernard, "that a touch of hell produces quite another response in a Chinese than the one you expected?" There was always that slightly bitter note in Bernard's words.

"He just closed up like a clam. But I don't think he'll up anchor and off now."

"Did you expect him to up anchor and off?" asked Bernard.

"You never know. Always an inclination to lam it when you're on a hot spot." Thompson had underlined the sentence. There was something of a temperamental conflict between these two, Alicia remembered. She had noticed it before when they met. Bernard's ironies galled the old policeman. And Thompson's blunt assumptions probably represented just that attitude which, in larger manifestations, had driven Bernard back from the world into his own soul.

"Better not bully them excessively, Thompson," said Buchanan. "The Chinese will be making complaints at Durabaya."

Thompson grunted heavily and went down the steps. And then he stumbled and swore furiously. "Blast the thing!" They heard him kick at something.

"Oh lord!" said Buchanan. "The saddle. Sorry, Thompson. If I've told those boys once, I've told them at least three times to put it away."

He picked up the saddle, the stirrups hanging from it, and hung it across the verandah railing.

"Did you hurt yourself?"

"No. But . . . well, if you ask me, a little bullying wouldn't do a lot of harm round here."

"Oh, I agree. Discipline's shocking. I must get out my skiing boots and go about kicking a few people." He smacked Thompson on the back. "You can help. Alicia, what are you doing now? Going home? Would you rather stay down here tonight? I have shooed your boys back to their duty, by the way."

Alicia laughed. "No, I shall be all right. But I'll look in on little Cooper before I go up. Perhaps he really has fever."

"I'm going across myself. Then I'll walk you home."

"I shall wait for Dr. Murray, if you wish," said Bernard.

"Yes, don't you bother, George. Bernard can drop me *en route*. Let's go and see Cooper."

The four strolled across to the row of bungalows.

Cooper was in bed, his chin muffled in blankets. He looked at them with watery eyes.

"Hawkesbury says you aren't fit," said Buchanan. "Apparently he was right for once."

"Have you a temperature, Mr. Cooper?" asked Alicia.

"No, no, I don't think so." For an instant she thought that he was going to dive completely beneath the clothes.

"Let me see?" She opened the little pocket-case she always carried and shook a thermometer.

"Oh, no, really I assure you, I am not ill, not really ill. This horrible business this morning distressed me a good deal." He blushed. "As a . . . a matter of fact, it made me violently sick. But I feel much better now, much better."

"Put this under your armpit," said Alicia, giving him the thermometer.

"Oh, really, I had no intention of putting you to any trouble, any trouble at all. It was foolish of Hawkesbury even to have mentioned it . . ." An arm in red and blue pyjamas wriggled out of the clothes, took the thermometer, and disappeared again. Mr. Cooper was a very modest man. Alicia wondered how she would manage him if he were ever taken seriously ill. One hand was clutching at the bedclothes now, as if he half suspected that she might snatch them from him and expose him in his pyjamas.

"I'd feel your pulse," she said, "if you'd let me have your wrist."

"Oh, this is too bad of Hawkesbury, too bad! I do assure you that I had no intention of troubling anybody, and that I am really quite well, quite well." A drop of perspiration formed on his forehead and trickled down to his nose. He burrowed and brushed it off on the blanket. Some people, of course, get into an immediate sweat at the sight of a doctor by their bedsides.

"That's time enough," said Alicia. "Let me see the thermometer."

It emerged from the barricades.

Alicia held it under the light. "You're quite normal," she said.

"Yes, yes, of course, I knew I was. Hawkesbury is a blundering fellow. Utterly absurd of him to send you over here, worrying about me. As a matter of fact, I thought of getting up presently. I've been lying in most of the day."

And yet, Alicia thought, he was not normal. He was given to these little spates of words, but he was usually collected and in command of himself. Now he was not. Smith's death had unnerved him.

"Were you very sick?" she said. "Would you like something to settle your stomach?"

"No, no, oh please! Please don't bother about me. I'm quite well, quite well, I assure you."

"All right then." Alicia smiled. "I shan't force my attentions on you. I shall go home now, I think, George."

"Yes, do, and for goodness' sake, get a decent night's rest." He opened the door. "Bernard is waiting there. I'll stay with Cooper for a few minutes. We'll have a drink."

"Good-night, then. Good-night, Mr. Cooper."

George stood in the doorway and watched her go. Then he turned back to Cooper.

"The whisky is on the sideboard in the dining-room. I should rather like a drink myself. And isn't that Thompson out there?"

Thompson came in.

"Think it's all right, sir, letting Dr. Murray go up there to sleep alone tonight?" he said softly.

Buchanan frowned. "I gave her the chance to stay down here. And I think I know when Alicia means what she says. And I've talked very earnestly to Ptai and Naqa. They'll be about, I trust. And you're only a couple of hundred yards or so away from the hospital, Thompson."

"I sleep heavy," said Thompson.

"Anyhow, why should she be more exposed to danger than anyone else? If there is danger. Why should there be? We lived in peace and safety until Smith came. I don't think the murderer has a grudge against anyone of us. And it will only put us all on edge if we start to take exceptional precautions. Alicia realized that."

Thompson nodded. Then he went to look for the whisky.

Buchanan told Cooper what had been told to the others. The little man did not say a word until he had finished and Thompson had come back with the whisky. Then he took it and gulped it down.

"What are you going to do?" he said and his voice was unexpectedly loud.

"I'm afraid we'll have to hold an inquisition," said Buchanan. "We can't conceal a murder, you know, and the consul chap at Durabaya is bound to insist that we make a proper inquiry."

Cooper's eyes, above the blanket, closed tightly. "Yes, of course," he said, and now his voice was hardly to be heard.

They sat and talked to Mr. Cooper for ten minutes longer. He hardly said a dozen words. Buchanan thought that he would be glad when they went. So presently, they went.

3.

Alicia and Bernard walked up the path together. The land breeze had only begun to stir and with it came the warm richness of the tropical woods along the lower slopes: a heavy sweetness, not cloying, but the breath of all that strong vegetable life, of sappy leaves and deep-honeyed flowers and aromatic barks.

"I had begun to think of Kaitai as my home," she said.

He did not answer for a moment. "As home? Home. How can the tropics seem home to one born to your soft, misty hills and the slow valleys of England? This, all this, is barbaric. It does not belong to our blood."

"Oh, I know all the crowded countries and cities of the East are foreign to us, but that is because the things of men there have grown in strange, different shapes. But in Kaitai, nature still shapes men, not men nature. Can't you smell those trees? In Ceylon, in China, in all the cities, one would smell men." She laughed. "I don't mean to be offensive. I mean, it is only in the really primitive places that one can sense the natural thing now. In England, nature has become a good bourgeois."

"It is an odd thought," he said, walking on beside her. "For my part, I do not much care. There is no place in the world to which I am more attached than to another. One can pass the years anywhere, and this earth is as good as that to make one's grave. I suppose there may be a certain patriotic argument for fertilizing one's native soil, but I have forgotten to what soil I am native. I shall bestow my nitrate on Kaitai. I hope."

"You sound rather like the man without a country," said Alicia, laughing, and conscious of an echo.

"I am the man without a country," he answered.

And in the warm breath of the land wind, Alicia suddenly shivered.

A man without a country is like a man dead, she thought. She had the swift, horrible fancy that she was walking with a man who was dead . . . dead long ago, in some other and distant place.

8

IN THE NIGHT

HE CAME to her verandah, but he would not come in.

"It is too late," he said, smiling. "We should be giving the native poets occasion for a long and probably very touching ballad. They have the fine flavor of romantic scandal in their nostrils. And how they sniff the wind."

But he stood on the step a while. Alicia felt that he wanted to say something more to her.

"Their love songs always seem to me remarkably lugubrious," she said. "And they have a nasty trick of continuity. I mean, they are not content to assume that all songs should end where happiness everafter begins. They pursue their inquiries further. Naqa was singing one here the other day, and it appeared to reckon four pigs ill lost for a shrewish wife. Their songs are really only cheerful at a funeral."

"You hear the drums then?" he said quickly.

And listening, she could hear the drums: a swift tattoo somewhere on the hills.

"They always drum and dance for death," he said. "And they dine handsomely too. Your boys will be off, Alicia, whatever Buchanan said to them. And they did not like the man Smith. They will speed him with an extra bowl."

"Isn't that a sign of merit?" She looked at the dark building across the compound. "You're right, I'm afraid. They have gone again." She came down the steps and walked across to the boys' quarters behind the hospital. She flashed her torch. The place was empty.

"It would be an awful bother to train other boys," she said, "but I'm half inclined to sack the pair of them."

"Any others would be just as faithful to their own inclinations," said Bernard behind her.

"Yes, I know, but it would be rather a nice feeling. They'd weep, of course. At the moment, I feel I could enjoy that, especially if they meant it. But they wouldn't mean it. It would merely be a gesture. Oh dear, really they are an annoying people."

Bernard laughed. "And subtle as the dove. You know, it is civilized people who are simple people. Native peoples are almost all subtle beyond our comprehension. They are—what is your phrase?—they are wheels within wheels."

"And they certainly grind slowly. George will really have to talk to them."

"They will like that. They all enjoy George a great deal. He tickles their sense of humor. There are more songs invented to honor George than ever there were for his ferocious great-uncle. Most of the poets can give a very good impersonation, too."

"Well, what does one do?"

"Resigns oneself to the conditions of existence on Kaitai. And, if it is at all possible, listens to the songs about George. There is one which describes him as the father of all Kaitai, with a good deal of physiological detail. And another, his descent from the gods, a very lively and impassioned descent indeed. The poet acquires considerable kudos by an illustration in mime of George stepping over the precipice of heaven."

They had walked back together to the verandah.

"I think I had really better go to bed?" said Alicia.

He paused, in the darkness. For the first time in all her knowledge of him, he seemed reluctant to leave.

"Alicia, when is the burial to take place?"

"Tomorrow morning. Didn't George tell you?"

"Tomorrow morning. Alicia, who was that man Smith?"

"I only know what we all know. You heard George, didn't you?"

"George said that he came to look for the asphalt deposits. I wonder. I wonder." He made a gesture which she felt rather than saw. "However, now, it is done. Will you be uneasy here alone, tonight?"

"I shall be all right." As she said the inane words, she turned her back to the mortuary and walked up the steps.

"You are nervous?"

"I am not."

"It is natural. Won't you go down again to the village? You could stay the night with Miss Roper."

"Oh, no, nonsense! I'm not afraid of a dead body lying . . . lying over there. It isn't the first time the mortuary has been tenanted, you know. And especially when . . ." She was going to make some reference to the post-mortem she had done, but she checked herself with a sudden horror. But why, why had she checked herself? Why had it suddenly seemed like that? She braced her shoulders. "I shall sleep perfectly well," she said. "Perfectly well. I'm hardened, you know."

"Are you?" he said.

She laughed: but her throat was dry. "Of course. You go along home yourself . . ."

"Alicia, go back to the village."

"No, once and for all, no!" She had not meant to be so emphatic. Resolutely, she swung round and stared at the dark shadow of the mortuary.

"Will you let me sleep here on your verandah?"

"No, no, you mustn't think of it." She knew that her voice was betraying her, but she could not wholly control it. "The dead do not walk, you know." She almost gritted her teeth. "One learns that in one's student days. The dead do not walk."

"Don't they?" he said softly. "I was dead. And I walk."

She laughed again, harshly. She wanted to ask him what he meant, but she dared not ask him what he meant. As they stood there together in the dark, he might tell her.

She flashed on her torch. The beam shone straight on the mortuary door. She had been holding the torch so. But the door was shut, locked. Of course it was locked.

"I am really going to bed," she said. "Good-night, Bernard."

"Good-night," he said.

She turned to her door. She did not know whether he had gone or not.

2.

She did not know what woke her: but she was awake suddenly, instantly, as one is when the nerves call an alarm. She turned sharply in bed and stared at the faint light of the window. There was, she knew, still an hour or more to dawn:

there was no lightening of the sky. And those are strange hours.

Far, in the hills, there was still the faint rhythm of drums. The natives would keep their watch all night, she knew. In the first night after death, the spirit is still bound to earth, it is still striving to grope its way back, back to the familiar things. It is struggling against all that draws it away. It is dangerous, on that first night. It rages. And sometimes it strikes.

It rages. How must the spirit of a murdered man resent his unnatural taking-off. All nature must cry out at murder. Naqa and Ptai had been wise to seek the fires and the dance and the songs tonight.

She swung out of bed. There was something. Something. A noise. Outside. And they strive to grope their way back to the familiar things. She could almost hear his voice: he had stood there at the door, and, "Hullo, lovely," he had said.

"Hullo, lovely," he had said, he, that grotesque thing into which she had cut this afternoon, cut and cut.

"Hullo, lovely."

She crept to the door of her room. There was no sound at all now. But presently, would she hear those slow, rolling steps on the verandah?

Her hand groped behind her for the torch. He would not face the light. He could not face light. That was why they kept the fires burning in the hills, why they knew, at dawn, that the danger was past. He could not come in the light.

She opened the door. She crossed the living-room. She turned the key in the lock. She threw open that door. She stood on the verandah. And she turned her torch on the white wall of the mortuary.

There had been a sound out here. She must know what was moving in the night.

The door of the mortuary was open.

She breathed deeply and steadily, counting her breaths. One, two, three, four. And her heart steadied.

She turned back, and she found her slippers. She put them on. She put on her dressing-gown. She went again to the door, to the verandah, and down the steps.

She knew that she was walking quickly, but each step seemed incredibly long, incredibly slow. And as she went on, she felt the darkness close behind her, close about her, a palpable thing, resisting her, through which she must force her way. Even the beam from her torch seemed strangely diffused, as if the air were thick, foggy. But there was no fog. Very far off, she could still hear the drums. Or was it the beating of blood in her ears?

Little Miss Muffet sat on a tuffet. . . . how utterly absurd! Yet how sensible of Miss Muffet. It was so much more comfortable to sit on a tuffet than to go across this dark yard in the night, to visit a corpse one had anatomized. She laughed . . . and to her horror she heard herself laughing. And something swooped in the darkness, with a scaly rustle of wings . . . a flying-fox, of course. They hung clustered amongst the trees all days, like rotting fruit, but at night they flew, evilly. They visited the dead too, it was said, and the natives loathed them. It was strange that all peoples loathed the bats. In the Middle Ages, they had given the wings and the shape of bats to Satan and his fallen angels, and one met the appalling tradition of the vampire in the most remote corners of the earth. What horrible racial memory was embodied in that?

She came to the first step. There was no sound in the mortuary. But the door stood open and it had been locked. The beam shone into a corner of the ante-room, where she kept her records. She must go through that room, and on, into the room beyond. Where Smith lay, beneath his rubber sheet.

With deliberate will, she stepped, one, two, three, on to the verandah. It creaked beneath her tread, and she stood, staring in at the half-opened door. A minute, perhaps two minutes, and there was no sound in the whole world. She could not hear the drums, the fronds of the dark trees were motionless. The warmth seemed to drain from her body, and she felt the cold run down through her arteries and veins and along the fibres of her nerves. And she stepped across the threshold, pushing the door wide.

No one was here. But that other door was closed.

Eight paces across the room. She seized the knob, flung the door open, and her light shone on the yellow sheet, and she knew that it was not as she had left it. And then, all the processes of her life seemed to stop, in one moment of incredible agony, as she swung . . . but it was too late. The world burst into flame, and then, darkness crashed in on her. . . .

3.

Naqa handed the tray to his second wife. "Take in the tea," he said, "and remember to draw the curtains first. And you will tell the doctor I am already very busy about our affairs, if she should ask. And if she should happen to mention that she missed me last night, express wonderment. Much wonderment. I was certainly sleeping between you and Elizabeth Marie Anne all night."

The girl, who was slim and young and very black and

newly promoted, nodded nervously. She crept across the kitchen.

"What is missing from the tray, fool?" snarled Naqa.

She stared at it. "Butter," she said, and saw at once that she had said the wrong thing, because Naqa made butter his personal responsibility.

He stamped on her toes. "My flowers are missing," he said, "that I present to the doctor each morning. Must I tell you of everything a thousand times?" But he put the butter on the tray, and then he kicked her with emphasis. "Go on, go on. The tea will be cold, and the doctor angry."

She pushed through the swing-door, and he looked in the cupboard for his private cache of aspirin. It had been an exceptionally distinguished wake, and his head was rocking. His eyes were like hard marbles in sockets far too small for them, and his tongue was coated with ashes and gritty cinders. His stomach too was queasy. Perhaps, after all, even a white man's death should be celebrated with less enthusiasm.

And then the girl came running, the tray still held out in front of her, like a battering ram.

"The doctor is not in bed."

Naqa snorted, and made for the bedroom. The doctor had a silly objection to him entering her bedroom, but if she was not there to see, the objection need not arise.

The bed was rumpled. She had slept in it. He scratched his head. The doctor usually slept until Elizabeth Marie Anne or this other one came with tea. But certainly she was not in now. Perhaps she had stayed at one of the other bungalows overnight. No, the bed had been used. And here were the clothes she had worn yesterday. He considered the matter. Perhaps she had been called up to a case. But no, there was her emergency bag in the corner, and, for that matter, Naqa himself would have known if anyone had been taken ill. He always knew. He had imposed his rules upon the islanders. Then perhaps she had gone across to the dead-house. She had not, perhaps, finished with the corpse.

He went off at a run, though neither his head nor his stomach approved his haste, but it would be as well to give some appearance of energy this morning. The door of the dead-house was open. He ran in. And both his second wife and Elizabeth Marie Anne, who was recuperating in her hut a hundred yards away, heard him scream.

4.

"Well?" said Buchanan. His face was grey and tortured.

"She has a terrific head, of course," said Miss Roper, "but I think she is all right."

"Don't like these head injuries," said Thompson.

"She wants to speak to you," said Miss Roper to Buchanan.

Buchanan crossed the verandah and went in through the living-room. Alicia lay back on her pillows, and her skin was dark against the white bandage. She opened her eyes, and he thought she smiled.

He dropped on one knee beside her. "Alicia!"

She did smile now. "It is you, George, isn't it? You look rather blurred. And you seem to be going up and down a good deal. But perhaps that's me, and not you."

"I feel rather as if it could be me. Alicia, what have you been doing?"

"Behaving like an idiot, I'm afraid. An idiot in a nightmare. Was it a nightmare, George?" She moved her head slightly, and he saw her eyes glaze with pain. "Naqa found me, didn't he?"

"Yes. And came yelling, with both his women, into the village. He kept shouting that you were dead. I . . . well, I'm glad you are not dead, Alicia."

"You actually look most annoyed. Unless that is the blur."

"I am annoyed. You gave me quite a turn. And I'd no idea I was so charged with sentiment." He grinned, and she smiled back at him.

"I think it is rather nice that I'm alive, too. Even though one does look as one does."

"You look entirely elegant."

"I do not. I'm going to have a black eye."

"You've been reviewing yourself in a mirror."

"Of course I have. My dear George, you do not imagine that I let you in without at least making sure that my bandage was on straight."

"It isn't, as a matter of fact." He caught her hand. "Alicia, what happened? Why did you go to the mortuary?"

"It was the mortuary, then. I wondered whether that was part of the nightmare."

"We found you sprawling across the floor, just inside the door."

She stared at him, biting her lip, in the effort to clear her mind.

"George, is the body still there?" she exclaimed suddenly.

"Good lord, yes! Why?" He was astonished.

"Because I . . . I dreamed that it . . . no, now I begin to remember. George, how do you think I was hurt?"

His jaw tightened. "We think that you may have fallen

against the door. Against the corner of the door. There is a smear of blood on it."

"Why should I have fallen?"

"You tripped, perhaps. Or something frightened you, and you fainted."

"Something frightened me, but I did not faint. George, you don't believe I just fell against the door."

"No, I don't. But hadn't we better leave all this until you have had some sleep. You mustn't get excited. . . ."

"I shan't sleep until I have straightened it out. George, someone hit me."

He nodded, grimly.

"Something woke me up. I heard a noise outside. I took my torch and went out. The door of the mortuary was open. I went across, went inside . . ." Her eyes glazed again. "Sometime before dawn. It was still dark, terribly dark. I went into that room. I thought the sheet on the body had been disturbed. Then something . . . someone moved behind me. I tried to turn. And then there was just pain, appalling pain. Coming down in great waves, surging, and I was fighting my way up through it for hours and hours and hours. And when I could see the light again, I was here, and there was Miss Roper sponging my forehead." She tried to shake her head. "That is all I remember, George, but I was struck. Someone was in the mortuary, someone had moved the sheet on the body, someone . . ." Her eyes closed. "Perhaps I had better stop."

She sighed and her whole body seemed to relax. He felt her hand droop tiredly in his own. He rose, and he bent over her and kissed her gently. Her blue eyes opened a little and she smiled at him.

"You are rather a comfort, aren't you, George?" she murmured. And then she went to sleep.

5.

"Someone meant to kill her, Thompson."

Thompson grunted.

"He was not content with his one murder, after all."

Thompson knelt down and looked under a chair. "Here's some of the glass from her torch. Do you think he meant to kill her? Seems to me she just walked in on him at an awkward moment, and he lashed out at her."

"She was surely showing her torch as she came across the yard. He could have slipped away before she reached here. He must have noticed the light."

"But he would have shown up in it if he ran out. The thing that interests me is what was he doing here. She says the sheet on the body had been disturbed." He walked across to the slab and pulled back the sheet. "And as she tucked him in, she ought to know. It's time he was coffined. You'll go ahead with the funeral this afternoon, of course."

"Yes. And the casket will be up at any time, now. Thompson, obviously the murderer came here to look for something."

"Or at something."

"At something?"

"He may have wanted another peek at the corpse, for instance."

"What have you got in mind, man?"

"Nothing to make sense of this. Yes, maybe he was looking for something. What?"

"Why should he want to look at the corpse? We all saw

Smith while he was alive, which should have been enough . . ." Buchanan paused, frowning. "What you are thinking is that someone may have wanted to identify Smith, aren't you?"

Thompson shrugged his shoulders. "All of us saw him alive, but I don't know that anyone saw him stripped. I thought there may have been a mark of some kind on the body that someone may have wanted to see. There isn't any peculiar mark, though. Not to notice. Anyway, it was only a vague sort of notion."

"I don't follow you."

"I don't follow myself." Thompson pulled the rubber sheet back over the body and they walked out again into the fresh air.

They sat down on the steps, and Thompson filled his pipe. Buchanan watched, abstractedly, the movements of his plump, hairy fingers. Thompson always looked clumsy until he did anything. Then his movements had an easy competence and deftness.

"This night attack rules out the natives, finally," said Buchanan.

"I was wondering about that. You know them better than I do."

"None of them would have gone within fifty yards of the mortuary last night, for any purpose whatsoever."

"The doctor's own boys?" asked Thompson.

"None of them. And anyhow, Naqa and Ptai were certainly at the funeral feast. They stage-managed the effects, having a certain prerogative in matters of the sort."

"You've checked on that?"

"I had a circumstantial report of the whole performance

while I shaved. From Benjamin. Before Naqa and his wives came roaring into the village."

"Actually," said Thompson, and his eyes narrowed a little, "it's pretty well impossible for anything to happen on this island without you knowing all about it."

"I used to think so."

"Do you still think that you would hear whatever the natives know?" Thompson stared at his pipe, rolling the bowl slowly in his palms.

"Unless there was a general conspiracy of silence, one or other would spill the beans. And I cannot for an instant conceive a general conspiracy of silence. Gossip is their art."

"If Smith had injured or insulted one of these people, would you have heard of it?"

"Inevitably. Kaitai does not suffer in silence. Naturally, I've considered the possibilities, Thompson. But the natives themselves are convinced that Smith was killed by one of us. It is partly why they are enjoying the whole affair with such gusto. No, taking one thing with another, I rule the natives out. I think they know a good deal less about it than we do ourselves. Not one of my boys has had a contribution to make."

"The murder was not a success," said Thompson.

"I doubt whether Smith would agree."

"I mean that the murderer did not get all he wanted."

"How? Why?"

"Because he is still looking for it. Unless he found it last night, of course."

"What was there to find?"

"That's what I'm asking. There wasn't anything of noticeable interest in Smith's clothes. They only amounted to his shirt and pants, anyway." Thompson stood up and went inside.

Presently he came out again. "And his shirt and pants are still there, with the three or four items from the pockets still neatly laid out on the table. I've re-checked them, though I already knew they were complete."

"And so you thought, just now, of a mark on the man's body?"

"There wasn't anything left to think of."

"A tattoo, or something like that. The plan of Treasure Island in pink and purple on his abdomen. Well, well. What about his papers, Thompson? The ones you brought off the lugger."

"In my safe. With the key on my ring and the ring on a chain and the chain on my belt." He pulled the ring of keys from his trouser pocket.

"Well, what do we do next?"

Thompson pulled his hat down on his nose. "That's the trouble," he said. "What would you suggest?"

Buchanan hesitated. That was a rather curious note in Thompson's voice. What exactly did it mean? It would be as well not to under-rate Thompson. Because he showed so little of his mind, one should not discount his mind. A man who has earned his pension at Scotland Yard is unlikely to be a simpleton. Yet one could easily fall into a habit of thinking Thompson a bit of an ass, amiable and solemn, but still assish.

"What about fingerprints? You've brushes and powders and things down below, haven't you?"

"I've an outfit in my pocket, and I've been blowing and brushing while you have been with Dr. Murray. Her own prints are all over the place, and Naqa's, and what I take to be yours . . ."

"I was here yesterday," said Buchanan quickly.

"Yes, of course." Thompson at last struck a match for his pipe. "I'll go over the woodwork later. At the moment, what about the path yonder?" He nodded towards the break in the wall of tropical growth. "If he left any traces of his passage, he left 'em there. You couldn't pick up an elephant's track on this hard clay in the compound." He rose, stretching. "I'll poke up and down the path a bit."

Miss Roper came out on to the verandah of the bungalow. Buchanan frowned. He had kept the others, Swan, Hawkesbury, Mitchell, Cooper away from the bungalow, but he had not been able to shunt Miss Roper. She was the only other white woman on the island, and she had insisted on taking charge of Alicia. It was difficult to see how he could have stopped her.

Now she put her fingers to her lips and walked on her elevated toes. Alicia was still asleep, presumably. Miss Roper began to clip some sprays of native honeysuckle.

Thompson was moving slowly down the path, pausing to peer on either side into the thick growth. No, Thompson was not a fool. How had he identified Alicia's fingerprints, and Naqa's, and Buchanan's own? He must have taken careful notice at some time. One left one's mark on almost everything in this sweaty climate, of course, but even so, fingerprints are not especially easy to collect. Thompson must have amused himself by watching for them on glasses and things of the sort. It would be interesting to know whether he had done it systematically.

A notion suddenly occurred to Buchanan. He rose and went inside and he drew back the sheet from Smith and looked at his fingers. Both thumbs and all the fingers and the heel of each palm were stained with ink. They were greasy. Buchanan dropped them back with a shiver of disgust. That had been sensible of Thompson. If any question of identification arose, the prints might be useful. Only, of course, if they were on record somewhere. Did Thompson think that they were on record somewhere?

He came out into the sun again. They would bury Smith in the evening, in the little cemetery on the first low hill behind. One must remember to hunt up the Book of Common Prayer. One would have to read the service oneself, presumably. Odd to think that there would come a day, inevitably, when one would be carried up there to the little hill oneself. If he had any preference in the matter, he would choose to die and to go to dust here in Kaitai. But who would read that burial-service? Who would stand there beside his grave as he had stood beside his father's grave? There was consolation in sons. Who would continue what he had done in Kaitai? If a man's work meant something more to him than a pay-check, if it had its own values, then a man would not want it to die with his death. If men are sterile, it is because their work is sterile, perhaps.

He walked across the compound to Miss Roper. "Have you seen Bernard this morning?" he said.

She looked up, sharply. "No. Why should I?"

"I thought you might have seen him. He walked up here last night with Alicia."

She stood, for a moment, very still, her garden-scissors open in one hand. Then she clipped another spray. "No. No, I haven't seen him this morning."

"He is probably up at his hut in the hills. He won't have heard of the attack, yet."

"As soon as he does, I'm sure he will be down. He is very fond of Alicia."

Buchanan nodded. "Has Thompson ever taken your fingerprints, by the way?"

She stared, startled. "Fingerprints!"

He smiled. "Yes, fingerprints."

"Good gracious, no! Why should he?"

"He seems rather familiar with Alicia's, and mine, and Naqa's. I thought he may have made a collection as a kind of joke, and that perhaps he had asked some of you others."

"I should not have taken it as a kind of a joke," said Miss Roper. "Did you give him yours?"

"No. I think he must have collected mine off a glass or something of the sort. One drops in for a drink with him now and again."

"We all do that. If he has been taking fingerprints from our glasses, I shall be very annoyed." She laughed a little. "Though I don't know why I should resent it really. Except that it is taking a liberty. Yes, and rather an unpleasant liberty." Her cheeks suddenly burned.

"Oh, I shouldn't be concerned about it, if I were you. He has been trained, you know, to read fingerprints, and he probably notices their points just as you or I would notice the meaning of a scrap of writing which happened to catch our eyes."

She bent to clip a rich, heavy spray, brushing the wild bees aside with her hand.

"Yes, one can understand that," she said. "But Thompson is sometimes very much the policeman."

And that, thought Buchanan, was a curious remark for a Miss Roper to make.

"You like the sober order of England," he said, "in which even policemen must keep their place."

"There are times when my whole soul yearns for Bath or Tunbridge Wells."

"It should not be altogether impossible for you to satisfy the yearning, should it?"

She looked up at him. "I have a divided allegiance," she said.

"Yet you might sometimes, surely, surrender to Bath. Or to Tunbridge Wells."

"I am not given to surrenders." Clip-clip-clip, went her scissors. "I am not really a good bourgeois. I have lived too many lives."

"You are one of those people who can make of their lives very much what you want to make of them. You do as you please."

"I used to think so. But is there anyone, really, who can do that? Circumstances can be . . . overwhelming. One can be caught up, whirled round, mangled in the wheels. And tossed aside, like a bloodied rag."

She swung on her heel, with an odd gesture; and he knew that she was angry with herself for that outburst. It had been like the harsh twang of taut nerves. Buchanan smiled grimly.

"Other people draw one in, of course, if one lets them. One cannot live on a pillar like St. Simeon Stylites. Or find one's landfall on an empty island, like Robinson Crusoe. I used to think that Kaitai was rather like Robinson's island. But it isn't, is it? Even here, one forges links, one grapples oneself to people."

She laughed. "You are trampling on my corns. Now, you seem to me admirably detached, George. I can hardly imagine anything which would seriously shake you. Unless it was your islanders. And even there, it is not that you are especially fond of your islanders, is it? Isn't it rather a kind of pride in your charge?"

She had shifted ground, quite skillfully. But Buchanan felt that he had scored a point.

"You have lived a lot in France, haven't you?"

"Yes. Yes, I lived in France during most of my girlhood." She began to gather up her sprays of blossom.

"Odd people, the French. I can never quite get on with them. They make everything so much an affair of personalities." She swept up an armful of sprays. "I must go and arrange these."

It was, decisively, a last word. Buchanan hoisted himself up to sit on the verandah, and felt for a cigarette. His oblique approach had been obviously too oblique. Should he have been more direct? But then, one cannot go about busting people open. If one is to apply the third-degree, one needs particular talents. And Miss Roper had a sinewy mind. She slipped from one's clutch. And it was always possible that she knew little or nothing. But Buchanan doubted that. Certainly, she had been under the screws at some time. When she spoke just now of being tossed aside like a bloodied rag, there had been a flash of incredible bitterness: and then she had made an almost frantic effort to cover the scar.

Thompson was coming up by the path. He was swinging something in his hand. Buchanan slid off the verandah and went to meet him.

"Well?" he said.

Thompson held up his find. It was a stirrup and a stirrup-leather, and the leather was knotted at the upper end.

"I found this thrown aside into the shrubbery," said Thompson.

Buchanan took it. "It's one of mine, of course. I told those blasted boys again last night to put that saddle away. But what on earth . . . ?"

He stared at Thompson, who grunted his heaviest grunt.

"You'll notice the knot. Gives a better grip. And makes a nasty weapon, Mr. Buchanan."

"Weapon? Do you seriously think it has been used as a weapon, man?"

Thompson grunted again. "The stirrup's pretty much the shape of Smith's injury. And," he held it up so that the light shone dully along the metal, "look at that."

There was, quite perceptible, a long smear on the stirrup.

"And that isn't rust," said Thompson.

Buchanan plumped down on a log.

"But it was attached to the saddle last night, man."

"Then it must have been detached. Unless it is from some other outfit."

"No, I recognize it. It is a leather from the saddle that you tripped over last night. I picked it up and draped it over my verandah railing. But, confound it all, why should anyone go to the trouble . . . !"

"If he used it once, perhaps he thought it might be useful again."

"Yes, but the thing's ludicrous. Why should he go to the trouble of taking a stirrup from my saddle, and returning it, and taking it again, when any sort of stick or club would be easier to hand and quite as effective?"

"This may have been at hand," said Thompson.

"How could it have been?"

"Has it occurred to you that you and Smith were probably followed down to the beach the other evening? Who followed you? Someone, to my way of thinking, who had listened in to your talk. Someone, that is, who was outside, on your verandah, while you were talking. And, perhaps, fiddling with your saddle while he sat and listened."

Buchanan stared at an ant, which was struggling up the log, half-pushing, half-carrying a seed twice as big as itself. He was tempted to pick up the seed and to do a job of porterage. But one could not be sure just where the ant would like it put. He felt, vaguely, that there was a moral in that somewhere, but then ants are always suggesting a moral of some kind, usually tiresome.

"Nicholas Swan, of course, says that he came on to my verandah while we were talking. But can you imagine Nicholas as a murderer?"

"I never went in for imagination, much. But someone killed Smith. Swan seems as likely as any of us. He's an inhuman little swine. And he works himself into silly rages." This was strong speech from Thompson.

Buchanan half-nodded. Swan did have an inhuman streak. By his own account, he had deserted his wife and daughters without a single qualm of conscience or compunction. It was true, too, that he developed the most furious fancies. He would quarrel over matters which would seem utterly inconsequential to most people, but which obviously were of consequence to Swan. The quarrel with Smith over Shelley, for instance. From his own experience of Swan, Buchanan knew that it could have been a furious quarrel. And his mind worked in queer ways. If he had used the stirrup once, he might find some fantastic reason of his own for using it again.

Somehow or other, his perverted sense of humor might be involved. Or his superstitions. The more one saw of men, the more one came to allow for singularities. We cannot plumb any man.

"I'm going to take another look at Smith," said Thompson.

They went back together to the mortuary.

"I wonder whether there is a spare pair of rubber gloves," said Thompson. He jerked back the sheet, and then took a corner of it and moved Smith's head. And then he whistled. For the back of the skull had been smashed, and smashed again. Thompson stared at it and then he stared at Buchanan. Buchanan swung away towards the window.

"Hell!" he said.

Thompson himself backed away. "What's loose on this island?" he growled. And he dropped the stirrup with a clatter to the floor.

"Well, that's not Dr. Murray's work," he said. He bent to pick up the stirrup.

Buchanan opened his eyes. He felt sick, and he always disliked himself when he felt sick. One's stomach should not compromise one's mind.

"What was it you wanted here, Thompson?"

"I wanted to see whether this stirrup fitted the wound in Smith's head. Rather looks as if someone has made sure that it won't."

"You think that's the meaning of this?"

"Well, what, then?" said Thompson.

"Looks more like some beastly form of mania to me. Let's get outside."

Thompson frowned. He walked across the room and opened

Alicia Murray's case of instruments. He tugged at a cupboard door and looked in. Then he poked about under the sink.

"The doctor does use rubber gloves, I suppose, when she's doing a post-mortem."

"Yes, of course. They were here yesterday. On that sterilizer."

"Where are they now, I wonder."

"This is her overall thing." Buchanan looked in the pockets. "What do you want them for?"

"I want to know where they are." Thompson went on hunting about the room. "Funny that they're not visible."

"Well, she wouldn't have taken them away from here. They must be about somewhere." Buchanan began to hunt too.

"I'm afraid Dr. Murray will have to look at the body again before we coffin it," said Thompson.

Buchanan nodded. "I suppose she must, now, poor kid. Why exactly are we looking for these gloves, Thompson?"

"Because it seems that they have been taken away."

Buchanan pursed his lips. "I see. The fellow probably put them on last night while he was doing this job here."

"And went off in them, by the look of it," said Thompson. He slammed the door of the last cupboard. "I'm willing to make a small bet that they are not here now."

"H'm'm'm. What could they tell you, anyhow?"

"Surgical gloves are usually pretty tight-fitting, aren't they?"

"Yes, I suppose they are."

"Then I should like to see whether they are split or not."

"I don't think they would split. We've all of us larger hands than Dr. Murray's."

"All of us?" said Thompson.

Buchanan wiped his forehead. "Well, no, not all of us, maybe," he said. Thompson was eyeing him.

"You don't expect to find them, if the murderer went off in them, surely. He is hardly likely to return them parcel-post."

"No, maybe not. But he seems to be careless. He threw his weapon away. Perhaps he just threw the gloves away too. Or was he careless?"

"Or was he careless?" repeated Buchanan. "It seems to me that he rather wanted someone to find that stirrup, Thompson."

"He took a lot of trouble to destroy the shape of the wound. And then he threw the stirrup into the bushes, just beside the path. Did he think we wouldn't hunt up and down the path?"

"I'm inclined to believe," said Buchanan grimly, "that he may have wanted to embarrass me."

"How do you mean?"

"Well, ever since you found it, you have been turning this and this over in your mind. It is my stirrup, taken from my saddle, on my verandah. The eyes of the audience are focused on me, so to speak. And I am a trifle ill-at-ease."

"This is beginning to get on your nerves, isn't it?" said Thompson.

"Of course it's getting on my nerves."

Thompson turned back to the sink. "The gloves were on that sterilizer, you say."

"They were when I came in yesterday afternoon."

"Dr. Murray may have left them there again then. I'll try the sterilizer for prints. He may have touched something before he put on the gloves. There's a pestle and mortar here. I wonder if he used the pestle to do this little job here."

Thompson stooped. "By gum, he did. There's muck all over it. H'mph. Then why the devil did he bring up that stirrup at all?"

"It doesn't seem an efficient weapon to me, anyhow," said Buchanan wearily. "The whole point about the stirrup, Thompson, is that it happens to be mine."

"The whole point? No, no, I don't think that," said Thompson.

Buchanan pulled a face and walked out. At the moment, he was on edge, and he preferred to control his temper. Miss Roper was sitting in the compound, on her shooting-stick, sketching with a pencil and a block of Alicia's writing-paper.

"I've never properly looked at the mountain from this angle," she said cheerfully, "but I really think this is the angle from which one should look at it. I'll ask Alicia whether I may set up my easel here."

Buchanan swore gently but fluently in the native tongue, which one can do without any noticeable movement of the lips. It is a language that meets most of the contingencies of life.

"I've been thinking of what you were saying," she said, "about the French. It isn't, of course, that they are an excitable people, but, just as you were remarking, that they have very strong personalities. Isn't that it?" She looked up anxiously.

But Buchanan had lost interest in French politics and even in English politicians. He was trying to discover, in this queer old maid, some likeness to the woman who had spoken with him here by the steps a half-hour ago.

"You are Miss Roper, aren't you?" he said suddenly, and surprised himself.

"My dear George!" She bubbled into a spinsterish chuckle. "And your father was a rural dean, no doubt."

"Oh, yes, considerable doubt. My father was a doctor at Wytcherley in Sussex. That is why I am so good at doing bandages and giving pills. He sold his practice though, when I was quite young and we lived for a number of years at Cannes. Long before it was over-run with all the horrid people who go there nowadays."

"I see," said George.

And then he went on up the steps. For Alicia was standing in the window and she beckoned him.

She sat down on the edge of her bed and smiled ruefully. "I feel better now," she said. "Did I mention when you were here before that I have a black eye?"

"You did. And, for goodness sake, get back into bed."

"My head feels like a lump of old iron if I lie down. My mouth tastes rather rusty, too. But if I sit up, it feels as it were charged with soda-water, and I prefer the aerated sensation. It is rather nice to be light-headed. I feel light-hearted too, queerly enough."

"That is because I kissed you."

"Did you kiss me?"

"Firmly," said George, "and I'm afraid I meant it."

"Do you always kiss young women with black eyes? And do they always have to have black eyes before you kiss them?"

"We're a grim race, we Buchanans, you know. We take our pleasures solemnly."

"Yes, you are a grim race, aren't you?" She looked at him curiously. "Your great-uncle must have been an exceedingly formidable man. He, I imagine, would have required two black eyes. George, I don't believe you have kissed a young woman since you were an undergraduate."

He blushed. "That's going back a long way, you know."

"Since the ship. Coming out. Is that it?" She laughed a little. "It is. You're rather disappointing, in some ways. I had quite expected to find you in a marble palace, with troupes of exotic dancing-girls . . ."

"I don't like the way our dancers wiggle," said George. "It seems to me highly vulgar, and I am a man of delicate sensibilities."

"You're a nice ass of a man, and I suspect that you actually have a conscience, which is an awfully unusual thing to meet nowadays."

"It is difficult to admit it, but I'm afraid that I have. At least, I am taken sometimes with uneasy twinges, a kind of moral lumbago. Or do I mean sciatica? It makes my lot very trying. Here, on the one hand, is Kaitai. Here, on the other side, is that mysterious She. Whoe'er she be. But what she, however mysterious, could bear to be called a Sultana? I mean to say! And then, Kaitai is hardly Wimbledon, is it? You can't pop up to town for a matinée of the January sales or a game of shove-ha'penny at the old Wig and Thistle. No Saturday nights in Soho, or Sunday mornings at the swimming-pool. By jove, I do lead a fairly miserable life, don't I?"

"I am filled with compunction. The January sales touch me most. That is nostalgic. And my toes are coming through my slippers." She wriggled them under his nose. "But there are better things in the world than bargain-basements, George."

"Yes, I feel that, too, but it is not always easy to be high-minded. I could, of course, call myself a Rajah instead of a Sultan. Like Brooke of Sarawak. Do you think that Ranee sounds more attractive than Sultana? A little less like trade, perhaps?"

"There are times when I almost take you seriously. I think that you probably would hesitate to ask a woman to marry you, because you'd feel that sooner or later she would become bored with Kaitai."

"Oh, not with Kaitai, but with me on Kaitai. There'd be so little comic relief. The days do drag, you know, and I shall probably grow into a curmudgeon."

"If you were exceptionally curmudgeon, the Sultana, or Ranee, as the case might be, could always turn you up and spank you. I think one can do that with curmudgeons, can't one?"

"With some curmudgeons, possibly. But I should probably be one of the thorny sort, with hard spikes, lacking in fortitude, patience, humility, longanimity. And inclined to snap."

"You hardly advertise your wares," she said.

"No. But it is at least some kind of a virtue in me that I am not deceived by my own appearances. I wonder what one would make of one's life if one were entirely free to arrange it, all its circumstances and conditions. A blasted mess, I suppose. I've very little confidence in myself. I should much have preferred, on the whole, that Buchanan the First had not uprooted us. I was meant to be fourth engineer on a Clyde tug, really."

"That sounds almost as if you mean it. Why, George?"

"I hate interfering in other people's lives. Any sort of authority frightens me. Especially the sort of authority that is thrust on me at this moment. How can one presume to judge?"

"Smith's murderer, you mean?"

He nodded. "No man is fit to be a judge. There is no such thing as human justice. There is only expediency. One has to enforce the law, of course, for the sake of the others. Anarchy, in fact, must be more horrible than tyranny. But I hate the job. And, in spite of myself, I have been going about it with a good deal of reluctance. I don't think I really wanted to uncover Smith's murderer at all. But now I have to, and I begin to realize how much I was shirking it."

"Now?"

"Since the attack on you. Until this morning, I suppose I felt that the affair was between Smith and his murderer and God. But if the murderer will drag other people into it, then we must take our precautions."

She shivered. "George, I am afraid. Are you?"

"Damnably."

"I thought you were, just now, when we were both trying to be funny. Trying hard. And . . . and not being so very good at it." She shivered again.

"I have been frightened, properly frightened, only twice in my life," he said soberly. "Both times, in the bright sunlight. Once, in a small boat, on an empty sea, with the familiar shore hardly a mile away. I had fished, alone, off that coast every day for a month. This day was like any other day. But suddenly, for no reason whatever, I was cold with terror. The sunlight was suddenly like a yellow curtain, the coast, though I could mark every tree and fold of cliff and rock, was suddenly alien, utterly, as if it were meaningless for me. I was in no danger. The boat bobbed placidly in the water. But the whole world seemed suddenly drained of meaning. I was in a void. There was just myself, and nothingness. One has something of the feeling at times in a nightmare. But this was in full day, under the sun. I've wondered sometimes whether it wasn't a moment of reality, whether, if for one moment, I broke through all the pretty symbols that our senses make for us, and found that there was actually nothing there at all." He wiped his forehead. "That's my temptation, as perhaps you've guessed. And it doesn't help me to go about kicking stones, like Dr. Johnson did."

She nodded, slowly.

He stood up and stared out through the window.

"Suppose that there is nothing there after all . . ." he said.

She stood too, and came beside him.

"When else were you afraid?"

"Half-an-hour ago, there by your verandah. With the sun beating down. But it was another sort of fear." He leaned forward a little. "I think that ghosts must walk in the sunshine, not at night."

"I think that too." Her hands clenched. "That was why I beckoned you just now, from here." She was silent for a long minute. "I knew what you meant when you said the sunlight was like a yellow veil. It seems to thicken. But I feel that something is moving behind it."

"I suppose one of us should try to remember a piece out of *Punch,*" he said.

"It will be better, I think, if we take notice of the warning," she said. "Wherever these alarms come from, they do mean something. I was afraid last night, but I thought it stupid, silly, ridiculous to be afraid. I was a fool. And now, I am very much more afraid than I was last night. Something horrible is loose on Kaitai, George."

"I think the Devil is walking the island," he said.

Thompson came out of the mortuary, and for an instant

he stood by the steps, and he seemed to look straight at the sun. Then he shielded his eyes with a queer, quick gesture.

"Alicia, where did you last leave your surgical gloves?"

"Gloves? Oh, I put them into the sterilizer."

Thompson was walking across towards the path.

"Alicia, the back of Smith's skull has been smashed in. . . . You didn't . . . ?"

But she was staring at him, her face grey and bloodless.

9

FUNERAL SERVICE

THEY BURIED Smith at the hour before evening, in the clearing circled by trees, on the first rise of the hills.

Buchanan stood at the head of the grave, Miss Roper, very straight and still, behind him. Nicholas Swan stood on the mound of earth. Only he and Miss Roper answered to the prayers. Hawkesbury stood uneasily a little way off, Bernard further away. Mitchell had only come to the edge of the trees. He sat there now on a fallen trunk.

The sea above the trees and between them was intensely blue, and dark . . . *the wine-dark sea,* Buchanan thought, as he stood there, the loose earth crumbled beneath his feet.

The four native boys who would fill in the grave were behind him, with Thompson. The rest, he knew, were crowded amongst the trees. They would not come nearer.

And he read: *I am the Resurrection and the Life. . . . We brought nothing into this world, and it is certain we can carry nothing out . . . and verily every man living is altogether vanity. For man walketh in a vain shadow and disquieteth himself in vain . . . and fades away suddenly like grass. In the morning it is green, and groweth up: but in the evening it is cut down, dried up, and withered. . . . So teach us to number our days: that we may apply our hearts unto wisdom. . . . Out of the depths I have cried unto thee, O Lord. . . . If the dead rise not, let us eat and drink, for to-morrow we die. Be not deceived. . . . Man that is born of a woman hath but a short time to live, and is full of misery. He cometh up, and is cut down, like a flower, he fleeth as it were a shadow, and never continueth in one stay. . . . Like as a father pitieth his own children, even so is the Lord merciful unto them that fear him. . . .*

2.

"It rather shakes you," said Hawkesbury, as they came down the hill.

"It is a very remarkable book, very remarkable," said Nicholas Swan.

Buchanan halted suddenly. "Where is Cooper?"

They all stopped. "Now I come to think of it, I haven't seen him all day," said Mitchell.

"He isn't in his bungalow. Wasn't this morning, when I looked in, nor this afternoon neither," said Hawkesbury.

Buchanan frowned. "I'd expected him to turn up."

"One does rather expect him to observe the rites," said Swan.

"Have you seen him, Bernard?"

"No. No, I haven't seen him since last night. I did not actually see him then, but I waited while you and Dr. Murray went in."

"Has anybody seen him since last night?"

No one answered until Hawkesbury repeated: "I looked in this morning and again this afternoon. Just to see how he was feeling. But he wasn't there. Neither time."

Buchanan turned back to where Thompson was supervising the filling of the grave.

"Thompson, have you seen anything of Cooper today?"

"No. He wasn't at home when I called."

"Then none of us has seen him today."

Thompson looked up. "What's that?"

"He hasn't been seen."

"Why not?" said Thompson. "Where is he?"

"That," said Nicholas Swan, "would appear to be the question under review."

Thompson looked uncertainly at the boys and then at Buchanan. Then he turned and spoke. "Finish this off properly. All that earth is to be thrown in or built up on top. And hammer it with your spades. I'll come back to inspect, and if you haven't finished the job properly, you'll do it all over again at midnight." He started down the hill with Buchanan.

"What do you think?" said Buchanan.

"I think we'd better find him," said Thompson.

"He's probably just wandered off somewhere on his own."

"He didn't have a fever last night, did he, when Dr. Murray took his temperature?"

"No. Why? You mean that he may have got light-headed and strayed away . . . ?"

"No, I don't think he was light-headed, and I didn't think he had a fever, and I don't think he has just strayed away. I don't think he was sick at all."

Buchanan stopped in his paces again.

"He wasn't sick," said Thompson. "He was frightened. That's why he took to his bed. And that's why I do not believe that he has just wandered off on his own."

"Frightened? How do you know?"

"First time I went to see him yesterday, he had all the doors locked. Had to get up to let me in. Same when you went too, wasn't it, Hawkesbury."

"Yes, that's right," said Hawkesbury.

"What the devil was he frightened of?" said Nicholas Swan.

"What we're all frightened of," growled Mitchell.

Buchanan saw Hawkesbury's jaw twitch. So he was feeling it too.

"I'm not frightened," said Swan. "Bah!" And then, as nobody responded. "What is there to be frightened of?"

"Oh, shut up!" said Mitchell.

"Who actually saw him last? You and I, Thompson?"

"No," said Hawkesbury. "I was in after you last night. Looked in to see if there was anything I could do. He's not a bad little bloke."

"What time was that?" asked Buchanan.

"Between nine and ten."

Thompson was quickening his steps as they went. They came down past the hospital, and Miss Roper, who had gone ahead of them, was there talking to Alicia, who was lying now on a seagrass lounge in the verandah. Buchanan hesitated.

"I think I shall stay for a word with Dr. Murray," he said. "You go on, Thompson. If you can find him, send a boy up to tell me. If you can't . . . we'd better organize a search-party, I suppose."

Thompson nodded and strode on. The rest went with him, excepting Bernard. Buchanan heard Nicholas Swan's excited chatter break out as they went by the woodland path. Perhaps

Nicholas was not so filled with the strong wine of courage, after all. Or perhaps his vessel had cracked.

Bernard and Buchanan walked across the compound together.

"This was an abominable thing, last night," said Bernard. "I tried very hard to persuade Dr. Murray not to stay here alone."

"Well, she is not going to stay here alone tonight," said Buchanan grimly. "And I hope you heard that, my girl."

"I did. With a great deal of pleasure." She smiled up at them. "Hullo, Bernard. Have you come to admire my eye, too? I shouldn't affront the day with it, if I were a truly considerate person. And I should have taken your advice last night, shouldn't I? I own up fully and freely, which should stave off *I told you so.*"

"Only a brute would say *I told you so,*" said Bernard.

"Dorothy has been saying how admirably you read the service, George."

It always gave Buchanan a slight shock to think of Miss Roper as Dorothy. "Oh!" he said. "You know, I meant that service. Its words seem to be the only sensible words that have been said round here since Smith died. *As soon as thou scatterest them, they are even as a sleep: and fade away suddenly like grass. . . . So teach us to number our days: that we may apply our hearts unto wisdom.* I mean, life is like that, if you see what I mean."

"It's rather disturbing," said Miss Roper. "It always unsettled me to go to church."

"I'm somewhat inclined to a nicely cushioned world at the moment," said Alicia.

"I am very much in favor of cushions myself," said Bernard.

"Unhappily, one sometimes persuades oneself that they are real. And sits down too abruptly."

Buchanan lit a cigarette. *"In the evening it is cut down, dried up, and withered.* It may be pretty grim, conservative, reactionary, but I'm afraid it happens to be true. I suppose one shouldn't go to funerals. They're so brutally frank. One can't help wondering. After death, the judgment. Distinctly embarrassing thought. Do you believe in damnation, Bernard?"

"Yes," he said. "Yes. For the man who knows what is true and denies it. He is damned here, and damned there." He took a cigarette from Alicia's box. "He is the only man who challenges God to God's Face. After death, the judgment. As you say." He shrugged his shoulders.

"And after a funeral there should be cakes and sherry, shouldn't there?" said Alicia. "I can manage the sherry, and I think there are some crackers." She rose from the lounge.

"Let me help," said Miss Roper.

"No," said Buchanan. "I'll help. I always know where the sherry is."

He followed Alicia inside.

"Was it very horrid?" she said.

"No. It wasn't. Really. I meant what I said. One did seem to get some sense out of things. And substance into them. Perhaps I should have been a parson. Anyhow, I feel a good deal cleaner. Where do you keep your sherry? Oh, I know. And I'll open that box. Is it one of the sort you can cut your hand on? If it is, I certainly shall. Alicia, you are coming home with me tonight."

"That sounds ominous."

"Yes, it did, didn't it? Well, well. There's a notion there

that grows on one, though. Corkscrew? Tha-a-a-ank you. If you think it more respectable, I shall come and spend the night here instead. Actually, that would be more sensible. It will save you the jaunt down. But you may prefer not to spend the night here."

"I don't know why, but it does sound more respectable, doesn't it? No, I shan't mind sleeping up here if you are here too." She blushed. "I'm thoroughly ashamed of myself. I'd no idea that I should ever feel grateful to have a man about the place. Oh dear, that's making it worse. I mean that I shall be glad to know there is someone about, and that if we feel like it, we can get up and make a cup of cocoa. Or something."

"That is establishing my status and putting me in my place, isn't it! Alicia, you are a positive pig on your occasions."

"Yes, I suppose I am," she said with some surprise.

"For my part, I am magnanimous. I wonder what Bernard and Miss Roper talk about together."

"I've often wondered. They talk a lot. She is almost the only person on the island he ever seems to seek out. He sits with her sometimes when she goes painting, you know. I've often wondered whether he was interested in painting. He's spoken to me several times, very knowledgeably."

"Yes, I know. He's talked to me once or twice. He seemed extraordinarily well-up in the French and Spanish seventeenth and eighteenth century people. And he let a few names of pre-War men slip, as if he knew them. But when I talked to him about contemporaries, he dried right up."

"But he always changes the subject, if one talks about anything . . . well, contemporary. I wonder whether he is afraid of saying something that would . . . you know, place him. Or whether it is that he just detests the whole world as it is."

"He does rather shake the dust off his shoes, doesn't he? If I were a curious person, Bernard would make me very curious indeed. However, he'll be getting curious if we don't take out the sherry."

She led the way back to the verandah.

Miss Roper looked up brightly. "Bernard was just telling me of a place on the mountain where one seems to look right down into the depths of the sea. The colors, he says, are most extraordinary. He's promised to show me the way."

"You are probably the only person to whom he ever surrenders his private perches," said Buchanan.

Bernard looked up quickly. "I am an unsociable. But Miss Roper and I are very sympathetic." He grinned mischievously. "Perhaps we have met in a previous existence. What is that dreadful English song of yours?"

Miss Roper flushed. "I am afraid that I remember it. And I do not approve."

"Why the devil do you stick yourself away up on the mountain, anyhow, Bernard?" asked Buchanan.

"I talk in my sleep. Loudly."

"Yes, of course, that is a problem."

A boy came running up through the trees. Bernard looked sharply at Buchanan who nodded and said, "Damn!"

"What is it?" Alicia and Miss Roper were at once on edge.

Buchanan stepped off the verandah to meet the boy.

"Well?"

The boy panted. "Mr. Cooper is not in his house, sir. He is gone. And no one, no boy or nothing, has seen him all day. Mr. Thompson make all boys go out and search."

Bernard stood up. "I suppose that I had better join the party," he said. "What about you, Buchanan?"

Buchanan turned back to Alicia. Her hands, he saw, were clutching at the arms of her chair.

"Missing? Little Mr. Cooper?"

Buchanan nodded.

"You must go, George. Of course." She turned quickly to Miss Roper. "And you had better stay here until the men come back."

"This sounds frightfully melodramatic," said Buchanan, "but will you promise to shoot anyone who makes trouble?" And he pulled a small automatic pistol from his hip-pocket.

She laughed, a strained laugh. "I shall certainly flourish it."

"Where are your boys?" He shouted. "Naqa. Ptai."

The two came running from the huts.

"Listen, you two! One of you will sit here on these steps, the other will sit in the kitchen. And don't break into the apricot-preserve. You will stay here until I come back, and if Dr. Murray needs you for anything at all, you will do at once what she says. This is one of the occasions when my voice is the voice of thunder. Do you understand?"

They understood.

"Do you remember when a boy was last flogged on Kaitai?"

Their lips trembled. They nodded.

"He was flogged before all the people, and he was shamed. Shamed. And you know why my father flogged him?

"Well, I shall flog you three times for each time that my father flogged Qu'na, if you do not obey what I tell you now. There will be no mercy in me, as there is no mercy in Tka, the blue shark. I shall flog until Tka himself may seem a friend. And then I shall have your shame sung each night, until at last men weary of you even as jests. And, heaven knows, that will be a long time on Kaitai. I shall give to the poet who makes the most shameful song about you, eighty-two pigs, a licence to re-marry, a case of preserved peaches, two bottles of the gin which is normally and properly forbidden to you, six copies each of *Vogue* and *The Sketch,* which vanquish the hearts of women. And I shall permit him to look three times, and even to take into his hands the top-hat of my great-uncle, the Hat that Shines. And I shall probably think of other favors to bestow on him as I go along. Your names shall be buried beneath the mud of oyster-beds. That," he added to Alicia, "should fix them."

"It was horrible," said Alicia.

3.

They met at ten o'clock in the clearing where the shoulder of the mountain thrusts towards the sea.

Thompson pushed back his helmet. "I'm pretty nearly all in," he said. "We worked right round to the further beach, and it's damned heavy travelling under the trees tonight."

"I feel fairly stewed myself," said Buchanan. "Where is Nicholas? He was with you, wasn't he?"

"He took a couple of boys and struck up towards the fishermen's lookout. That hut on top there. He'll be down presently."

"No sign, of course?"

"No. We're wasting time. Useless to keep at it tonight. We're only wasting energy we can employ better in the light."

Buchanan nodded. "Any of you got a cigarette?"

Mitchell held out his case.

"Thanks. What do the rest of you say?"

"I can keep going a while longer," said Bernard. "I'll go over the top of the rise here on my way home. But I think it is useless for us all to go on. Much better, as Thompson says, to wait for the light."

"I think we ought to keep searching as long as we can stand," said Hawkesbury. "Poor little devil, he may have got bogged somewhere, or something like that."

"I pushed as far as I could towards the swamp," said Buchanan. "And turned out every native on the route. None of them had seen or heard of him. I've told them to work right round the swamp at dawn."

"What about the beaches?" said Mitchell.

"I've told them to cover the beaches too. Hawkesbury, we'll actually do much better to get some sleep, and start fresh."

"I'm going home, anyhow," said Thompson. "Or it might be better if we all doss at the hospital, together."

They all turned and trod wearily down the hill.

There was a sudden crash ahead of them.

"What's that?" shouted Hawkesbury.

Their lights shone down the path.

"Oh, it's Swan," said Thompson.

The little man was sitting cross-legged, on the ground, grinning.

"I fell through a tree," he said. "One should never try to walk down a precipice."

Buchanan looked at him curiously. How extraordinarily tough the man was. Though he was by far the oldest of them, and though he had just gone over a difficult spur in the dark, and though he actually had, by the appearance of the broken bough beside him, just fallen through a tree, he looked the freshest of them all.

"Are you hurt?" he asked.

"I've a bruise or two where it won't show." He looked up at the high clay bank. "I miscalculated the grade. But a shaking-up is good for one's liver. If you'll look in those branches there, I think you'll find Cooper's coat. It caught in something as I came down."

One of the boys swung into the tree and threw down the coat. Buchanan caught it, and they all turned their lights on it. It was torn and muddied.

"Where did you find this?" said Buchanan, his heart sinking.

"I didn't find it. It was given to me. By that old man . . . what's his name? Huna, Hwan, something like that."

"Hwan," said Buchanan.

"Who lives in that long grass-hut on the spur. He has a sweet-potato patch down near the swamp, and he went along this evening to do a little hoeing. He did not attend the funeral. He is an unsociable old man. He found this in the middle of his patch. And he is very annoyed. Cooper had apparently been running all over the spuds, in the most eccentric fashion. I am afraid the poor fellow is out of his senses. He had torn off his coat and thrown it away."

"But he could not be lost near Hwan's potato-patch. He must have walked up past it dozens of times," said Buchanan. "Why didn't Hwan come straight down and report this?"

"He has several reasons, all of them good. He was tired. It was late, almost dark. If white men care to throw away their coats, he saw no particular cause why he should be expected to return them. And he was indignant with Cooper for trampling down his potatoes."

"It is queer that Cooper should have done that," said Buchanan.

"It sounds," said Bernard, "as if he had lost his way in the dark and was not certain where he was walking."

"Running," said Swan. "Old Hwan says that his prints in the soft ground looked as if he were running, half-running, half-stumbling along. Hwan remarks that they remind him of the footprints of a man who is pursued by a demon in the dark, and has a nasty suspicion that the demon is gaining ground. The probable presence of a demon in the vicinity is another reason why Hwan preferred not to venture abroad again."

"Did he notice where the tracks finally led? Which way did Cooper run from the patch?" asked Thompson.

"Towards the swamp."

"That sounds bad," said Thompson.

"If he was running round in the dark," said Mitchell, "it must have been last night, not tonight, surely. What did his houseboy say, Thompson? That Cooper was missing when he first went in this morning?"

"Yes. The boy turned up there as usual at about half past seven, and Cooper had already flitted. Unless he has been running round in a frenzy all day, it does look as if he made his tracks in Hwan's patch last night and not tonight." He grunted. "I suppose we'd better go up and try to get a line on them."

"Better to divide," said Bernard. "Let some people go and sleep, so that they will be fresh in the morning. And let those who are least tired now go to the place. If he ran down towards the swamp in the dark, I do not think that we shall find him. No."

"I'm afraid so, too," said Buchanan soberly.

"Anyhow, the mystery seems to be solved," said Nicholas Swan.

"What mystery?" growled Hawkesbury.

"The Great Kaitai Mystery," said Swan.

He had spoken what was obviously in all their minds. There was a moment of difficult silence. Then:

"I don't believe it. I don't believe little Cooper had it in him," said Hawkesbury. But he did not sound wholly convinced. And Buchanan noticed that he had used the past tense of Cooper.

Bernard trimmed the wick of his storm-lantern. "Thompson, you had better get some sleep. Buchanan, you should go back to the ladies. They will be anxious. Who will come with me? I shall prefer, on the whole, to travel alone. I shall travel faster. And I have these boys, if I need assistance. But I do not think it will be possible to find Cooper tonight." He had taken on an air of authority, slipping into command as if it were his natural habit.

"I shall go with you," said Swan.

"I'll come too," said Hawkesbury.

Bernard did not argue. But he gave Buchanan the impression that he would make the pace.

"Are you going to sleep at the doctor's, Buchanan?" asked Thompson as they turned down the hill.

"Yes."

"What about you, Mitchell?"

"Someone ought to go back to the shore," said Mitchell, "just in case Cooper has come home. I'll sleep at the club."

They walked in silence down the rough paths. When they came to the hospital, they turned aside. There were still lights in all the rooms. Naqa rose, beaming, from the steps. Alicia and Miss Roper came out on to the verandah as they heard the voices.

Buchanan shook his head. "No," he said. "But the others have gone off to pick up a track that has been found. You had better take your coat, Thompson." He passed Cooper's muddied jacket to Thompson. He did not want the women to see it. Then he stepped up into the light. "You will stay here tonight, Miss Roper?"

"I should much rather go home, if Alicia does not mind."

"Better stay here, I think."

"You'll be here to look after Alicia," she said. "I suppose you ought to be chaperoned, but I should very much prefer to go home, if I may. Mr. Mitchell or Mr. Thompson will escort me, perhaps. If I do not go home, goodness knows what tricks my girls may play. Cook has taken an unfortunate fancy for that boy, Mota, and he seems to me an opportunist of the most cynical kind. She has already given him most of my mustard pickle, and I don't for an instance imagine that she will stop at that if his opportunity occurs. But while I am in the bungalow, she would never dare to have him in her hut."

"Your cook's morals had better look after themselves for one night," said Buchanan.

Miss Roper shook her head decisively. "My cook has no morals. She merely has a healthy respect for my powers of observation." She grasped her shooting-stick firmly in one hand, her bag in another. "In any case, I have started a run in my stocking, and if I do not do something about it before morning, they will be quite ruined."

"You can take them off between now and morning," said

Alicia. "And I can lend you a pair. I can probably lend you a needle and thread, too, if they are of any use."

"They are not," said Miss Roper, obviously determined to be gone. "Thank you, my dear, but one has one's own little habits which one does not care to disturb, as one grows older. It is foolish of me, I know, but there it is. I shall really be much more comfortable at home."

Buchanan did not quite know what to do. His whole mind was in a turmoil. This afternoon, he had thought that he began to see the shape of things, the pattern into which all this abominable business would fit. But now his pieces were scattered. The running feet of little Mr. Cooper had dashed them away. This afternoon, he would have been willing to let Miss Roper go to her bungalow. Now, it was a different matter.

"I think you ought to know," he said, "that Cooper appears to be . . . well, running wild."

"George!" Alicia stared at him. "You don't mean. . . .?"

"I mean that Cooper seems to have run off in some kind of frenzy. I'm afraid that he may have—" he hesitated— "gone out of his mind. I am not very happy at the thought of Miss Roper spending the night alone."

"I shall lock all my doors and the windows," she said, though her voice shook a little. "Surely you cannot mean that Mr. Cooper. . . ?"

"I shan't be very far away," said Mitchell, "at the Club. If Miss Roper is good at screaming."

"I am certainly going home." Miss Roper stiffened. "I am perfectly capable of looking after myself."

They were all ill-at-ease, and as Buchanan knew, people are least rational when they are afraid. But was Miss Roper afraid? She was obviously at a high nervous tension, but was it fear? Anyhow, one could hardly hold her here by force. Confound the woman!

"Are you two coming?" She set off across the compound, Mitchell in her wake. "Good-night, Alicia, good-night, George," she called.

Thompson looked after them and hesitated at the foot of the steps. "I'm going home, after all," he said. "I need a bath. But I don't think you need worry about Cooper. We'll find him in the swamp, if we find him at all."

Buchanan stared. "Then I think that we might very well worry about him. What do you mean, Thompson?"

"His nerve has snapped. He's run for it."

"Thompson, you're not seriously suggesting . . . ?"

"I think he's run for it," said Thompson.

"But where the devil can he run to?"

Thompson shrugged his shoulders. "I searched his place this afternoon. I haven't had a chance of speaking to you, away from the others, since. In a drawer, tucked between two shirts, I found a couple of pages torn from a notebook. They are in Smith's handwriting. And as far as I can make out, they are an analysis of your pitch deposits."

"Good Lord!" said Buchanan.

"One has the day before yesterday's date. With a bearing, or I take it to be a bearing, on the location of the specimen. The other is dated the day before that, with a different bearing. It looks as if Cooper and Smith had a common interest, doesn't it?"

"Yes," said Buchanan, "I suppose it does."

Thompson lit his pipe. "Think about that. And then you'll agree with me, I reckon, that Cooper has run for it."

"Yes, but what the hell is *it?* Where has he run to?" Buchanan smacked his hand on the railing. And then his eye caught a distant light. "By jove, he couldn't have gone off to the lugger, I suppose."

"I went off again myself this afternoon," said Thompson, and there was just the slightest hint of self-satisfaction in his voice. "And I've left Rata and that other boy, Murphy, there. And I think I reduced Mr. Sym Lung and his friend to a state of order. Now, if you'll excuse me, I'll go and take a kip."

"Wait a minute!" shouted Buchanan. "Thompson, what do you make of this?"

"Where there is a common interest," said Thompson, "there is ground for a quarrel. I think that Cooper quarreled with Smith. And I do not think that Cooper was ill last evening. I think he'd taken to his bed because . . ."

"Because what?"

"Because," said Thompson, "he was afraid of us."

He strode away, across the yard.

"Mr. Thompson!" called Alicia.

"Yes?"

"Oh, I don't know. But be careful. And don't be too sure."

Thompson laughed. "I'm a very careful sort of man," he said. And he went on. They heard his footsteps die away into the night.

"He was very anxious to be gone," said Alicia.

"He is very anxious," said Buchanan, "not to say a word more to me than he can help."

"Why?" said Alicia.

"I don't know. Unless he regards me as an accessory after the fact," said Buchanan grimly.

Alicia suddenly trembled. "Is it cold?" she said. "Or is someone walking over my grave?"

10

THIRD NIGHT

SHE HAD been asleep. She had not meant to sleep. She had not thought that she could sleep. The house had been appallingly hot, airless, as it was when the first dark storms were gathering at the beginning of the rains. Instinctively, one looked at the sky, looked for the dark to close in, purple and sullen. But the stars were yellow in heaven, and no clouds gathered. The menace was *here,* not *there*. It was not the time of thunder or of the icy rain that lashes tortured trees and changes the face of mountains: this was another Thing that brooded now over Kaitai.

She flung herself out of bed, felt for her dressing-gown.

"George," she called. "George!"

There was no answer.

She threw open her door. "George!"

He was not in the living-room. He was not on the long settee, where she had left him.

"George! George!" She ran onto the verandah. She cried out. "George!"

There was a queer, distorted echo from the shroud of trees.

She steadied herself against the verandah post. He was gone. Where?

She ran back into the house and found her torch. She turned up all the lights. She went out again. She had found the front door open. But he had locked it before she went to bed. Here was the key, still inside.

There was a patter of feet in the compound. Naked feet. She swung with her torch. Naqa leaped up onto the verandah.

"Naqa! Where is the Master?"

"I heard you call. I came." His eyes were like white balls in his face. He was clutching a heavy stick. Suddenly, he bounded like a cat. "Someone is running," he said.

Now she heard it. Someone running, up through the trees. Naqa leaped back towards the door. "Inside!" he cried. "Oh, please, inside!"

She turned the torch across the compound to the path. Whoever it was, he was coming by the path. Running very hard. But uncertainly.

"Stand there, Naqa," she said. "We shall see who it is."

He came, a shadow, a man. And as he ran he kept shouting: "Alicia!"

She ran to meet him. "George. George, what is it?"

And then she saw that his shirt was slashed with red from the shoulder to the waist.

He was sucking in tremendous breaths. "Alicia, you must come. At once. Bring your gear. It's Thompson." He collapsed on the verandah.

"My bag, Naqa. In my room. Shoes." She dropped on one knee beside George.

"No, no, that's Thompson's blood. He's dying, I think." He doubled over, panting.

2.

She stood up. "He's gone," she said.

Buchanan nodded and wiped his forehead. He stared down at the heavy face, strangely composed now.

"He looks as if he has found the Peace," said Alicia softly.

"*Requiescat,*" said Buchanan. "Shall we put him on his bed?"

"Yes. George, have you noticed that there is this same mark on his head as Smith had? There was one blow and then another, perhaps three, I think. One wound at least has the same kind of arched shape."

"Yes," he said. "I've noticed."

They carried him to his bed.

When they were done, they went back to the sitting-room. It was in the doorway, between sitting-room and bedroom that Thompson had died. Buchanan stooped and gathered the bloodied cushions.

"The bathroom is through there," he said, "if you want to wash."

She nodded and went through. Her pyjamas and dressing-gown were stained. She called through the door. "If Naqa is outside, tell him to fetch my clothes. A linen suit and the bundle of things on the chair in my bedroom."

"Would you like to go back? No, I daren't let you go back alone."

"Someone has to stay here. And I do not intend to leave you alone, either." She came to the bathroom door, and looked about at the room.

"What happened?" she said.

He waved at an overturned table, a smashed chair. "Thompson was hit, as he came out through that door. He must have been wakened. He was in bed, obviously. He wasn't knocked out at once. He must have dived at the man. And he cried out. I heard him. I was sitting on your settee, staring through the window, watching the compound. And I heard his cry. I ran straight out. He cried only once. I think he must have made one effort to get at grips. That's how the chair was smashed, the table overturned. But the second blow must have silenced him. He was still alive when I reached here. . ."

"How long did you take?"

"How far is it? Three hundred yards, by the path. I knew I couldn't get through the scrub, though it must be less, direct." He glanced at his watch. "About ten to two, it was."

"You saw, heard nothing of the other?"

"Nothing. He must have heard me coming."

"Thank God he did not wait for you."

"He may have known that I had a pistol," said George.

And then, she screamed. "George, look! Oh, look!"

The light in the lamp was failing.

And he laughed. He moved away towards the door, laughing and laughing. She crouched back, watching him, and her mind was in that instant like ice.

He saw her, and he stopped. "Sorry, Alicia. I'm a trifle rumpled, I'm afraid. But it did seem rather funny for a moment that the oil should burn out, now. I'll fetch the standard-lamp from the other room."

He brought it in and set it on the mantelshelf. "Alicia," he said quietly. "Will you go back into the bathroom and lock the door. There is someone outside. I thought I saw a shadow when the light failed. And I have just heard a board creak."

"You are not going out?"

He released the safety-catch of his pistol. "I am going out. Through the kitchen window. Lock that door. Please!"

She backed into the bathroom, and drew the door to her.

Buchanan took three casual steps towards the kitchen. Then he leapt across it and wrenched up the window. He swung over the sill, and dropped into the shadow. Then he went round the house as silently and as swiftly as he could.

And he said, "If you move your hands I shall put a bullet through you, Mitchell. Stand exactly where you are."

Mitchell, one foot on the porch step, turned his head.

"Is that a pistol or a pipe you've got there?" he growled.

"It's a pistol," said Buchanan, "And it shoots. Bullets."

"Are we playing something?" said Mitchell.

"What are you doing here?"

"I'm going to call on Thompson."

"Thompson is dead."

Buchanan saw Mitchell, against the pale reflection from the window, stiffen.

"What are you doing here?" he said again.

"When did Thompson die?" Mitchell's voice was harsh.

"Fifteen minutes ago."

"How? Murdered?"

"Murdered."

"Were you here?"

"I was here when he died."

"Who killed him? You?"

"I do not know who killed him. Yet. Now, perhaps you'll tell me what you are doing here?"

Mitchell relaxed. "It's a reasonable question, in the circumstances. I've just been prowling about. I couldn't sleep, so I came out to get some air." He stopped.

"Yes?" said Buchanan.

"Sounds pretty silly, doesn't it? It's true, though. Foul night, indoors. I came out and sat on my verandah for a bit. Then I began to wander about. Came towards the hospital, wondering whether you'd be up. And I saw a native running like hell from this direction. I bawled at him, but he shot off among the trees, towards the hospital. So I thought I'd wander down here and see if Thompson was holding a levee or something."

"How long ago was this?" snapped Buchanan.

"Just a few minutes ago."

"That would be Naqa. I sent him back to fetch the doctor's things." He moved forward. "Keep one hand up, Mitchell, and open that door with the other. We may as well go inside. But I'm taking no chances, and you'll have to forgive me if I appear discourteous. But sure as eggs are eggs, and they are, I'll shoot you if you play tricks."

"Don't apologize," said Mitchell. "I'm not arguing. But I've got nothing more lethal than a hammer in my pocket."

"Why have you got a hammer in your pocket?"

"I thought I might find some use for it. There seems to be a low character loose on Kaitai." He pushed the door with his foot, and Buchanan followed him closely as he went in.

He halted just over the threshold, and looked at the overturned table and the broken chair. "So Thompson fought for it, did he?"

"Get on," said Buchanan. "Sit in that chair. Facing me."

Alicia came out from the bathroom.

"Mitchell has a hammer in his pocket. Will you take it out, please?"

"It's in my hip-pocket. I'll have to stand up again."

Alicia pulled out the hammer.

"Let me see it, please," said Buchanan.

Alicia handed it to him, and he looked at it. It was clean.

"See what he has in his other pockets, please."

She emptied Mitchell's pockets.

"One packet of cigarettes," said Mitchell, "a dirty handkerchief, three pennies, a box of matches, a rusty screw . . . oh, yes, I forgot the piece of twine."

"That is all," said Alicia.

"Good. Then I can put this down. Sorry to be so investigatory, Mitchell. . . ."

"As I said, don't apologize. I'd offer to search you, if you'd agree."

"That might be as well," said Buchanan grimly. "Turn out my pockets, please, Alicia."

She turned out his pockets.

"I'm afraid I haven't anything to contribute myself," she said, "except a handkerchief and a box of matches from my dressing-gown."

"Mitchell, your explanation is thin. That's why I'm inclined to swallow it. If you had killed Thompson, you would hardly have back unless you were prepared to kill us. And if you were prepared to kill us, you would hardly have blundered about outside like an overgrown calf."

"That's what I have been thinking myself," said Mitchell, "only you put it more clearly. As a matter of fact, I didn't know whether to knock or not. I saw you and the doctor here through the window, and I wondered what was up. I was still wondering when you slid round the corner."

"How long have you been prowling, as you put it?"

Mitchell looked at his watch. "It's half past two now. I went home and went to bed some time after eleven. I kept the light burning. I've been feeling nervous, and I don't mind telling you so. I had the door locked. Round about midnight, there was a banging on it. I got up and looked for the hammer. Didn't have to look far. Had it under the bed, where I could reach it. Then I yelled out, 'Who's there?' It was Hawkesbury."

"What did he want?"

"A drink. And company. He was nearly all in. And scared. Said that Bernard had pushed on ahead of him and Nicholas. Hawkesbury grew a blister on his heel and couldn't keep up. Nicholas sort of got ahead of him, trying to keep in touch with Bernard. Finally, they both got away from him. He sat on a rock for a while, and then he found that the trees about him were starting to move. So he ran. By the time he reached me, he was in a sweat, I can tell you. I reckon he must have run all the way home. I gave him a trebel whisky, and after a bit, he eased off. But he'd had a proper attack of the willies, and he wasn't arguing about it, either."

"Is he still at the Club?"

"No, after a while, he began to feel ashamed of himself, and he said he'd go off to bed. I got up then and pulled on my pants. I walked across with him."

"Why?"

"We went to see if Swan had come back."

"Had he?"

"No."

"Was there any sign of Miss Roper as you passed?"

"Only a light burning. You could just see it. Her curtains

were drawn. I saw Hawkesbury into his place, and I bet he looked under the bed. Then I started back again. But I didn't feel much like going home. I wasn't very keen about going to sleep. I sleep heavy. So did Thompson, you know."

"I know. I've thought of that," said Buchanan. "And I think that whoever killed him knew it."

"I think that whoever killed him did not expect to find him here," said Alicia quietly.

"He did say something about sleeping at the hospital," said Mitchell. "But why the devil did his murderer come here at all if he didn't expect to find Thompson?"

Buchanan walked across the room and looked at the old, flimsy safe that stood behind Thompson's desk. It was actually little more than a strong-box.

Mitchell whistled.

Buchanan stooped. And then he tugged something from the lock. It was a strong piece of wire.

Mitchell whistled again. "Well, that's interesting. I didn't think we had a wireworker amongst us, Buchanan."

"No," said Buchanan. "Neither did I."

Mitchell stretched over and took the wire from him. "That's the sort of trick you learn in stir. During recreation, from the experts. Which of the local inhabitants has been in the jug?"

"I didn't know that any had," said Buchanan slowly.

"So, there he was, working away quietly at the safe, when he heard Thompson on the move." Mitchell glanced at the bedroom door. "And he laid for him as he came out. What with? Have you found the weapon?"

"No," said Buchanan, "we have not found the weapon."

Alicia glanced at him. "There was more than one blow.

One was with a heavy piece of wood, I think. There were splinters in the basin after I had washed the wounds. The other blow was with something curved."

"Like Smith's?"

"Like Smith's."

"And then he ran for it, leaving his bit of wire in the lock. What is in that safe, Buchanan?"

"I do not think we shall open it just yet."

They sat silent for a few minutes. Mitchell, Buchanan noticed, kept turning his eyes to the stain by the bedroom door. Each time, he wrenched his eyes away. Each time they returned.

"Are we going to sit here all night?"

"I rather think we are," said Buchanan.

"Buchanan!" Mitchell raised his voice. "Have you thought about those boys in the lugger?"

"What do you mean?"

"What in hell do you think I mean?" He kicked at the chair. "That Chink. He's a nasty item. And Thompson had been giving them some attention. He went out this afternoon and ramped all over the deck." Mitchell straightened in his chair. "Gave them both a kick in the pants before he left."

"How do you know?"

"Because I went with him. And I can tell you, he made them sore. I thought he was pretty hot myself, though I agreed with him on general principles."

"What was he after?"

"Whatever he was after, he didn't get it. But he would have got a knife between the shoulder-blades if that Chink had had a sympathetic joss. The other fellow, the cross-breed, just curled up on the deck, but the Chinaman got more and more wooden. And didn't Thompson bring some stuff off the lugger after your first visit?"

"Yes." Buchanan found himself looking at the safe. "Yes, he did."

"It's in there, is it?" Mitchell swung round to it. "It is, eh? What exactly is it, Buchanan?"

"Only the ship's papers, and some of Smith's own personal papers. And a sample of the stuff from the swamp."

"Have you examined them?"

"Only casually, on the lugger, as we checked them."

"Had Thompson looked them over?"

"I don't know."

"I'll bet he had."

"Are you suggesting that the Chinese boy came ashore, tried to pick Thompson's safe, and then when Thompson interrupted him smashed in Thompson's head?"

"Doesn't sound quite so probable put like that," said Mitchell. "But the heathen had it in for Thompson."

Buchanan frowned. Was it so unlikely, after all? Smith, he imagined, would not have been an amiable master. By the time the lugger had reached Kaitai, his boys may well have been ready to murder him, if an opportunity occurred. And they would certainly be aware that an accident, in a small boat, at night, off a windy beach, could seem very plausible. Had one of them slipped ashore that night? How? Smith had the dinghy. But it was not a terrific swim for men bred to small craft in tropical waters. The cross-breed had, quite probably, been a bare-skin diver in his time, while the Chinese had lived all his life with the sea.

And the business last night at the hospital had at least as much meaning if you attributed it to Smith's boys as it had now.

And if Thompson had bullied and threatened them, this raid on his house was not inconceivable. Perhaps there was something in Smith's papers which threatened them, or promised them some profit, or jarred their superstitions. The difficulty all along had been to uncover the workings of the murderer's mind. It had seemed alien from any on the island. But if the mind at work was the mind of Sym Lung, the very incomprehensibility would become comprehensible, so to speak. One would understand why one could not understand.

But what of Cooper, in that case? What of Cooper's flight? And what of the papers, Smith's analyses, in Cooper's house? Had he stolen them? Or had they been planted there? Could Sym Lung or Charlie Lord Nelson have planted them there? Or someone who had noticed Cooper's absence before the rest discovered it and who was ready to incriminate him?

Cooper's absence itself was so ominous. That was the difficulty. Why had he broken for the wildwood unless he had a guilty conscience? The mere fact that he had, apparently, run was incriminating. But if Smith had been murdered by Cooper, then Cooper had presumably murdered Thompson too. He had come back for that. Surely, if all this were true, the little man must be mad.

Why should he have killed Smith, what conceivable quarrel could he have with Smith? Unless, of course, as Thompson had suggested, some common interest had made common ground for a quarrel. The analyses and the pitch deposits. Was Cooper somehow involved with Smith there? How had Smith come to the island, how had he first learned of the deposits? Had Cooper prompted him, had he come here on Cooper's tip?

Oh, but damn and blast, could one live, day by day, with a man like Cooper and so mistake him?

Wasn't it much more likely that Cooper had just lost his nerve and bolted, like a timid rabbit, blindly? First he had taken to his bed, in sheer fright; then he had streaked for the nearest horizon. He would probably crawl home, sooner or later, thoroughly ashamed of himself. Or some of the natives would pick him up. Unless he had gone into the swamp.

One was reluctant, anyhow, to believe that the pleasant little man, with his pathetic, puppy-like friendliness, was anything but what he had seemed, in spite of Thompson's last hints.

It was very trying indeed to be a detective, especially if one thought too much. Detectives are stern men who deal with facts. They have a simple faith in facts. But what are facts? One can never isolate a fact from the context of the mind which observes it, and even mathematicians are given to whimsy. Yet he obviously must take up the burden of Thompson. He must attend to matters of fact. Even if he did hang poor Cooper, finally, on some silly piece of evidence which would utterly fail to explain Cooper in any serious sense at all.

But where did one begin?

One should begin, presumably, where Thompson left off. But where had Thompson left off? He realized now that Thompson had spoken very little of his mind. But he had had nearly two days to worry at the problem of Smith, and a man from Scotland Yard would almost certainly make something of something in a couple of days.

What would Thompson have made, how would Thompson's mind have worked?

He would have gathered all the facts. Facts about the place, about the method of the crime, about the people. Well, Buchanan surely knew all the facts about the place himself. And about the method of the crime. But what of the facts about the people?

He had flattered himself that he knew a good deal more about the people than anyone else on the island. But did he? He was so damned fond of entertaining himself with subtleties. Perhaps he missed the simpler things just because they were simple.

What sort of facts would Thompson have looked for in all these people. Physical facts? The police always attended to physical facts. Biometric measurements, and footprints and fingerprints, and things of that sort.

Fingerprints. Thompson had been interested in fingerprints.

His jaw dropped a little.

"Thought of something?" said Mitchell.

"Mitchell, did Thompson, when he went off to the lugger, take those boys' fingerprints?"

"Yes, he did."

"How did he take them?"

"An inked roller and some sheets of paper. Ruled off. Just like the police use."

"What did he do with them?"

"Brought them ashore, of course."

"H'm'm. He didn't send any message off on the radio, I suppose."

"No. No. But I think he may have intended to. He asked me whether I'd had any trouble getting through to Durabaya.

And when was the best time to send out a call. Then we went up to the funeral, and after that we hunted all the evening for Cooper. He didn't mention it again."

"I see." But what did one see?

He rose, and went into Thompson's bedroom. He did not look at the thing shrouded in its sheet. But he found Thompson's belt, hanging loosely from his trousers. And he unfastened the ring of keys.

He came back to the living-room, and he walked across to the safe. The third key opened it. He swung back the door. He heard Mitchell close behind him. He stood up.

"If you don't mind, I should prefer you to sit in your chair, Mitchell."

"Don't trust me altogether?" Mitchell grinned.

"At the moment, I cannot afford to trust anybody."

"Suppose I reciprocate? You forget, Buchanan, that you may seem just as likely a suspect to any of us as we do to you."

"I don't forget it," said Buchanan. "The point is that someone has to use authority, and, on Kaitai, authority happens to be mine." He turned back to the safe.

It was almost full. Neat bundles of bills and receipts, clipped in rubber bands: a cash-book: packets of letters: a book of newspaper clippings. All these on the top shelf. Buchanan took them out, one by one, and set them in order against the wall. He turned a few pages of the pasted clippings. Reports of old court-cases, cases presumably in which Thompson had been interested. Yes, here was his name . . . P.C. Thompson, Sergeant Thompson, Sub-Inspector Thompson.

The second shelf: a passport, a warrant-card, an album of photographs, the Thompson family album, presumably. A wedding-group, the bridesmaids bustled, the bride rather plump, the gentlemen in winged ties and whiskers. The bride again, no longer a bride, but staring stiffly at her infant off-spring. Was that Thompson in a frock? A shop-front, with the bridegroom of the wedding-group, aproned now and wearing a bowler hat . . . *John Thompson, Grocer and General Storekeeper*. Pathetic, in its way. Were there other Thompsons to whom all this could be returned? There was a brother, who sometimes wrote.

There was an envelope. Yes, here were Smith's analyses. He read them, and his face darkened.

There was a small cardboard-box. It appeared to be full of photographs. Photographs taken on the ship, photographs of Naples, and the Grand Harbor at Malta, and the breakwater at Port Said, and the railway-station at El Kantara, and the harsh mountain mass of the Suez coast, and the dark rock of Aden. One or two skittish ones of passengers on the ship. A gentleman showing his suspenders, three girls against a life-buoy, Thompson with an officer who, as one's experience of shipboard photographs ran, was almost certainly the Chief Officer. Another officer, rather bibulous in general effect, and probably the ship's doctor.

Photographs on Kaitai. The island from different aspects. All neatly marked and dated. Several oddish blotches: *Sunset* 12.4.38, *Sunset* 5.8.39, *Sunset* 7.26.39. Thompson had had his poetry then, even if the photographs were not particularly successful, unless in a surrealist sense.

And then he grunted. For here were other blotches, but unmistakable ones. They were photographs of fingerprints, not very complete, not very good, but still, sufficient for an identification, no doubt, if a man knew the job. One could see the materials on which they had been developed. This was a gin bottle. Several prints showed black on the white label, others grey against the dark glass. He turned it over. It was dated, too, with one initial, *H.* Hawkesbury, perhaps. And this set was developed on a glass. *N. S.* Swan. And another set from a glass, a sherry-glass this time. Sherry is sticky. *D. R.* Dorothy Roper. Another on the dark, shiny surface of the overturned table there. *M.* Mitchell did sweat a lot. He was sweating there now, beside the lamp. And his arm was resting on the table, hand and fingers spread, as he canted his chair sideways. He often sat like that. *G.B.* Blast! When had he ever looked at the *New Yorker* with filthy fingers? It is extraordinary, of course, what graphite powder will bring up on a smooth surface. His fingers had probably been spotless, really. And here were Alicia's, from a metal surface, it seemed. All of them here. Except Bernard's. But Bernard did not give so many opportunities, perhaps.

He slipped them all back amongst the other photographs, and bent to the third shelf. There was a large white envelope, with yesterday's date in pencil. He opened it. Here were the inked prints: Smith's, taken from his dead fingers, and two other sets marked *Nelson* and *Sym Lung*.

There were photographs too.

"Alicia, when did Thompson photograph Smith's injuries?"

"When the body was carried up to the hospital. In the mortuary. Didn't you know?"

"I didn't," said Buchanan grimly.

If the skull had been shattered to destroy the original shape of the injuries, the murderer had been too late. Did he know that? Was that why he had broken in here tonight? Or had he discovered that Thompson had been searching for fingerprints? Both, perhaps.

Buchanan felt, with a queer sense of resentment, that Thompson might at least have troubled to leave some notes.

He put these things into their envelope again and the envelope into his pocket. What had Thompson made of it all? Had he found any prints at the hospital? There were no more photographs. But he had taken these photographs of Smith's battered head the day before yesterday. He had only searched for prints at the hospital yesterday, after the attack on Alicia.

"What sort of a camera did he use, Alicia? I know he had that large thing he used on a tripod. Was that it? Didn't he have a small pocket camera as well?"

"Yes. That's what he used. A small Zeiss, with a very good lens. It does extraordinarily fine work. I've seen some of the photographs he has taken with it."

"I wonder where it is? Where did he develop? In the bathroom, I suppose."

He went into the bathroom, but there was no camera there. He recrossed the living-room and went into the bedroom. He turned out Thompson's pockets. And then he looked under the bed. And into the wardrobe. He found it on the shelf. Inside Thompson's topee. So Thompson had had it with him yesterday. He had taken it out of his pocket when he reached home and dropped it into his topee when he put his topee away, as one might drop one's gloves into one's hat.

He turned the camera over. It was loaded. The number on the spool stood at 10. He had taken nine photographs. Nine photographs, waiting to be developed. And Buchanan had never developed a photograph in his life. What did one do about that?

One of the others might know how to develop. Mitchell,

for instance, had a remarkable series of photographs of the natives. But was it safe to give the film to Mitchell to develop? Alicia used a camera too, sometimes. But this must wait. One did not want to broadcast news of Thompson's shots. He dropped the camera into his own pocket and went back to the living-room.

"Any luck?" said Mitchell.

"No." Truth must sometimes cover her nakedness.

Mitchell sniffed. Perhaps Truth looked a trifle awkward in her chemise. "What are you going to do now?" he asked.

"I wish Naqa would come with my things," said Alicia.

"I probably frightened him out of his onions," said Mitchell. "Would you like me to go and fetch him."

Buchanan frowned.

"We can't sit about here waiting for the dawn," said Mitchell. "Or can we?"

"Are you cold, Alicia?"

"Good heavens, no. I just feel like something out of *La Vie Bohème*, that's all, sitting about in pyjamas and wrap." She looked appallingly tired. Her face was drawn and peaked, and her bandage had slipped. She should certainly be in bed. But if he took her home, he must leave the house unguarded, and it was possible that Thompson's murderer was watching for another chance at the safe.

"There is a rug in Thompson's wardrobe. Won't you lie down, if we stack those cushions a bit?"

"If I shut my eyes, I shall just go to sleep. And I am afraid to go to sleep." She smiled at him. It was a very good effort on the whole.

"I could go and get your things, you know," said Mitchell.

She shook her head. "No. No. I wouldn't think of it." Her

eyes turned to the drawn curtains. "As it is, I keep thinking I can hear somebody, something at the window." She shivered suddenly. "No, no, I can't hear anything really, but . . ."

"It isn't exactly a pleasant situation, is it?" said Mitchell.

"There!" She stiffened in her chair. Then she laughed. "No, it's stupid of me."

But Mitchell was staring at the window and his eyes were wide.

"Douse that lamp!" he whispered.

Buchanan snapped the shutter. Mitchell was across the room, crouching at the window. He pulled back the curtain and raised his eyes to the sill. And they heard, strange in the night, a heavy sigh. And then something, like a dead weight of flesh, dropped on the verandah.

"My God!" whispered Mitchell.

"Look!" said Alicia.

The verandah door was moving, slowly, with incredible slowness. In the faint light, in the crack, the widening crack of the door, was something white. It was near the bottom of the door, it was sliding down, its slow pressure was moving the door, inwards. And then they saw it was a hand, a human hand. It fell flat on the floor, and was still.

Buchanan leaped.

11

THE RETURN OF COOPER

"IT'S COOPER," said Buchanan.

"Get him here. On this sofa thing. Quickly." Alicia turned. "Mitchell, get a basin of water. The bathroom there. Behind you. And towels. And put on a kettle. We may need it. Let me feel his pulse, George."

He lay, utterly limp. One shoe was gone, his foot swollen, blistered, bleeding through the torn socks. His shirt and trousers were in tatters. He was muddied to the knees, there was mud on his arms, on his face, in his hair.

"Get his clothes off, George. There's a scissors there. Don't turn him. Cut them away. There's iodine in my bag. He's badly scratched. Mitchell, more towels. There's a pile in that cupboard in the bathroom. We'll need compresses. George, my bag! That capsule. There in the metal container. And a glass. Water. My syringe. In the container too. Two of those tablets in the glass. Now, water. About a tablespoonful. Let them dissolve. Yes, yes, for the syringe. Have you put the kettle on? An inch or so of water. I want it quickly. Yes, boiling."

Buchanan slit the shirt and drew it and the trousers gently away. They told their own story, and so did the torn flesh.

Cooper had evidently wandered off into the reaches of the swamp, and then, somehow, had struggled back, through the low, thorny scrub of the marshy levels. He must have realized his danger before he had fled too far. If he had gone into the heart of the swamp, he would never have struggled out, alone. There were quagmires, green and treacherous.

"What do you make of him, Alicia?"

"Shock and exhaustion."

"Will he live?"

"Yes, of course. Unless there are complications." She listened to his heart. "I wonder what his history is. His breathing is a shade better. Are his clothes very wet? There is always a chance of pneumonia."

"They've been wet and dry and wet and dry, I think. The upper mud is caked, but down here, below the knees, he seems to have been paddling again."

"Let's hope he hasn't poisoned himself in any of those cuts. Is the kettle boiling? Good." She dipped her syringe. "Now fill it and put it on again, please. And if there is a saucepan you might fill that and put it on the other jet. There are two burners, aren't there? We'll have to wash out these scratches. Oh, dear, his legs are nearly in ribbons at the back. Poor little man!" She raised her hypodermic.

Buchanan stood back. He felt in the pockets of the trousers. There had been nothing, he remembered, in the pockets of the discarded jacket, lying now in Thompson's bedroom.

There was little enough here. A box of matches, a crumpled handkerchief, a pocket compass. The trousers were filthy. He picked up a leg. Scorched, too. Three distinct burns, here by the cuff. Presumably Cooper had made himself a fire during the night.

He tried the hip-pocket. There was a soiled, creased envelope. He turned it over. It was addressed:

George Buchanan, Esq.

2.

My dear Buchanan,

I hardly know whether you will receive this or not. I doubt whether I have the courage to give it to you. I know now that I have not the courage to say to your face what I have written here. That is why I write it. I may screw myself to the sticking-place, as Hamlet says. It was Hamlet, was it not? I cannot think properly tonight.

What I must tell you, what I should have told you today, is that I am, in a sense, responsible for the visit of the man Smith to Kaitai. Let me hasten to add that I am innocent of his death in any other sense than that my indiscretion brought him here. I feel that I can contribute nothing to a solution of the mystery. But that hardly eases my conscience.

The truth of the matter is that I informed a friend of mine, a person in the City, of the asphalt deposits on this island. I had no intention of making mischief. I was hardly aware that it could provoke mischief. I mentioned it more or less in passing, when I was writing to him some months back. I was speaking of your solicitude for the natives, of your remarkable disinterestedness, and I cited your refusal to exploit this particular resource of the island, as an evidence.

To my inexpressible dismay, I learned from the man Smith that my erstwhile acquaintance had used my letter to interest a number of people and to form an investigatory syndicate. The man Smith was employed by them to visit Kaitai, to take samples of the material, to test it, and if the circumstances seemed favorable to open negotiations with yourself. All this I learned from Smith only yesterday, when he handed to me copies of his analyses and demanded my co-operation in his approach to you. I cannot adequately describe to you my dismay. I feel like a traitor to you and to the island, like (if I may be permitted a vulgar expression) a mongrel which bites the hand that has fed it. I am especially distressed because I see no way to convince you that my indiscretion was innocent. It must seem to you, surely, that I was myself moved by some hope of profit, when I communicated this information to my correspondent, especially as Smith disguised the purpose of his visit from the first. The affair bears all the outward marks of a conspiracy, and I cannot tell you, my dear Buchanan, how deep is my distress. I fled yesterday to my bed, hoping that I could, in seclusion, find the courage to speak to you. But my courage has failed me utterly. If it had not, I think I might well end my life. There is little in it which persuades me to prolong it, except that strange, instinctive clinging to existence which is natural to the most miserable of earth's creatures. Since my dear wife died, I have lived out my days without zest or pleasure. Often I think that I might well end it all, and now the prospect of having to face you with this story intensifies the temptation. It would be so easy to walk out into the sea.

Yet I cannot forget Smith's eyes, those horrible sockets where the crabs had fed. God help me, I feel utterly alone in this world.

I shall send this letter to you by the hand of a native, perhaps, unless, indeed, my courage fails even for that.

There are times when I seem to myself to be magnifying

the importance of it. I find it very difficult now to think clearly. I should certainly be better dead.

If I find the resolution to remove myself from this life. I can only trust, my dear Buchanan, that I shall be less trouble to you in death than I have been in life.

It is difficult indeed to discover the right course. I am only aware of this crushing sense of the trouble I have, however unwittingly, brought on Kaitai. What an ungrateful return for all your kindnesses to me! ! !

It has taken me several hours to compose this letter, for I have paused often to consider it all. And a resolution to end my life grows in me. If you receive this letter, I shall have acted on that resolution. You will find the analyses of which I spoke thrown into one of my drawers, together with my other papers, my will, the name and address of the correspondent to whom I have referred, and so on.

If this indeed is my last communication to you, permit me to thank you and all my friends here again and again for many consolations and kindnesses.

I am, my dear Buchanan,

Most sincerely yours.

3.

Buchanan put the letter back into its envelope. He crossed the room to Thompson's desk, and took some gum, and carefully pasted down the flap where he had torn it. Then he wet his finger and rubbed it in the mud of Cooper's trousers, and he smeared it over the mend. He put the letter back into Cooper's pocket.

The letter had been intended only for post-mortem publication, so to speak, and it must embarrass their future relations if Cooper learned that he had read it. Buchanan felt distinctly uncomfortable, as it was.

Cooper had been stupid to make so much of the affair. Yet it was like him. One could understand his distress. But suicide was a heavy penalty to set himself.

Happily, however, he had changed his mind. He had struggled back from his swamp.

One could sense in his stilted phrases something of his strange agony.

How odd it was that a man should come out of Balham or of Brixton, after all his sober years as a London clerk, to fight his fight in a tropical swamp. Our ends are strangely shaped.

4.

"How is he?"

"He is in a normal sleep now," said Alicia.

Buchanan walked out on to the verandah. There was a faint streak of pink in the dull grey, and here and there in the bush birds called, silver and remote.

Mitchell tapped out his pipe. "How is the little man?"

"Sleeping."

"Good." Mitchell pointed with the stem of his pipe. "That's his mark on the verandah."

There was a muddy impression from a rounded iron heeltap.

"It comes straight up from the direction of the swamp," said Mitchell. "I picked it up in that dug soil at the bottom, where Thompson tried to grow his cabbages."

Buchanan nodded. "Yes," he said. "Yes." He looked about

at the hard clay for signs of any other prints, but there were none.

He swung under the railing.

"Good!"

Mitchell shifted along, and Buchanan plumped down beside him.

"Strenuous night," said Mitchell.

"Damned strenuous. Got a match?"

Mitchell held a match to his cigarette.

"Mitchell, who exactly are you?"

Mitchell grunted. "I wondered when this would come. Aren't you satisfied with my original story?"

"As far as my own inclinations are concerned, I do not care very much. But this is a situation in which my own inclinations are, to say the least, irrelevant. My inclination, at the moment, is to retire to Surbiton. But Providence has appointed me another vocation. Did you have a vocation, by the way?"

Mitchell was startled. "What made you say that, Buchanan?"

"Oh, I'm not such an idiot as I look. Not always."

Mitchell dropped his pipe to the ground. He stooped to pick it up. His face was red. And his voice, when it came, was curiously muffled.

"I thought I had a vocation, once," he said.

"You ran away from it?"

"Ran? Maybe."

Buchanan saw the white of his knuckles and kept silent. It was a long silence.

"I came here," said Mitchell at last, slowly, "because I wanted time to think. To think."

He paused again: but after a minute, Buchanan said, even while knowing it a stupid thing to say, "Think about what?"

Mitchell looked up. "Buchanan, you have always taken me for a good deal of a fool, haven't you? You've recognized, of course, that I can do this silly little job you have given me here more or less efficiently, but otherwise and in general, you think I'm a . . ."

"No, I don't!" Buchanan interrupted. "That's just it. I have always thought that you wanted to be mistaken for a fool. And that provoked me. Why should you want to be mistaken for a fool? Only two kinds of people are normally willing to be thought fools, the wise and the humble. And I don't suppose they are two kinds of people at all. Wisdom and humility are the obverse and the reverse. Yet you didn't seem to me a humble man, or a wise man, in the senses which I mean. I thought you were a shrewd, experienced, man of the world, making quite a stubborn effort to disguise yourself. I thought something else of you. I thought, and I think, that you did feel yourself to have a vocation of some sort, and that . . . well, you have not satisfied yourself in it."

Mitchell nodded. "That isn't bad diagnosis. I am certainly not humble. My pride was my sin, probably. And I have tried to appear something other than I am in sheer self-protection. You've seen a mountain-devil, funny little lizard thing. It looks as ferocious as it can, though it is quite harmless. I shouldn't say that I'm harmless, but it's much the same instinct."

"You are a clergyman, of course," said Buchanan.

Mitchell stared. "Good lord, no! What on earth made you think that?"

Buchanan blushed. "Sorry. I don't know, really, except that I've always had just a shade of a notion that you might be a clergyman."

Mitchell grinned. "Defrocked, eh? That's funny. Didn't someone say that of Swan? Well, I'm damned!" His grin widened. "No, as a matter of fact, I was a Member of Parliament. I used to play football, too. That was how I became a Member of Parliament."

"Yes, of course," said Buchanan, a trifle bewildered. "One thing just leads to another, as De Quincey pointed out."

Mitchell shook his head. "De Quincey did not know what football can lead to," he said, "in Australia."

"I am not quite sure," said Buchanan, "whether I have committed an unpardonable gaucherie or not."

"I've nothing against clergymen," said Mitchell, "when they'll only make up their minds what they believe in. And stick to it. Nowadays, it seems to me, there are too many of them who let down their own side. And a clergyman playing up to the grandstand is a nasty spectacle. It's bad enough in a politician, but then a politician is a public performer and it is expected of him."

"And you were a public performer?"

"The trouble with me was that I began to take myself seriously. I began to think that if one were a Member of Parliament one might begin to do something about it. It? The way people live, the food they eat, the prices they pay for it, the wages they get. Most people's lives seem to me one succession of kicks in the pants. I tried to do something about it, and I got kicked in the pants myself. Heartily. Maybe I ought to have padded my pants before I started, but there you are. And here I am. Unbloodied, maybe, but considerably bent.

I've retired from the scenes of my triumphs, like the Emperor Charles V. He had exceptional facilities, with rack and dungeon and screws and headsmen, but even he had enough of it. His intentions were good, too."

Buchanan flicked his cigarette across the yard. "What happened?"

"It's a dull story. I was a pretty good footballer, a better footballer than I ever was a politician. That gave me a pull with the lads about the place and presently I found myself on the district committee of the Party. Then I began to grow ambitions. I did some night classes at the University. Then I took a saloon. That's the way you rise in the world. The pub was in a pretty poor district, waterside, just, of course, where a beer-merchant can acquire most influence. But the poverty began to get under my skin. I began to take the planks in the platform seriously. And . . ." He shrugged his shoulders. "It was the same old story. Just like little Alice, the village maiden. She learned from experience, but she learned too late. She was left to lump the baby. So was I. Taking one thing with another, I don't care if I never see a ballot-box again."

Buchanan stared across the veil of trees. "You never met Smith before he came here?"

"No. I did not kill Smith, Buchanan. I realize it isn't much use protesting. It's proofs you need, not assurances. I've papers to prove my identity, if you care to look at them, but they aren't particularly relevant, I suppose."

"Oh, I believe you," said Buchanan, "as much as I believe anything at the moment. Mitchell, when you and Miss Roper went home last night, what happened? Did you look into Cooper's place to see if he was there? You said you would, if I remember."

"Yes, we did. At least, we went up and pushed the door—it was open—and called out. There wasn't any answer. The whole place was in darkness. We stood there talking a minute or two."

"What did you talk about?"

"The affair at large. Miss Roper asked whether Thompson had taken my fingerprints, and we talked about that. And then she asked whether Thompson was spending the night with you at the hospital or whether he was going home. I said I thought he was staying at the hospital. He changed his mind, didn't he? And then I said something about him gathering Cooper's papers and taking them off to his place for safe-keeping. She said that he must have felt certain that Cooper was dead, to do that. And then she came back to the fingerprints. What could Thompson do with fingerprints? And I said that he could ask various police forces to check them, if there was need for that."

"You knew that Thompson had removed Cooper's papers then?"

"Yes, he asked me to witness it. He said that anyone might come and rummage round, if that way inclined, and that it would be safer to take charge of the stuff."

"Did he look at any of it closely?"

"Only a couple of loose bits of paper lying on top of the drawer. He didn't go through the bundles of stuff. No, I don't think Thompson was just prying. He expected to find a suicide note, I think. He as much as said so. Sounds rather a rotten thing to say, now that little Cooper has turned up, but Thompson was fastening onto anything that looked like a note."

"I see. Then you and Miss Roper both knew that Thompson had removed Cooper's papers. And you both thought that Thompson would be away from his bungalow tonight."

Mitchell's jaw came forward, ominously. "Trying to make a case?" he said.

"No," said Buchanan wearily. "Trying to make sense, that's all." He stretched himself. "I've said that I believe you as much as I feel justified in believing anyone or anything at the moment. Perhaps you'll go and see about a grave for Thompson. And a coffin. Here are his measurements." He walked a few paces to the corner of the house and looked out across the morning sea, steel-blue in the early light. And then he leaped. "Mitchell!" he shouted. "Mitchell, the lugger's gone."

12

ONCE ABOARD THE LUGGER

THE BOY, Rata, quailed.

"How did it happen?" snarled Buchanan.

"They kicked us overboard. With their boots."

"Were you drunk?"

"Not drunk, no."

The second boy suddenly began to howl, terrific wailing cries.

"Stop that!" yelled Buchanan. "Stop it! Here, Benjamin, smack his head."

Benjamin smacked his head.

"Now, you two, I want this story straight." Buchanan was very grim. "If there are lies, I shall peg you out in the place of the ants, and they will feed on you, slowly, at great length, and your thirst will be more terrible than the thirst of Iqua, who swallowed the volcano of Bu, and erupted all the days of his life. And even he did not have ants in his pants. I left you in authority on the lugger, Rata, because it was my foolish belief that you could be trusted. You have failed me. My confidence was misplaced. All the people are aware that my servant has betrayed me. And if there is one thing more than another for which the Buchanans are rightly distinguished amongst men, it is for their just wrath. The voices of my fathers are in my ears, and they are angry voices. It was not thus and thus that they were used by their servants. When they said go, their servants emphatically went. And when they said stay, their servants were as men changed into stone, immoveable as the mountain. But I said stay, and you did not stay. At this moment, my heart burns with anger. The volcano of Bu is, by comparison, a most inferior affair, a mere pot-boiling kind of fire, such as the women keep in the grass houses, without any fear of consequences. Why have you betrayed me, you utterly inferior and detestable products of unbelievable lapses on the part of your parents?"

Rata shook in the morning breeze. He recalled, he, in his old age, Buchanan the First: and here was the authentic note. It was very terrifying to an aged man, who had hoped to eat his last rice where he had eaten it for forty years, in the shadow of the Palace; and he had hoped too that his service would commend to the Sultan his sons' sons, who were now almost of adult age and singularly indisposed to arduous toil.

"They kicked us overboard," he quavered, "with their boots. They are men of terrible aspect, and their knives flash in the light like the fin of the white shark as it turns, like the silver belly of that water-snake which is deadlier than the white shark, like the teeth of a woman in the night. The yellow man is a man of death, he has consorted with magicians, the lightning strikes for him, his knife was thrice washed in human blood before the temple of Ipata, and his boots, with which he kicked, were like the leaden boots of the White Man Who Dives in the Sea."

"None of that impresses me in the least," said Buchanan. "If the present threat of the House of Buchanan is not greater than that of a remote and highly improbable Ipata, it is obviously time that I pulled on my own boots. And there are also the boots of Mitchell, who once played centre-forward for Richmond. He has a kick coming in any case because you have broken into his stores. And stolen gin to regale the detestable Sym Lung."

"His claws are more ferocious than the claws of the Divine Crab, Ataqi. And he had threatened to tear out our throats and the throats of our daughters if we did not obey him."

"What were your daughters doing on the lugger?" demanded Buchanan, his brow thunderous.

"They had come off to the lugger in my canoe, with food for their fathers."

"It sounds rather like a new version of *Dan, Dan the Signalman,* and the Fish and Chips Express," said Buchanan. "By the Hat of my Great-Uncle Buchanan, it is time and more than time that discipline was re-introduced into this community. What, may I ask, you things born out of season, did your daughters do when Sym Lung and Charlie Lord Nelson kicked you overboard?"

"They laughed," said Rata, and now his brow blackened. It was plain that he would have words to say too if his occasion arose.

"And what did you do?" said Buchanan.

"We swam ashore."

"And then?"

"When we look back, the lugger is going."

"And your daughters are probably laughing on the further side of their faces now. The fact is, Rata, that you and this howling thing here whose soul is the soul of a frog went on a bender with the terrific Sym Lung, and as soon as he had got you drunk enough, he dispensed with your presences. But why has Sym Lung fled, and where? Can you answer that?"

Rata shook his head forlornly.

"Did he not understand that the arm of Buchanan reaches out to pluck men from the decks of ships a thousand miles away?"

Rata shook his head again. Sym Lung, regrettably, did not understand that.

"Then you should have made it clear to him. What time was it when he pitched you overboard?"

Rata's head continued to shake, more and more dismally. "We had not the machine which informs one of the passage of time."

"You mean that you were too drunk to notice."

"We were sleeping on the deck," said Rata miserably.

"And you woke in the water. I thought as much. And it is my one regret that Tka, the blue shark, seems also to have been neglecting his responsibilities last night. One looks to him to keep the bay clean of offal. Of offal, you understand." Buchanan wiped his forehead. It had been a strenuous interview. He spoke in English, for Mitchell. "I'm afraid that is all the sense we are likely to get from them. You had better go and send out that call to Durabaya. They may be able to suggest something. I hope so. My own mind has withered."

He turned back to the shivering boys. "There is a corner yonder in the sun. Near the bush that attracts flies. You will stand there, and you will continue to stand there until I remember to tell you not to stand there. It is unlikely that I shall remember. Nevertheless, you will remain. You will receive one bowl of water four times a day, and a bowl of rice, without bamboo shoots, at evening. And you will oblige me by mixing mud . . ."

Rata raised his hands in horrified protest.

"Yes," said Buchanan, "by mixing mud and putting it upon your head and smearing it on your cheeks, so that you will ultimately come to look like mud-pack treatments in a beauty-parlour. And if you do not know what a beauty-parlour is, I can only say you have been saved much. You will smear the mud thickly. And I shall send messages through all the villages that Rata and Murphy are here exposed to the public mock and scorn, and that I, Buchanan, shall take it as a personal favor if any of my subjects will favor you with their frankest epithets. They shall not, however, throw stones at you. Or lumps of coral. Or crabs, Stinking seaweed and dead jellyfish, yes. I shall consider whether you are also to wear the hats of paper."

Rata's head fell to his breast, in an abyss of shame.

"My great-uncle was of a pedagogic turn of mind," explained Buchanan to Mitchell. "His most fearsome punishment was to stand them in a corner with dunces' hats. They disliked it very much, and I always reserve it as my final threat. Do you know how to make a dunce's hat, by the way? You have to do complicated things with the paper, I imagine, and I was never very good at that sort of thing."

Dorothy Roper came behind them. She held out her hand to Buchanan. "George, I cannot tell you how sorry I am. For your sake as well as Thompson's. I do, truly, realize how terrible this must be for you. Thank heaven little Mr. Cooper has returned. And to think that it was these men from the lugger after all. We hadn't suspected that."

"I think Thompson half suspected it, anyhow," said Buchanan.

"And that was why they killed *him*. What are you going to do?"

"Send a call to Durabaya. There may be a Dutch gunboat there. I shouldn't imagine that the lugger will get far. We purposely did not let them fill their tanks. They'll probably make for one of the native villages on Guya. With any luck, the Dutchmen should collect them there."

She breathed deeply. "The air feels cleaner. What a tremendous relief it is not to suspect, any more, one of ourselves. I feel that the Devil has left the island."

"According to Rata, Sym Lung thinks the Devil has a permanent residence here. He walks the island, and it shakes under his tread."

2.

Swan was asleep in Thompson's deckchair. Hawkesbury sat, moodily, on the step. He was paring a stick, stripping its bark, and his yachting cap was on the back of his tousled head.

"Has Dr. Murray gone home?" said Buchanan.

Hawkesbury nodded. "About half an hour ago. Cooper was awake at seven. Wanted to see you. She persuaded him to go off to sleep again. He's sleeping now. You can hear him. What happened to the lugger?"

"They persuaded Rata and Murphy to steal gin out of Mitchell's store. They then got them thoroughly pickled and threw them overboard. With knives, apparently, as an added inducement. How is Swan? Is he all in?" Buchanan looked across at the little man, who appeared to be having a pleasant dream.

"He's a trifle tired, he says." Hawkesbury lowered. "He's got the constitution of a snake. He is peeved with Cooper. Wanted to wake him up and tell him what he thought of him. What's the strength of Cooper, anyhow, Buchanan? Did he just get lost? Or what?"

"Or what, I should think."

"Looks to me as if he killed Thompson," Hawkesbury growled. "I'd like to know how exhausted he really was when he fell across the doorstep last night."

"Dr. Murray must be our authority on that," said Buchanan.

"Yeah. Well, Dr. Murray may know her stuff all right, and I'm not saying that she doesn't, but she's a woman, and she hasn't seen the things I've seen. There's depressants and things as'll reduce or quicken a pulse-rate and set the heart knocking. Ever eaten cordite? I remember once a fellow in a jug at Aden. They'd picked him off a dhow in the gulf. Got blown down the Red, and bumped into a sloop of the Indian Marine. Had a cargo of Somali girls for the sheikhs across the water. They'd been after him for years. The people at Aden, I mean. Guns one way, girls the other. The two most profitable trades in the world, and whenever you sit sentimentalizing about the milk of human kindness, you want to remember that. Girls and guns. And that goes for anywhere, any of the seven seas and the five continents, from the Malabar Coast round and back again to Cape Comorin, *including* Timbuctoo and Regent's Park." He produced a plug of tobacco and began to shave it.

Buchanan watched him curiously. "I suppose you started to smoke plug when you were before the mast."

"When I was a lad of eleven. Ran away to sea, I did, because my old man wanted me to be a boy soprano. Smuggled aboard a five-masted American schooner, in the lumber trade, at Birkenhead. Stowed away. Sick as a dog for two days, then scoffed all the food I'd brought with me, in one go. Cook caught me raiding the galley that night. First Officer took a tarred rope to me next morning. After that, I cleaned the cook's pots. And he was a greasy cook."

"What were you saying about Aden?" asked Buchanan.

"Oh, this fellow was landed into the clink there. After three days he was took seriously ill. Fever of 104°. They shifted him across to the isolation ward. Barbed-wire round it too, on top of palings about eight feet high. Temperature dropped a bit during the night. He went to sleep. Nurse left the ward for a bit. When she came back, he was gone. Through the window and over the palings, barbed-wire and all. Not a sound or a smell of him left. Got away off to the oasis—what's the name of that place? Just across the Arab border—joined a caravan and disappeared into the big sand. Never a word of him for four months, until a British patrol came on him hanging in chains up near—what's the name of that place again? Anyhow, there he was, meat for vultures. But that was over another affair."

"Yes, I think I read that story somewhere before," said Buchanan. "Where was it now? I've forgotten. But was it Aden?"

"It's a damnably poor story, anyhow," said Nicholas Swan, opening his eyes.

Buchanan strolled towards the corner of the house. "Oh, Hawkesbury," he said.

Hawkesbury lumbered after him. His feet were still sensitive, presumably.

They crossed the little clearing and Buchanan sat down, on the slope overlooking the sea.

"I'm sorry, Hawkesbury," he said. "I never like barging into anybody's private affairs, but the circumstances are exceptional, you'll agree. I've heard you give several different versions of your early history and I've always admired your virtuosity. But now, I'm afraid, I must ask you for the truth."

Hawkesbury glared. "What do you mean, the truth?"

"I mean that I want to know who you are and why you came here. My dear chap, I recognize your talents. Your stories always seem to me to have a good deal of energy and fire. But you are a bit short on your facts, you know. Still, I gather you've done the best you could with the material at your command. But now, we must come down for a minute or so to the dull, pedestrian truth. You are not a sea-captain at all, are you?"

Hawkesbury deflated, slowly, like one of those dying pigs which sometimes amused our elders.

"Come now," said Buchanan in his most avuncular vein. "As I said, I've always enjoyed your stories. I am grateful for them. I hope that I shall hear many more. But you know, there happens to be a register of people who have taken their masters' tickets. You are weak on the factual side, you know, Hawk. A good atlas would help you quite a lot. You are inclined to get Asia tangled up with Africa, and Nome is not in Siberia. Where do you come from, really, and what was your job, when you had one?"

Hawkesbury was scarlet.

"What business is it of yours, anyhow." Hawkesbury flushed slowly, from his bull neck upwards.

"My dear chap, must I go into that again? You are not a

sea-captain. You are not even a seaman. You are always getting your terms muddled. Remind me to lend you the *Yachtsman's Vade-Mecum* sometime."

Hawkesbury's jaw dropped.

"You used to work in a shop, didn't you? You have a pretty hand with parcels, I've noticed. By the way, do you know how to make a dunce's hat?"

"No," said Hawkesbury. "I don't."

"That's a pity. I am going in for strong, centralized government in future, and I must do something about dunce's hats. Was it a grocer's shop, Hawkesbury?"

"If you want to know," said Hawkesbury surlily, "I was a radio announcer before I came out here."

"Where?"

"In Seattle."

"That must have been interesting. Why on earth did you give it up?"

"They objected to my voice. Said it had gone out of fashion."

"Really, that's too bad."

Hawkesbury glowered. "They said it was a sissy voice."

"That's almost incredible." Buchanan clucked. "You've been in films too, haven't you?"

"How'd you know that?"

"Extra parts, I suppose, or we should have heard something about it. Oh, I don't know, except that you always wear your cap on the back of your head. And you smoke your pipe so aggressively. And there's the general quality of your imagination."

"It was a hell of a life anyhow," said Hawkesbury. "I've always wanted to have adventures, real adventures."

"I imagine that you could have a much more adventurous life in Seattle than on Kaitai. Piccadilly and the Strand seem to me the heart of romance. Funny, isn't it, how we always want to be over the hills and far away?" He sighed. "Whenever I feel that I should like to be D'Artagnan or Mr. Bunter or Father Brown, I always think of a foggy night in London. Wild cries from Kensington Gardens, and things like that. Were you ever actually a boy soprano?"

Hawkesbury breathed through his nostrils, loudly. "Yes, I was," he said.

"And I've never been able to sing a note myself. Hawkesbury, I suppose I can really take your word for all this? Because, if I can't . . . oh well, I've said it all before." And he walked off into the trees.

His legs were like lead, and his eyes ached, and his shirt clung damply to him in the morning heat.

He wondered vaguely what Buchanan the First would have done. Been thoroughly grim and Old-Testament, no doubt. There was a good deal to say for the Old Testament, as a text for men of affairs.

He said a prayer for all administrators and those in high places. He could not imagine why anyone should care for power. It was difficult enough to manage one's own life with any satisfaction to oneself and one's neighbors, without presuming to superintend the others. What had Thompson discovered? Had he discovered anything? Anything of real consequence? There was the camera. He hit his pocket. Yes, it was still there. Perhaps Alicia could develop the film. She seemed to be able to do most things. She could probably make a dunce's hat.

He turned and started back. As he came into the clearing

about Thompson's bungalow, Mitchell left the steps and walked to meet him.

"I've spoken to Durabaya," he said. "The gunboat sailed yesterday. They will wireless her. But the Consul is coming over. By seaplane. He'll be here in the early afternoon."

"In time to take the burial service then," said Buchanan.

Mitchell raised an eyebrow. "Getting stale?" he said. "Oh, Cooper's awake. And he wants to speak to you."

Buchanan nodded. As he walked up the steps, Swan grinned. "What've you been saying to Hawkesbury, George? He offered to punch my head just now."

"Did you take the offer?" asked Buchanan.

"Hardly."

"That's a pity," said Buchanan, and went indoors.

Cooper was still lying on the long settee. He looked painfully worn, but there was color in his cheeks again.

"Ah, good morning," he said. "Good morning."

"Hullo," said Buchanan. "How do you feel?"

"Very much rested. Thank you." His eyes were evasive.

Buchanan noticed that his trousers were lying across Cooper's feet. So he had looked for the letter. And found it, no doubt.

"I cannot say how sorry I am to have put you all to so much trouble. And how grateful. Especially to Dr. Murray."

"We are all extremely annoyed with you," said Buchanan, "What on earth became of you?"

Cooper blushed. "I . . . I'm afraid that I missed my way. I walked off, you know, in the middle of the night. I felt that I needed some fresh air. Perhaps I was a little light-headed. I may have had a touch of fever after all, a touch of sun. I am not at all clear, really, as to what I did. But I seem to have wandered away towards the swamp. And when I . . . ah . . . realized my predicament, I found it difficult to find my way back. So I slept during the heat of the day. And I over-slept. It was quite dark again when I awoke. And I was very hungry. I started off. And then I found myself going into the swamp. I fear that I became alarmed, very alarmed, and I began to run. I threw my coat away somewhere, I remember. It was too hot. And I thought someone would find it if I were really lost. My watch is missing, too."

"No, I took it off your wrist. Here it is." He passed it to Cooper. The glass, he noticed, was cracked, and the watch had stopped at one-fifty.

"I must have damaged it somehow," said Cooper, holding it to his ear and shaking it.

"You may have knocked it on a tree or something," said Buchanan.

"I seem to remember falling several times. I have made a dreadful fool of myself. As if you did not already have enough and too much to trouble you."

"Well, we are relieved to have you back."

"I cannot imagine why I ran to Thompson's. It must have been the nearest of the houses when I came out of the trees. Perhaps I saw the light."

"Perhaps you did," said Buchanan, and for an instant wondered whether Cooper could be making a play upon words.

"It's very kind of Thompson to take me in. I haven't seen him about though."

"No. No, he isn't about. Anything I can do for you? Fresh clothes? We'll bring some over from your place. And a shave? But you don't really need a shave." He looked at the little man's smooth pink face. "I'm afraid these clothes of yours are hardly worth cleaning, but I'll give them to your boy, shall I?"

Cooper's eyes lit, and he clutched at his trousers. "Oh, no, you mustn't trouble yourself. I'll take them home when I go." His hand, Buchanan noticed, was gripping the hip-pocket.

"Buchanan," he said, "Buchanan, I . . . I have something to say to you. Something I should have said to you before. But I hadn't the courage. I haven't the courage now, but I must tell you. Must." The sweat suddenly began to run on his forehead. "Buchanan, I was, in a sense, responsible for Smith. For Smith coming here."

And then it came out, in a rush of words: the friend in the City, the letter, the appearance of Smith.

"I did not suspect for one minute, not for one minute, that Smith had come here because of what I had written. Not until he told me. I don't know whether I can expect you to believe me. . . ."

"Why not?" said Buchanan.

"But, really, I'd had no part in it at all, except that first foolish reference to the deposits. I had not imagined that my acquaintance would think twice about it. When Smith told me that a syndicate had been formed, that he had been sent to investigate, I was flabbergasted. Flabbergasted. I didn't know what to say."

"What actually did you say?" asked Buchanan.

"I hardly know. I was exceedingly angry, exceedingly. And Smith laughed at me. It was, he said, a little too late in the day for regrets. That may have been true, but it did not make my distress any less . . . less sharp. I felt that I had betrayed you, in a sense."

And Buchanan felt, as he had felt before when he read

Cooper's letter, that Cooper was piling up molehills to make a mountain. But people of Cooper's temperament are often given to that sort of feat.

"I was particularly angry that he should have lied to you. Why could he not have come openly and frankly, and said what he wanted, and asked your permission to investigate . . . ?"

"He had been doing some investigation already, I take it," said Buchanan, "and had discovered that I should certainly have ordered him off the island if he had come in his proper guise."

"But to call himself Goulburn!" protested Cooper.

"It was the name of the man he bought the lugger from," said Buchanan. "He thought, I suppose, that he might as well use the same name. When we identified him with an author of the same name, he thought it something of a joke. And he let us believe it. He was rather notorious down the coast under his own name, anyhow."

Cooper wagged his head. "He was a confirmed liar. Doubtless a qualification for his mission here. My dear Buchanan, I cannot say how upset I am about all this. Believe me, it was my distress over the matter that sent me wandering off. I did not know how to face you. I knew that I should tell you of it, but I lacked the courage to face you. I could not screw my courage to the sticking-place. As Hamlet said. It was Hamlet. Wasn't it?"

"No, it was Lady Macbeth. But never mind that now," said Buchanan. "Cooper, when did you first find out about Smith?"

"On the afternoon of his death. He came to me and showed me the analyses he had made, and said, 'These will interest you, I suppose. Now, how do we put the screws on Buchanan?' "

"Oh, he did, did he!"

"Yes. You see, I'm afraid he had assumed that I was somehow involved with these people who had commissioned him. He thought that I was one of them, as it were. It must have seemed likely. And that has made it especially hard for me to speak to you. You would surely suspect the same thing." Cooper looked up with pathetic, anxious eyes.

"But why on earth did you run off?"

"I was in the most dreadful distress of mind." He passed his hand wearily over his forehead. "I hardly knew what I was doing. And I was afraid."

"Afraid," said Buchanan, "that if you admitted your knowledge of Smith, we should think that you had killed him?"

It went home, on a nerve-centre. "Yes," said Cooper. "I was afraid of that."

For one moment, Buchanan thought that he was going to speak his thoughts of suicide. His lips trembled. Then they tightened. And his hand closed on the hip-pocket of his trousers.

He suddenly shoved his feet off the side of the couch.

"I think I had better go home," he said.

Buchanan was ready to let him go. He was not eager to tell him of Thompson's death until they had gone from Thompson's house.

Cooper pulled on his torn, scorched, muddied trousers. Then he looked woefully at his shirt.

"I'll get your jacket," said Buchanan. "Thompson brought it home with him. We found it, you know, up near Hwan's clearing, towards the swamp."

"I threw it down, I remember," he said vaguely, "in case I was lost."

"As a kind of pointer," said Buchanan.

"Yes, as a kind of pointer."

Buchanan fetched the jacket, and Cooper pulled it on. He drew it tightly across his chest.

"You're short of a shoe," said Buchanan.

"Yes, I must have pulled it off when my foot began to bleed." He looked at the punctured blisters on his heel. "Perhaps I might borrow Thompson's slippers. I don't think I could get a shoe on, in any case."

So Buchanan found him Thompson's slippers, and remembered Thompson's talk of sandshoes. Two mornings ago, though it seemed like years.

"You fought your way through to this eastern side of the swamp," said Buchanan, "last night. Your scratches all seemed fairly fresh."

"Yes. I was lost all day yesterday, but I slept most of the day. That was part of my incredible stupidity. But I was almost exhausted. I had not slept all the previous night, and I had wandered about, hardly knowing what I did or where I went. I have never been in such a state in all my life before." The lack of precedent especially agitated Mr. Cooper.

"Well, come on now, and I'll see you home. Then you had better go to bed again and really sleep it off."

They went out on to the verandah. Swan, rocking in Thompson's chair, uncoiled his legs.

"Can we depend upon you for hare and hounds regularly, Cooper?" he said.

"I'm terribly sorry that I have put you all to so much trouble," said Cooper. "I cannot say how sorry I am." He blinked.

"It was a pleasure," said Swan, "except that you seem to have outrun us. And now we are in the same difficulty as before. Who killed Cock Robin?"

"Oh, shut up, Swan!" said Buchanan, and Cooper blinked again.

"I'm afraid I don't quite understand," he said.

"It was entirely a provocative remark," said Swan.

Mr. Cooper looked bewildered. He sometimes found Swan very difficult to follow.

"Where is Thompson?" he asked.

"Dead," said Swan.

"Dead?"

"Dead," said Swan. "Murdered."

Buchanan caught the little man's elbow. He had swayed. For an instant Buchanan thought that he was going to faint. His muscles were rigid. They heard him swallow. Then he pulled his arm away, and turned down the steps. Buchanan went with him. He only spoke once before they reached the village.

"George," he said, "what abominable thing has come amongst us?"

They went into his bungalow. The door still stood open, as Mitchell had said. Cooper dropped on to his bed. Buchanan picked up his green-and-white pyjamas from the floor. "Get into these," he said. "Do you feel like something to eat?"

"No," said Cooper. "I feel sick. Horribly sick. No, no, I'm all right, really but this kind of thing takes me in the pit of the stomach. George, how was poor Thompson killed?"

Buchanan told him.

There was a long silence when he had finished. Cooper had changed into his pyjamas and crawled between the clean sheets.

"Buchanan," he said at last, "you'll find those reports that Smith made in the drawer over there. The analyses, I mean. If you care to look at them, now."

"I am afraid they are not there," said Buchanan, and felt something more than discomfort. "You see, Thompson gathered up your papers and took them across to his place."

Cooper flushed slowly. "That was . . . officious of him," he said.

"Yes. If I'd known that he intended to do it, I should have stopped him. I don't think he meant to be heavily officious, though. He believed that something serious had happened to you, and he probably thought it best to remove your papers from the empty bungalow. He put them in his safe."

"In his safe?" And now the color ebbed in Cooper's face. "Buchanan, do you mean that?"

"Yes."

"But . . . but Thompson's murderer tried to break into his safe."

"Yes," said Buchanan again.

Cooper's lips trembled. "Don't you see, don't you see? Someone is trying to fasten these murders on me." And he burst into tears.

13

VERSUS BUCHANAN

ALICIA MURRAY walked slowly down the path, the knotted leather in her hand, the stirrup hanging from it.

Her heart was dead. It had died, long since, in the remote Maytime, under other stars. May and June and July: life came so quickly to that mid-summer height: and how quickly does the curve descend. Already she felt a wintry breath.

Now, at all times,
And in all these places and before all men,
I shall put off this harsh, particular pride
Which I had thought my natural habit then.

She had put off her pride, as trees put off their leaves, in her season. It was dust now, and she trampled it. How odd of God.

Lately, it had seemed for a moment that there was some stirring of life beneath the dust and mold. The heart may know another spring. She grimaced. Had she really wanted another spring? All that to endure again, the ache of growth, the fever of sap, the putting out of leaves. Better to own a dead heart, and a dulled mind, and to live, while one lived at all, by the *lex scripta*. By the time-table and the orderly clock. By the text-book and the rules of good behavior. Always wash your hands before meals, and never forget to carry a clean handkerchief. When offering a handkerchief to a lady, be sure that . . .

Yes, unquestionably, she was a trifle mad. But she was struggling back to respectable sanity. There had been a moment when the world turned over, but now it was coming right again. Yet how appalling that what was right should look so wrong. She was a little giddy from the revolution, perhaps.

This was a bad mood. But it was a real mood. It was that other which had been false. This mood was compelled by facts, its context was reality.

She knew he was walking behind her, but she did not slow her steps. Nor did she quicken them. He would overtake her, presently, and then she would have to spit out this bitter seed. Seed? Was it, then, new life she must spit out, new life, however bitter?

She swung the stirrup-leather in her hand.

"Alicia!" he called.

Now she must stop. She must stop, here by this tree. Her feet were stubbornly reluctant to stop. Her heart was stubbornly reluctant to die. Lie down, heart. One felt that there ought to be a Shakespearean tag appropriate to the occasion. Something out of Pyramus and Thisbe, that most lamentable comedy and cruel death. *That will take some tears to the performing of it.*

"Alicia!"

She turned to meet him. "Yes?"

"Confound it, woman, you walk on like inexorable fate. Or a woman policeman in the Park. I wonder if anyone has ever tried to pick up a policewoman in the Park. My dear child, you do look grim. Apart from your black eye, I mean."

"Have you a cigarette, George?"

"Yes, I think so. Yes, here."

"Thank you." She bent a little to his match.

"Can you develop photographs?" he asked.

"Yes. Yes, of course."

"I knew it would be *of course*." He sighed. "I've never known a woman who could be put to such various uses. You can probably make paper hats. Would you develop the film in this camera?" He took it out of his pocket.

"Thompson's?" she said.

"Yes. He was using it yesterday, at the mortuary. I take it that if he found any fingerprints of note he recorded them here. Though as the murderer walked off with your gloves . . ."

"I've found them," she said. "Jammed down behind the beam under my verandah. Perhaps he thought I hadn't a second pair." She was terribly tired. Her legs ached, almost as much as her head. She wished it was all over. But how could it ever be all over? Whatever she did now, it would never be ended. Whatever she did, she would always ask and ask herself whether she had done the right thing, the best thing. . . or whether she had been the whole world's fool.

"He doesn't seem a very particularly considerate sort of bloke to me," said Buchanan.

"I think he has been as considerate as he could," she said, "except for one moment. I even think he was considerate when he hit me."

"Well, that is turning the other cheek with a vengeance. Isn't there a suitable song? *Two Lovely Black Eyes*."

"He didn't want me to see who he was," she said, and her voice seemed to come from somewhere outside her, from someone she was listening to. "For my sake as well as for his own."

His face had fallen, oddly. "You know who he is then, Alicia?"

"I think I know who he is, George."

"Well, if he sets you brimming over with loving-kindness, I can only say that he seems to me a singularly happy murderer."

She was silent for a moment, and then she said, "Do we have to talk in this way?"

"I haven't any way of talking. I just say what comes in to my mouth, and God knows, I hope I shall not be judged by it. Alicia, why do you think you know this man?"

"Because I know why he came the other night." She raised her hand.

He stared at the stirrup. "Yes, I've noticed that, but I was carefully avoiding it as a subject of conversation."

"He came to destroy the marks that this had left on Smith's head. He did not want this to be identified as the weapon."

"Well?"

"It is yours, isn't it, George?"

"Yes, of course it is. But wait a moment. Alicia, do you seriously think that the stirrup caused the injuries?"

"They were this shape," she said, and she met his gaze. "As if this had been swung at the end of its leather, again and again and again. We thought of a rowlock, remember. One could recognize some shape. Just, I said, as if this stirrup had been swung by its leather. The leather is knotted to give a better grip, you see." She knew that her voice was steady, that she was saying the words which had to be said.

"Yes, I see. My attention has been drawn to it before. You found this in Thompson's bungalow, of course."

"Yes." She looked at him sharply. "I found it in Thompson's bungalow. And the marks of it on Thompson's head."

"Thompson found it in the bushes along here, you know. It seemed to him a queer place to find it. I thought so too. I mean, it would have been much more sensible of me to put it back with the saddle, wouldn't it?" His tone was searing.

The pain in his face shocked her.

"Now I know," he said, "what you mean. And so, I was as considerate as I could be. Except for one moment. The moment when I kissed you, Alicia."

"Yes," she said. "It is the only thing in all this for which I hate you, George. You wakened that much, just that much of a silly girl in me, enough to hate you now because you kissed me. I . . . I think I can be adult about the rest of it. And somehow, I think you must have had reasons, what seemed good reasons to you."

"It is clearly a case in which justice will be served if I am mercifully detained during his Majesty's pleasure. I shall call you for the defence."

"I know what the reasons are. I know the first reason, at least. And it was a good reason. Up to a point."

"Obviously a case in which a skilled alienist may work wonders. A padded cell will hardly be required, and strait jackets are abhorrent to a modern sensibility."

"George, it is not like you to twist the knife." She closed her eyes. This was all utterly beyond belief, that she should stand here in the sun and accuse George Buchanan of murder.

Yet she must, must get the truth out of him. "And it is not like you to deal in ponderous irony."

That struck him, as she had known it would strike him.

"You have brought out your whips and scorpions, haven't you, Alicia?"

"Yes," she said, "all of them."

He took a cigarette from the packet he still held in his hand, and the hand, she could see, was shaking.

"You believe I killed Smith. And Thompson."

She steadied herself. "I want you to consider a case, George. And to tell me how it can be answered. It must be answered, you know. It must be answered to the world."

He made a wry face. "I shall need powerful advocacy."

Her hands were gripping the leather. "You know, of course, what the natives believe."

"I am told, on good authority, that they have three new songs about me. Rather in the mood of the Border ballads. A good deal of blood and . . ." He broke off.

"They say that you killed Smith because he was going to destroy their villages."

"As I said when it was reported to me, they take rather a melodramatic view of Smith. He would merely have set them to work. That, undoubtedly, would destroy them and their villages in the long run. They have direct minds, of course."

"We put our feet on sparks in Kaitai," she quoted. "Do you remember that, George?"

"Certainly. It is number three in my list of cautionary sayings."

"I can imagine one thing only in this world, George, for which you would do violence. For this charge of yours, the people of Kaitai."

"Oh, I sometimes go fishin', you know."

"Don't! Please! I . . . that hurts, George."

"Well, you are not entirely a solace and a balm yourself, you know."

"George, I hate what I am doing so much that I could almost kill myself. But someone has to say what I am trying to say. There are facts that must be faced."

His face was so strange that for a moment it seemed transformed. "Facts!" he said. "Facts! There, I knew it. I knew that the facts were going to do somebody in before we were finished with this affair. And I actually told myself that I must attend to matters of fact. This is a hoist with one's own petard, if you like."

"One cannot entirely ignore facts. One can explain them."

"God help us, so one can. In this sense and that. Who'll be the judge and who'll be the jury? Yet there was one judge whom I've mentioned before. He was a very exceptional judge. *What is truth?* he asked. There are not many wigs on the Bench with his training in philosophy. Or humility, maybe. But look at the major event of his career. What is one to hope of Mr. Justice Buzfuz? Or of oneself?"

"Pilate refused judgment," she said, and she was fighting with every ounce of her will to keep her command. "He saw the Fact and he would not recognize it. He washed his hands."

"And afterwards he jested," said Buchanan. "Well, that is in the modern judicial vein. Though I think his jokes were probably better. And I think I know what desperate need he had to jest."

"He washed his hands," she said. "We cannot wash our hands, George."

"Not all the perfumes of Arabia. And I hope you won't read that for a confession of guilt. All right, let's have your facts, even if I do hang poor Cooper."

She stared at that.

"Sorry, it's all right, no libel intended. I was merely retreading an earlier line of whimsical thought. Where were we? You could only imagine one thing in this world for which I would do violence."

"Yes. For Kaitai. For your people and their happiness."

"I begin to see the whole rueful pattern. Smith was breathing fire, so, like a workaday St. George, I picked up my stirrup and slew him. I didn't happen to be on my horse at the time."

"But the stirrup happened to be on your verandah. When you went out with Smith."

"Being the last known person to see him alive. I've been a bit uncomfortable about that all along. All the best authors make such play with it. But I'd rather hoped that my author was going to pedal on it less."

"You had been drinking together, you had quarrelled, you went down to the beach together, you say that you then left him to push off his boat alone. What would a prosecuting counsel make of all this?"

"Very much what you are making of it, no doubt. Alicia, when did these things occur to you, in just this fashion? When did they come together and make this very horrid pattern?" He made a movement towards her, and then dropped his hands. "You did not see it like this yesterday, when I kissed you."

She flushed, in spite of herself. "No. Nor last night. But this morning I heard Naqa singing. And then I found the stirrup.

And then I realized, George, that there was motive, and opportunity, and that the weapon was yours. And I saw it . . ."

"Yes, I know. As a judge would see it. I'm very annoyed with Naqa. He shouldn't have been singing about the place this morning. I suppose he woke you up. Anyhow, they might reserve their musical testimonies for a happier moment. It's damned embarrassing to have this cheerful carolling going on all over the island. It would be embarrassing if I had killed Smith, but as it is I feel that I am all too undeserving. So you have taken a stirrup and a song to hang me with. Figuratively speaking. Because I don't see how I am going to be hanged for this. Or how anybody else is going to be hanged for it. It has been troubling me a good deal."

"George!" She twisted the leather in her hands. "It has cost me more to say what I have said to you than anything else in my life has cost. Immeasurably more. Please try not to be so bitter."

"Well!" he said. "Well!"

"George!"

"But, my dear lady, the problem is a real one. You know, you say, who the murderer is. But how, on Kaitai, do you propose to bring him to justice, to try him, to carry out the sentence? Who, to be brutal, puts on the black cap, and who fixes the halter, and who pulls the trap? It's very difficult. I can't try the cause, judge, pass sentence and execute it."

"Can't you?" she said.

"No, I'm damned if I can. This is an acute problem. You see, you are not the only person who knows the murderer. I know who he is, too.* But what am I to do with him? The

* We take it that the reader does too. We are sorry to give away our secrets so early in the game, but we are an ingenuous author.

only thing I have been able to think of so far is an appeal to his better feelings. But is he likely to respond?"

"Yes," she said. "I thought of that, too."

"There are all sorts of difficulties. It would be bad for the native morale to execute a white man on Kaitai. It would be even worse to ask anyone of the natives to assist in the execution. However, all this is hardly your concern. It is part of the burden of government."

She shook her head, as one might shake it to clear one's mind. "You know who committed the murders, George?"

"Of course. Very much better than you do. And I wish with redoubled fervor that Great-Uncle Buchanan had stayed at home on the Clyde, where there are police to look after these matters."

"George, Thompson was still alive when you reached him, wasn't he?"

"Yes, he was. And I know how that adds to your score. Alicia, are you seriously proposing to accuse me before a jury of my countrymen, if we can find a jury of my countrymen?"

"I am afraid that it may not be left to me."

"But if it were?"

"George, don't you see how you have been mistaking this whole situation? You must try to look at it as . . . well, as other people will look at it."

"Men have been hanged on less evidence than this, you mean. I haven't mistaken it. I've been acutely conscious of it. But I imagined that you, at least, were prepared to take me on trust."

"Does it matter very much if I am? Will this consul take you on trust?"

"It matters a good deal to me whether you are or are not prepared to trust me."

"George," she held out her hand, "I've spoilt our friendship. I knew I would. I'm giving you my resignation, and I shall leave Kaitai as soon as it is possible for me to leave. But someone had to say this to you, someone had to bring reality into your dream-world here. You've forgotten, you know, how the affairs of the real world are conducted. You have forgotten the judgments of men, and their habits of mind."

"On the contrary, it seems to me that I have remembered them only too well."

She shook her head. "It has been this that I have loved on Kaitai. It seemed an idyll come true. Life conducted with tolerance and grace and a sense of humor. Order without compulsion, government without brutality. Unhappily the world has intruded. And you cannot act in the face of the world as you have acted in the face of your islanders. The world is not sufficiently civilized. If you do not judge, it will judge you. And if I have destroyed our friendship," she raised her chin, "I have destroyed it in the one cause which can make its ending bearable. Your cause, and Kaitai's."

"But do you or do you not believe that I murdered Smith and Thompson?"

"It is for you to prove that you didn't."

He laughed suddenly. "Well, I'm jiggered! Your resignation is accepted, by the way." He took the leather and its stirrup from her hand. He held it up. "We can assume that the medical evidence is satisfactory on this point. Smith's injuries were produced by something more or less of this shape and size."

"I'm not very certain about the actual size. It was impossible to determine that. The weapon could have been a little larger or a little smaller. It was curved like that."

"So is a rowlock. As we noticed, at first. Why are you so emphatically for the stirrup, Alicia?"

"Because I was able to get a wash from it. And I made a slide. There was . . . well, there was brain matter on it."

"I wondered about that. Yet, Alicia, I do not believe that Smith or Thompson was killed with this stirrup. Doesn't it occur to you that the clue is just a little too good, too obvious?"

"Was it so very obvious?"

"Someone paid a visit to the mortuary on the night after the murder. He smashed up the dead man's skull. Why? Surely to destroy the particular character of the original injuries. He wanted, in short, to destroy evidence which might point to the weapon. But next morning, almost without effort, Thompson finds this stirrup in the track to the mortuary. The stirrup has brain-matter on it. I believe it acquired the brain matter when the basher paid his visit to the mortuary. Then it was planted for one of us to find. In short, it was hoped that we would mistake this stirrup for the real weapon. Someone, in possession of the real weapon, was very anxious to mislead us."

"It sounds a long shot," she said.

"Then how else do you explain the midnight incursion? What other sense can it possibly have?"

"I don't know. But I do think it may easily have another sense."

"My dear girl, suppose that you were in the habit of carrying about with you, every day, the real weapon. And suppose that its absence would be noticed. Wouldn't it be rather sensible—and comparatively easy—to suggest some alternative weapon to the public mind?"

"Put like that, perhaps. But who carries the real weapon about? And what is it?"

"What else is there in the familiar scenery of this island that is more or less shaped like the stirrup, which could produce much the same impression of a curved instrument?"

"Dozens of things, I suppose."

"I haven't been able to make it dozens. I've a list which I shall read you sometime. But several, anyhow. There is the good old rowlock again, of course. It seemed a likely gamble for the moment. You know, I don't think that the gentleman who pilfered my stirrup was with us when we discussed the rowlock. He would have been satisfied to let the rowlock carry the guilt, if he had known that we suspected it. But I do think he may have been about the place when Thompson tripped over my saddle the other evening. Something put this trick into his head. Certainly, my stirrup only disappeared after Thompson had tripped."

"George, you can't mean . . . ?" She stared at him, and her hands were clenched.

"I don't want to mean anyone or anything yet. Suspect everything that I say to you. Be very mistrustful of evidence. I am. There is only one safe guiding principle: human beings are extraordinarily queer people, and they do not behave according to a logical pattern. Especially when they are frightened. And several people have been badly frightened on this island lately."

"It seems incredible to me that anyone should have taken the risk of coming to the mortuary . . ."

"If he knew that your boys were away, and that you were sleeping behind locked doors?"

"Even if he knew that. And it was such a horrible thing to do. And for what was, after all, not a very important element of the case."

"If he was in possession of all the facts of the case, yes. But suppose that he was not. Suppose that he was bewildered too. Suppose . . ."

"But it was such a stupid thing to do. He would have given himself away, entirely, if he had been seen."

"That, of course, is why he hit you. He was naturally reluctant to be seen."

"Then why take the very real risk? I proved that it was a very real risk. He would have put his head into the noose if I had seen him."

"Perhaps he cared less about his head than about somebody else's head."

"I don't know what you are talking about!" she cried.

"No, I agree it all sounds pretty improbable. But then, this sort of affair is improbable. And human beings are highly improbable, when you think about them. This raid on the mortuary seems to me like the act of a frightened and bewildered man, who is trying to do what he thinks best in circumstances which he does not understand."

"What he thinks best!" she repeated, and there was real horror in her voice.

"It wasn't an apt phrase, perhaps. And what I am trying to say isn't really clear to myself yet. I can just see some dim sort of pattern taking shape. I'm afraid I shall have to go and talk to people. I'm not very heartened by the prospect."

"Whom must you talk to?"

"The people who heard me talking to Smith as he and I walked together down to the beach."

"George, why?"

"Because I think that he frightened someone then. Someone who heard him threaten me. I don't think I told you that Smith had threatened me. It seemed, in my delicate circumstances, an item better left unsaid."

She nodded wearily. "I was afraid of something like that. And that you had been overheard."

"Another nail in my coffin, eh? Or a twist in the hemp?"

"Why did he threaten you, George?"

"He wanted to force a concession out of me. A concession to work the asphalt deposits. The threat itself was interesting. He told me that he would put Kaitai on the front-pages of all the newspapers in the world, as a haunt and refuge of jail-birds and crooks. Allowing for the hyperbole, it was a disturbing remark. I did not like it. Someone else may have liked it considerably less."

"It could only mean that someone on Kaitai was a criminal, wanted by the police."

"Quite so. And wanted in a large way, unless Smith was being exceedingly hyperbolic. As a matter of fact, it was that remark which made me leave him. It gave me a very nasty jolt, and I needed time to assimilate it."

"And you believe that someone in the row of bungalows overheard him."

"If anyone was awake, he must have been overheard. He was shouting, drunkenly. By the way, Alicia, how drunk was he? Did you do a blood-test for alcohol or anything like that?"

"Yes. He had been drinking a great deal."

"He was rocking, as we went down the road. If he had met anyone, and stopped to talk, he would probably have sat down."

"Why do you say that?"

"I was thinking of the direction of the blows. And the opportunity. And of the person who struck them. It would be so much easier to kill a man of Smith's height and bulk and fighting-strength if one caught him sitting down or lying down. He may even have gone to sleep. I'm almost certain he was lying down or sitting down."

"Why? How do you know?"

"Because there were little holes in the sand. Have you ever, when you are sitting on the sand, pushed your fingers into it? Well, someone had pushed four fingers and a thumb into the sand at about the place where Smith might have sat down if he had been overtaken on his way to the dinghy." He spread out his own hand. "Like this. He would plump down at a spot just above high-water mark. Where the sand was softish and dry."

"Swan overheard you talking, while you were still in your house," she said slowly. "And Swan always hints that his story would make a tremendous stir in the world."

"Yes, I've naturally thought of that."

"And Swan had already quarrelled with Thompson."

"About Shelley."

"So he said."

"Nicholas does not amuse you, does he, Alicia?"

She shivered. "If it must be one of us . . ."

"It may as well be Nicholas. Well, he is a useless old man. But I should be sorry to lose Nicholas. He is a rod to my spirit. He chastens me. He reminds me that this is a vale of tears, that man is born to trouble. It is all very salutary."

"George! What is that?" She clutched his arm. "Listen!"

He listened.

"That," he said, "is a seaplane. Blast! I had meant to look up the exact extent of the consul's jurisdiction before he came. There are circumstances in which, under our treaty, he can set up a kind of a consular court. You know, just like the old arrangement in China. Do you mind if I skip along? I'll take this with me." He waved the stirrup. "And do you think you could develop that roll in Thompson's camera? And do you know how to make dunces' hats?"

"Dunces' hats?"

"Because if you do, there may be still a job for you on Kaitai, even though you abandon the Medical Service."

14

INQUISITION

"DO YOU think the machine will be safe there," said the pilot, "or are your natives of a thieving turn of mind?"

It floated at its buoy, a hundred yards offshore.

"They got off with a lugger from here," growled the consul. "Now I'm glad to say, Buchanan, she's on a reef. And I want to be sick, if you do not object."

"On a reef?"

"I gave the man a paper-bag too, as we came along," said the pilot. "Yes, she's on a reef. We circled round her. That lump of coral about eight miles s.e. They must have gone on during the night, and under their power, for she's wedged like a cork in a bottle. And there she'll stay. We circled round her several times, and there were your bold buccaneers on her deck. It was difficult to be sure at the distance, but they seemed sorry enough for themselves. So I went up and let out my aerial and wirelessed to the Dutchmen. They'll come along and do what's needful to be done presently, no doubt."

"Finishes your case, Buchanan," said the consul.

"What? Oh, yes. Did you see anything of the two native girls? They were carried off, you know."

"They appeared to be doing the gentlemen's washing," said the pilot. "So they must have made some progress in domesticity before the shipwreck. Buchanan, you'll see to it that none of your boys climbs into my craft."

"I'm sorry," said the consul, "to intrude my private troubles, but could I lie down somewhere for a while, with a basin handy? My constitution is not adapted to travel by air. Unless there is anything you want of me at once, Buchanan. And I only say that for politeness' sake. When are you burying poor Thompson?"

"At sunset."

"And I suppose the Chink killed this fellow Smith, all right." The consul's little eyes were sharp.

"Let's talk it all out later," said Buchanan. "Come along up to my place now, and I'll give you a drink. And a basin, if you must have one." They were surrounded by pop-eared natives.

"He's a disgusting spectacle when he's sick," said the pilot, "and I hear you've a club on Kaitai renowned for its hospitality. I'll put my foot on the bar, if I may."

"Come along with me," said Mr. Cooper eagerly.

Buchanan and the consul walked up together to Buchanan's house.

"This is a bad business, Buchanan," said the consul soberly. "I've had a question from my people at home already."

"Yes, I know. I mean, I know that it is a bad business."

"You look all in yourself. What's the procedure exactly? What happens next? I've a right to claim a court of inquiry, and to sit on it myself."

"But you are not entitled to try a prisoner. I wish to heaven that you were. I'd like nothing better than to pass you the buck. But old Buchanan the First was very jealous of his prerogatives."

"I'm entitled to demand that justice is done," said the consul.

"Even that is a trifle doubtful, in my reading."

"De facto. I shouldn't presume too much on your treaty rights. My Government can be very snooty when it wants to snoot. And Smith wasn't the only one with his eye on your asphalt. That is meant as a friendly and entirely irregular tip from one who knows. What do you mean to do, Buchanan?"

George groaned. "Apply for a mandate under the League of Nations, probably."

"It's as desperate as that, is it?" The consul frowned. "Why actually did the boys run off with the lugger, Buchanan? And if you suspected them, why did you leave them free to run off in the lugger? I don't believe they were the killers, though I was being tactful on the beach just now. You don't believe it either, or you would be less rattled."

"Of course I don't believe it. I wish I did. They skipped because Thompson had been out bullying them. Perhaps the girl friends had something to do with it, too."

"Who did it? Do you know?"

"My good chap, will you please go and be sick for a while, and give me time to do what I have to do?"

2.

"Here are the photographs," said Alicia. "I've compared the fingerprints as well as I could with those that Thompson had recorded. I think I can identify them all. Except this one. On the stirrup, you see."

"How did you learn to identify fingerprints?"

"In medical school, of course. We had lectures on forensic jurisprudence, with something about fingerprints, and we used to practise with one another's, naturally. Fingerprints are quite easy, once you know what to look for. Here, in this photograph, is the specimen cupboard. They are my prints. And Naqa's. And I shall want to know why his are there at all. And this is the sterilizer. Mine, yours, Thompson's. There are blurs here and there, you see, which are probably old ones of mine. Thompson took a good deal of trouble to bring these up clearly, George."

"Yes. He had a fingerprint sort of mind, poor chap. Personally, I detest this concrete sort of evidence. It can be made to seem so convincing. This is the stirrup, unmistakably. It isn't a very clear print, Alicia."

"No. But you can count the ridges here on this one little bit. See that whorl. There's a little island. It's from a middle finger, I think. Well, I can't identify that convolution with any of the prints Thompson had recorded. I think the man who made it was sweating heavily."

"Perhaps he was nervous," said Buchanan. "It could, of course, have been anyone who has handled the stirrup. And it could be the person who took the stirrup from my saddle. In either case, I think it may prove a useful bargaining instrument. Alicia, do you feel that you could bear an unpleasant experience, a very unpleasant experience?"

"If it is necessary." But she felt her spirit shrink.

"I need a witness. I do not want it to be the consul. And I may need a doctor." He walked across to the window and looked out. Bernard was walking down the little street. Buchanan followed his course. Then he said, "I don't think there is any considerable physical danger, but I can't be altogether sure."

"I don't mind that," she said.

"Come along then. U'm'm, wait a moment. Perhaps I had better take a flask of brandy."

3.

Miss Roper stood in the doorway.

"What is it?" she said.

"May we come in? Have you anyone here, by the way?"

"No. My girls are down admiring the seaplane. Such exciting things, aren't they? I wonder where invention will really end. I always remember the first airplane I saw. It was at Hendon, I think, somewhere about 1912. Before the War, anyhow. Yes, please do come in. Alicia, my dear, you should have had a beefsteak for that eye."

"It feels rather as if it were a beefsteak," said Alicia. "Very raw."

"What have you done with the consul, George? I thought he looked a very pleasant man, even though he was a trifle green."

"He's reading *The News of the World*. Industriously. He says it takes his mind off things."

Miss Roper bustled with cushions. "Put this one behind your head, Alicia. You will feel more comfortable. Will you take a glass of sherry, either of you?"

"No, thank you."

George leaned forward a little. "Miss Roper, I'm afraid that I want to talk seriously. Very seriously."

"Oh dear, I was afraid of that when I saw your face. What about, George?"

"You."

"Well?" The syllable was curt, as if she had hardly trusted her voice.

"Miss Roper, when Smith and I walked down the other night, past this row of houses, did you hear us talking?"

"No. No, I didn't."

"Didn't you hear Smith? He was talking very loudly."

"No, I didn't hear Smith."

"But you can hear people talking when they pass by. Listen now."

A group of natives was coming up from the beach.

"You can hear what they are saying?"

"Yes, of course. But I was asleep, I suppose, when you passed the other evening. Yes, of course I was asleep."

"That is not true, Miss Roper. I'm sorry, but it isn't true. Your light was burning when Smith and I came past Swan's place. We saw it go out. And I believe that you turned it out when you heard us coming."

She sat very still in her chair. "It is not pleasant to be called a liar, George."

"It is not pleasant for me to call you one. But you have left me no option, Miss Roper."

She bowed, stiffly. "We shall not dispute."

"I hope not, fervently. Are you willing to admit now that you heard Smith speaking as we went by to the beach?"

"I have said that I was asleep. You must have been mistaken if you thought you saw my light."

"We were not mistaken. Miss Roper, the fact that you deny having heard us convinces me that you understand very well the significance of Smith's talk. May I see your shooting-stick?"

"My shooting-stick!" Her eyes went involuntarily to the corner of the room.

Buchanan rose and took the stick from the little umbrella-stand. He brought it back and handed it to Alicia. "Would you look at the curved metal frame of the seat and tell me whether you think it could have produced the injury to Smith's skull."

Dorothy Roper stood up. "I think," she said, "that you had better go."

"Alicia!"

Alicia took the stick. She had almost cried out against George. But she had driven him to action. This was his revenge, perhaps.

"Yes," she said dully, "I think it could possibly . . ." Her voice broke. She stared at the curved metal.

"Miss Roper, where was this stick on the night of Smith's murder?"

"Here. Here on this stand." She sat down again. Her aspect has changed. She was tense. It was as if she had suddenly determined to fight. "On this stand. Where it always is when I am at home. Are you accusing me of murder?"

"Did you leave this house after Smith and I passed, that night?"

"No. I did not leave this house."

"Did anyone leave it?"

"Who was there to leave it?"

"Miss Roper, on the evening after Smith's death, when we were gathered at my house, you made an odd slip of the tongue. You said, 'Who was this man Goulburn? He was not Goulburn the writer, was he?' Do you remember that?"

"I remember it. What of it?"

"How did you know that he was not Goulburn the writer?"

"He seemed very unlike any possible conception of Goulburn the writer that one could have. It was not a slip of the tongue. It was a question, which I asked because I had already suspected the man."

"Of what?"

"Of assuming a name and reputation to which he had no right."

"Miss Roper, you are fencing with me. Three people knew from the first that Smith was a liar. I knew it myself. Dr. Murray knew it. She told Bernard. And Swan and Cooper learned it on the night of Smith's death. But who told you?"

"I have said all that I think it necessary to say on the matter. I am willing to answer your reasonable questions to a reasonable degree. I recognize your rights. You apparently suspect me of murder. You are entitled to question me. But you are not entitled to badger me. I have given you an answer. What is your next question?"

"I shall put it in the form of a statement, then. It was Bernard who told you."

For one instant, she flinched: for one instant only, but it was enough.

"Miss Roper, I asked you once whether you really are Miss Roper. Are you?"

"Yes. Yes. I do not understand you."

"How would you prove it?"

"I have my birth-certificate in my trunk, I believe."

"A birth-certificate. Well, I don't dispute that you may have been born a Miss Roper. But have you your passport?"

"I have a passport, yes."

"May I see it?"

"No."

"If I insist?"

"How can you insist?"

"By placing you under arrest and searching your house."

She rose again, and walked across the room, and looked out over the sea. Alicia saw that Buchanan was clenching the arms of his chair. And then she realized that her own hands were clenched, and that the handkerchief in her fist was wet.

Buchanan spoke. His tone was unexpectedly gentle. "I am going to get the truth of this matter, Miss Roper, however I get it. It will be easier for us all if you help now."

She was silent, it seemed to Alicia, for a very long time.

"If I tell you that I have no passport . . ."

He waited before he answered her. "I might believe that. It would mean that you have destroyed it, because you have resolved never to leave this island again. Has he told you, then, and have you believed him, that he will never be taken alive?"

She cried out. "How did you know? How did you know?"

He moved in his chair. "There are seven thousand natives in Kaitai. They all have eyes. And they all have tongues. You were very careful. But not careful enough."

"God!" She flung round. "We had to meet sometimes. Sometimes." Her face was convulsed, as she struggled to command herself. It set now, in terrible lines, that revealed the agony of long years. "What is it you want with me and him?"

"The truth. I am afraid that nothing less will serve us now."

She turned again to the sea; and again, there was that long silence.

"Will it be enough," she said, "if I tell you that I killed the man Smith?"

"No," he said, and Alicia felt that he was reproaching himself, "it will not be enough, now."

"What else do you want to know?"

"Everything, I am afraid."

"Everything!" She laughed and her laugh was like a sword. "As if one could tell you . . . everything. As if it could be said. Or understood, if it was said. Everything!"

She turned back to them and her ravaged face was now curiously calmed. "I am married to him," she said.

"I did not doubt that."

"Married to him. *Therefore now they are not two, but one flesh.* I have believed that. Until death parts us. I shall go with you and be by your side. What else is there for me to say?"

Buchanan was white. Alicia, though she hated him for this, could also pity him. Perhaps Dorothy pitied him too, a little. They were women, and they knew him better than he could know himself.

"It is a long time ago now," said Dorothy. "A very long time ago when we were still young. They arrested him on the anniversary of our marriage, its fourth anniversary. At Dom, where they were building the new forts. He was in the Corps of Engineers, you know." Her tone had lost its urgency. It was remote, almost as if she spoke across distances in space and time. "They charged him with espionage, with selling secret information to a foreign Power. Charged him, Bernard, with that!" The old agony and shame and indignation cried in her voice. "Bernard!"

Buchanan nodded slowly.

"They tried him as quickly and quietly as they could. They remembered another *affaire*. Even so, all the world heard of it. . . ."

"I remember," said Buchanan, "I remember." And he spoke a name.

"He was innocent, innocent, I know with every fibre of my soul that he was innocent. But they sentenced him to twenty-five years, twenty-five years of imprisonment and exile. In New Hibernia."

Buchanan thought of that lovely island whose seas are walls and whose ports are barred gates, where men's souls rot.

"He served fifteen years. And in those fifteen years, I crossed and recrossed the Pacific. I know every harbor and waterside where there are men for sale. But it was fifteen years before I could buy the man I wanted. In all that time, I did not once dare to go to New Hibernia. They would have discovered me. And in all that time, I did not rest. I did not go home. His exile was my exile. I planned and thought and prayed. Always to one end. I had only one thought and one prayer. Do you wonder that I grew old and withered? A wife who was not a wife, a woman who could bear no child."

The thin lips moved soundlessly for a moment.

"I thought and I planned and I prayed always to one end only. It was fifteen years before I did what I had set my whole life to do. I had to learn to wait. Always to wait. There could be no mistake. One mistake and there might be no chance again. But I found a man at last who knew the place, who was willing to try, who did try, who succeeded. He brought Bernard away." She looked at Buchanan and he raised his eyes to hers. "What do you think I would do to save him from being taken back?"

"Then," he said, "you did hear Smith that night?"

"Yes," she said. "I heard Smith. And I knew what he meant. When my husband escaped, his story was in every newspaper in the world, I believe. We had fled to China. His photograph was there, even in a vernacular newspaper of Shanghai. And this man Smith had been a journalist. I understood him when he spoke to you. Only too well."

"Why did you come here?" said Buchanan.

"We separated. We thought that would be safest, for the time. They would be hunting me, perhaps, as well as him. And Bernard came down to the islands, where there are no police regulations and where men travel without passports. He came here. And after two years, two years in which I had gone back to Europe, to Europe and America, always trying to cover my tracks behind me, he wrote. And he said that here on Kaitai, he thought, we could both be safe. As if there is any place in the world where the hunted hare may hide."

"I am sorry," said Buchanan.

"I do not know what you will do now," she said, "but I say this to you. I have prayed God each night to bless you because you made us welcome here."

"Thank you." Buchanan breathed deeply. "So, Bernard still had ten years to serve."

"They would not be content with ten years now," she said.

Better to die than to be taken, thought Alicia.

"What happened after you heard Smith and me pass?" said Buchanan harshly. He had brought himself back to the task.

"I thought," she said, "that you knew."

"You followed him to the beach. You took your stick, as a matter of habit. You talked to him. And . . ."

"No!" The voice came from behind them.

Buchanan swung on his heel. "Ah, I thought we would draw you sooner or later," he said.

"I will not let my wife say this thing." Bernard closed the door from the bedroom behind him. "She did not kill Smith. I was here when we heard you pass."

Buchanan turned on Dorothy again. "Well?"

"He did not stay with me," she said desperately. "He went away. Then I hurried out. . . ." But she understood what she had said, and she cried, "No, no, that was not it."

"He went away. He did not stay with you. Well, Bernard?"

"She is right. I went out. It was I who went. And I took the stick." He laughed savagely. "Do you think I was going back to that place? Do you? I knew that this man Smith had recognized me. He came talking to me that day. He talked round and round the truth, he would not say it openly. He was not certain when he came to me, perhaps, but he tried to make me betray myself. When I heard him speak to you, I knew that he had succeeded. I had come that night to my wife because I was afraid, because I had to tell her what I thought. It was as well I did come." He laughed again. "There is the whole story now, Buchanan. What are you going to do? Before you do anything, remember this. I shall not go back to New Hibernia. And it would be foolish of you to try to hold me now."

"You took the stick. You know, you really owe an apology to Dr. Murray, Bernard."

"Yes. Yes, I am sorry for that. More sorry than I can say. But I had to destroy the mark on the man's head."

"Were you sure that it could be identified with your wife's stick?"

"I did not know. You talked as if the mark . . ." He stopped and stared at Buchanan. "We are saying too much."

"Far too much," said his wife wearily. "George, and you, Alicia, you have known Bernard now for . . . how long? Can you believe this?"

"You believed it," said Buchanan. "You lied to protect him."

She made a hopeless gesture. "If I thought he needed protection, that is not to say that I thought him guilty. And I say this to you. I shall go into any court to which you drag him, and I shall swear that I, not he, killed the man Smith. And how will you prove that I did not?"

"I shall not be dragged to any court," said Bernard. His face reddened. "We shall say this, though, to you now, and you may see how you could break it down. We did not separate. We were here, together, all that night."

"If you insist on such a story," said Buchanan, "I am afraid that you will be tried together. And see what could be made of it. Your wife may insist that she struck Smith down, at her meeting with him on the beach. In that case, the prosecution will suggest that you came down to the beach too, and that you, alone or with her help, put Smith into his boat, pushed it off. hoisted the sail, steered it out, lashed the sail, pulled out the plug, and swam ashore. You are delivering yourselves into the hands of a prosecuting attorney. He will entertain a jury tremendously. My personal problem is, of course, what jury, what counsel, and where. However, that is a trifle premature. Why did you take the stirrup from my saddle, Bernard?"

"I . . . I did not."

"You're an awfully bad liar, you know. There is a fingerprint on the stirrup. Are you willing to let us compare it with your fingerprints?"

The man drew back. "No. No. No, I shall not give you my fingerprints."

"Then will you own up to the stirrup? And to the visit to the mortuary? And to blacking Dr. Murray's eye?"

"I have already owned up to it. I was afraid that the mark of the stick would be identified." He wiped his forehead with the back of his hand.

"You've been reading up the crime articles in the magazines. Bernard, if you killed Smith, why did you kill Thompson?"

The man rocked, as if he had been struck. He stammered. And then he shouted. "Oh, have done with it, have done."

"I'm doing my best," said Buchanan. "But I must get things straight. You know, there seems to me to have been a very good motive indeed for you to murder Thompson. It should have occurred to you a moment ago, when you quivered at the suggestion of fingerprints. Thompson was collecting everybody's fingerprints. If this affair had prompted him to circulate them amongst the police forces in various places, some one or other of them might have been recognized. As it happens, he doesn't seem to have acquired yours. But how were you to know that? Your wife did not know that he had taken hers off a glass until I told her. Now, did she tell you what Thompson had been up to?"

"There was no opportunity," said the woman in a voice utterly flat and staled.

"The odd thing is, however," said Buchanan, "that when you want to own up to the murder of Thompson, you cannot think of that excellent motive. So I believe your wife. You did not know about the fingerprints collection. Why, then, did you kill Thompson?"

"What is there to say?" Bernard swore softly. "You will think of a reason, no doubt, and it will serve as well as another."

"But that is my difficulty. I can't think of a reason. Bernard, you're good deal of a fool, aren't you? You are a man who jumps to stupid conclusions, a man who cannot think clearly in an emergency. If you had been able to think clearly, they would never have pinned that charge of espionage on you long ago."

"I was innocent." He drew himself up angrily.

"Then you strengthen my point. You were innocent, but you did not have sufficient gumption to prove your innocence."

"We know what happened," said his wife, still in that terrible, flat voice. "It was another officer in the Corps. He made Bernard his scapegoat. He escaped himself."

"Further confirmation of what I'm saying. The trouble with all this talk is that we have a murderer too many and a murder too many to fit Bernard's story. You did not kill Thompson, Bernard, and you did not kill Smith. But you did something nearly as bad as killing Smith, and I hope that it does not kill your wife's love for you . . ."

"Nothing could do that now," she said. "I understand what you are going to say. He did not kill Smith, but he believed that I had killed Smith." She suddenly clenched her hands. "And I would have killed Smith too, if only I had thought of it."

"All this silly affair of the stick and the stirrup," said Buchanan, "is the sign of a man who loses his head. Who loses his head because he does not understand what is happening. When you understand what is happening, you can take command, Bernard, as you took command in old-soldierly fashion last night, when we hunted for Cooper. But where you cannot grasp a tangible fact, you are lost. It appears in your chess playing. I've found that the one way to dish you is to do the irrational thing. To make a move out of any reasonable gambit. It throws you into a flummox. That is much what has happened in this case. When you and your wife heard Smith and me on the path, you turned out the light. And then you slipped away. But next morning, you heard of the murder. And you heard that your wife, with some odd whim, had gone off to paint on the mountain at dawn. . . ."

"I went," she said, "because I hoped to find Bernard. What you have said of him is true. He ran away that night, when he should have stayed to talk out with me what we had heard Smith say. I went up to the mountain at dawn to look for him."

"And he jumped to this conclusion: he thought that you had gone out to talk to Smith. To plead with him, perhaps. And that . . ."

"I thought it possible that Smith had attacked her," said Bernard, "and that she had struck at him. I did not believe it altogether. But I thought it possible. I was terrified. I am a fool, but my wife is a woman who acts . . . acts. I was afraid. When you spoke of the injury, I thought at once that you might suspect her. I did not know what Smith had told you. And it seemed that you must think of her stick. I could not stop thinking of it, myself." He buried his head in his hands.

"Well," said Buchanan, and he snorted, "you're a damned odd pair. One of you thinks the other a murderer, and the other is not so certain about the first."

"We have been through things," said the woman, "that could make the killing of a man seem a small enough matter."

"Well, we seem to have untangled your part in it now," said Buchanan, "though it has given me a headache. Let me just be finally clear on this. You do believe, Bernard, that Smith recognized you?"

"Yes," he said. "I believe that he recognized me. That is why I came in the night to talk with Dorothy."

"What did you say to one another?"

"We asked," he said, "whether it would be necessary to kill the man."

"And you decided against it," said Buchanan. "I'm glad of that, on the whole."

The woman backed against the window. "Why are you so sure that we decided against it?" she said.

"Because," said Buchanan, "I happen to know who our murderer is. And now, if you'll excuse me, I must go and write him a letter."

15

ITEMS OF CORRESPONDENCE

"ONLY just got him done before dark," said the consul. The sky outside was already changed from green to violet.

"What?" said Buchanan absently. "Oh, the funeral." He took up the long envelope from his desk and looked at it curiously.

"Everyone was there," said the pilot, "except for the little man Cooper. He showed me the greatest hospitality all the afternoon and then he went off and buried himself in a great tome of a book."

"He usually avoids funerals," said Buchanan.

"I agree with him," said the consul. "Morbid affairs. Much better if they just stuck us out in the dustbin."

"I'm beginning to dislike funerals myself." Buchanan slit the envelope. "And I'm afraid we may have another yet to come." He drew out the papers.

"Good Lord, you don't say!" The consul's cheeks swelled, and he whistled. "What exactly do you mean by that, Buchanan?"

"Would you care to read a letter? I wrote it myself, so I can answer for its interest."

The consul guffawed. "Not turning literary, Buchanan old boy, I hope."

"Oh, no. It's the matter rather than the manner which will interest you. Here!"

2.

My dear. . . .

I am rather at a loss to know how to address you. I do not know your real name. It occurs to me that it may be Smith. Now that I have all the facts, so to speak, I seem to recall some faint resemblance about the eyes.

I am rather at a loss about this letter altogether. I shall probably find it a very difficult letter to write. One has to be so careful of the consequences, but I cannot help feeling that however well I manage it, this letter will inevitably invite you to a sticky end.

I should not write it at all if we lived in a community where one can refer one's dirty work to the police and the judiciary and the common hangman, and leave it all to them. But on Kaitai, I am, apparently, the police (now that poor Thompson is dead) and the judiciary and, unless you have some adequate alternative to suggest, it looks as if I may become the public hangman too.

I am not charmed at the prospect. In that, no doubt, we share a sentiment. I trust that we may be found to share other sentiments.

The fact of the matter, my dear sir, is that you have put me into an uncommonly nasty hole. What am I to do with you? A private execution is out of the question. A public execution would be extremely bad for our prestige as a ruling race and for the general morale of my native subjects. It ap-

pears, after a careful examination of the treaties under which my rights are internationally recognized that I am responsible for the administration of justice here; and the consul, on whom I had placed some hopes, now firmly declines to go beyond his authority.

What am I to do? I feel that my first recourse, at least, should be to your better feelings. I am sure that you do possess rather better feelings than you have lately revealed; and that, as the necessities of the situation and the general circumstances become clear to your mind, you will permit them to operate.

May I now proceed to develop the necessities and circumstances for your consideration?

Let me begin with my conclusion. I have now no doubts whatsoever that you are responsible for the deaths of both Smith and Thompson; and while I am somewhat doubtful whether I could establish your guilt in a court of law for the murder of Smith alone, I am positive that any judge would hang you on the evidence of your responsibility for the joint crimes.

I propose to set out here my general view on the course of events. You may possibly be kind enough to correct me if I am wrong in minor details, but I do not anticipate any emendations on the major score.

Whatever your original connection with Smith, I do not believe for one instant that he came to the island without your knowledge or without immediately making himself known to you. You may be a retired clerk. I doubt it. You have always spent a great deal more money than Hawkesbury or Mitchell or any of the others, and spent it in a way which suggests that you are used to spending money. It did not occur to you to be niggardly where a retired clerk would necessarily be economical. I imagine that you are a retired business-man, perhaps, and that when you smelt out my asphalt deposits here, you could not resist the temptation to make more money, more and more money, if you could manage it.

The arrival of Smith was a consequence. A journalist with some smattering of chemistry, I gather. Enough chemistry to analyze specimens, enough journalism to write a prospectus.

I very much doubt whether there ever was a syndicate. A syndicate of any capital and common sense would have sent out an expert, if it sent out anyone at all before it had approached me. This affair, I take it, was entirely between you and Smith.

You probably found him difficult from the start. My impression of Smith is that he would play his own hand, with very little regard for his partner, unless, of course, his partner was dummy. But you were not disposed to be dummy, especially when you discovered that Smith was taking a line of his own, and that the one line which you most wished to avoid at the moment. For you realized quite clearly that I was the snag. Smith realized it too, but he thought he had found a method of removing my snag. He was rather clumsy about it. You heard him as we went down to the beach that night.

You were very annoyed that he should have opened out to me. And on me. You followed him down to the beach. In your pyjamas, I imagine. But you pulled on your shoes. And you quarreled with him, of course. The quarrel became heated, because you kicked him. You kicked him in the head. He was probably lying down, perhaps sitting. Otherwise, I do not see how you could have kicked him in the head. He moved his head at the last moment. And so it was your heel and not your toe that struck him. Your iron heel-taps. I only noticed that you wore protectors last night. If I had noticed before, of course, matters might have taken another course.

I imagine that you may have made some effort to revive him. Or perhaps you got blood on your pyjamas while you were dragging him down to his dinghy. (You slipped up there a bit too. After going to all the trouble of putting on his shoes to make us believe he had walked down to the boat alone, you found you had to drag him, and of course made a track.) You must have got a good deal of blood on your pyjamas, because there was enough, evidently, to stain the sheets after you went back to bed. Your effort to create the impression of a boating accident was commendable, but you should have left the plug in the boat. And you should have taken it further out before you abandoned it. But then, you are not a very good swimmer, and the wind and tide were against you.

Your pyjamas and your sheets were messy. You had no real opportunity of destroying them in your bungalow. Your boys would have thought it rather odd if they had found you at the grate, and it would have been reckless to start a fire in the middle of a tropic night. On the other hand, if you had permitted your bed to be made, it would have been difficult to hide the sheets. And the boys would have been curious if your pyjamas were missing. So you went to bed and stayed there all day, from the moment when you discovered that Smith had been washed back onto the beach. You had probably popped back into bed before your boys arrived for the morning chores. Domestic labor was a little unsettled, in any case, that morning. And you stayed solidly, firmly, and decisively in bed all day. You were reluctant even to put your hand up out of the clothes, and you kept your sheets gripped under your chin.

But when all the rest of us had gone off to bed, you got up. You dressed, and you gathered your sheets and pyjamas into a bundle. And you remembered to take your pocket-compass with you, and a box of matches.

I do not believe that you got lost that night at all. But you were going into the loneliest and most deserted part of the island, and you thought it as well to leave your coat as a pointer, in case you really did lose yourself. You also ran all over H-wan's potato patch, to enlarge the effect. Further, if you chanced to be missed, as was likely, it would be well to suggest that you had lost your way in some kind of a nerve storm. It would save other and perhaps more difficult explanations.

You found your way, during the night, down to the edge of the swampland. But you did not dare go into it until there was some light. Moreover, a fire at night is much more likely to be noticed than a small smoke in the grey dawn. So I take it that you burnt your pyjamas and your sheets at dawn.

All this has been conjecture, you suggest. But may I point out that:

(1) *Your trousers were scorched, though you said nothing of lighting a fire for food or warmth.*

(2) *When we left you on the night before, you were wearing red and blue pyjamas, and your sheets were rumpled. when I returned with you this morning, although you professed not to have been at home since you went off on this excursion into the swamp, there were clean sheets on the bed, and the pyjamas thrown down on the floor were green and white.*

Admitting that you probably put clean sheets on the bed when you took the dirty ones off (you would not have wanted anyone, your houseboy, for instance, to find the bed sheetless), it still appeared that the green and white pyjamas had been put on and taken off again. In short, that you had been at home.

You denied, in effect, that you had come home, and I should have thought of some other explanation for the pyjamas, no doubt, if I had not already noticed that you did not need a shave. Now, I ask you, my good chap, could even the most minor of Samsons have gone for two days without showing some signs of a whisker? The conclusion I drew then was that you had been home between the time when we had last looked for you in your house and the time when you fell across poor Thompson's doorstep.

It was sometime in the evening that you reached home, while we were searching for you, and the village was more or less empty. What you did during the day, I do not know, but I have a suspicion that you may then really have got lost. Or you may have been exhausted and slept, as you said. At any rate, you came home and, as you would, you shaved. You are that sort of man.

You did not know whether you had been missed or not. You did not propose to go out and ask about it. Far better to minimize the excursion, and go off to bed and to sleep, if you could sleep. By the way, does a murderer's sleep come easily to him, or did Lady Macbeth know her stuff?

You had actually put out the light when Mitchell and Miss Roper came to your door and shouted. I wonder why you left the door open. For the draught, I suppose. I always leave mine open on the hotter nights. But you had kept yours stubbornly shut all the day before. Then, you had something in the house to hide, of course, and you were not encouraging visitors.

That conversation of Miss Roper's and Mitchell's, at your door and on to her door (I take it that they lingered; none of us was eager to separate last night, except poor Thompson, perhaps) was your first news of what had been happening in your absence. And it was startling news. They talked of your flight, of Thompson's collection of fingerprints, and of the papers he had removed from your house. They added, too, that Thompson was spending the night at the hospital. They were, unhappily, mistaken in that. Thompson had only half suggested it.

I believe that you gave yourself time to think. You realized that you would need to explain your absence, and you realized too that you would have to explain whatever papers Thompson had taken, or any, at least, that he had read. And he would almost certainly have read the analyses.

So you wrote a letter to me, which would cover the contingencies. Whether you had really settled then that I was to read it or not, I do not know, but it was a useful thing, perhaps, to have about. If the situation demanded it, you could produce it. It was disarming, in the matter of Smith.

What you went after in Thompson's safe, I do not know. It may have been only the analyses, but I doubt it. You already had your explanation to offer for them. It may have been the fingerprint records. You seem to have had a deft hand with a piece of wire, and one does not customarily learn that sort of trick in a London clerkship. Or it may have been that Thompson had taken other papers of yours beside the analyses. Mitchell is pretty clear that he did. For safe-keeping,

Mitchell says. Whether Thompson had read any papers of yours beside the analyses, I do not know and you could not know. But you wanted something out of that safe, and what better opportunity would there be than that night, in Thompson's absence.

You waited until the middle of the night. But Thompson was not absent. Did you hear him move before he could surprise you? I think you did. You hit him as he came through the door, with a piece of wood. He hit back at you, once, I think. And you guarded the blow. You took it on your forearm. That was how your wrist watch was cracked and stopped. At ten minutes to two, the minute in which I heard Thompson's last wild shout.

What did you do then? If there were papers you wanted in the safe, you took them out or you had already taken them out, because the analyses were the only things of yours I found there. And then you ran into the dark. But before you left, or when he first fell, you kicked Thompson's head. As you had kicked Smith's head. That was why you came back with only one shoe. Did you find blood on the other, Cooper?

You ran, I believe, down through the brambles to the swamp again. Did you bury the shoe there? And whatever you had brought from Thompson's safe? We shall know. I have sent two parties of boys out, one to find the place where you burned your sheets and pyjamas, the other to follow your course last night.

When you broke back again to us, I think you were very near to genuine exhaustion. It would have been strange if you were not. But you did not talk in your sleep.

And that is my case against you, Cooper. In what court is it to be tried?

3.

"This," said Buchanan, "is his reply. It may interest you too."

My dear Buchanan,

Thank you for your letter, undated. There is no need to assure you that I have given it the most serious consideration.

My name, oddly enough, is Smith, though I do not recall that the resemblance was ever noticed before. Smith actually was my cousin. And I am a retired clerk, but of some competence. There are other resources than his salary open to a senior clerk in a position of trust, and I may remark, in passing, that I have long been familiar with the uses of a piece of wire.

Your general reconstruction is shrewd and adequate. There is just this point I should like to enlarge. I did not intend, in cold blood, to murder either Smith or Thompson. Smith lay on the beach and was very insulting to me. Very insulting, indeed, and very contemptuous. When I protested, he made a clutch at my legs, and tried to pull me over, in a drunken jest. I lashed out instinctively with my feet, and I kicked him several times. Until, in brief, I discovered that he had ceased to move.

Thompson fell when I first struck him with a piece of heavy wood which was lying (symbollically, perhaps, considering this climate) in his fireplace. But he too clutched at my legs, and I am afraid that I kicked him too.

What I really wanted from Thompson's safe were the papers he had brought ashore from the lugger. I had reason to believe that Smith had brought with him, foolishly, the letters in which I first proposed that he should come and see for himself. I hoped that Thompson would not have read them. It seemed, at least, an excellent opportunity to recover them. Whether they are actually there or not, I do not know. Thompson, poor fellow, interrupted me before I found out. I really should have looked in his bedroom before I began work.

He did take other papers from my bungalow, but they are of little consequence, and I think you may find them in one of his packets.

I have, as you see, freely admitted your charges. I am not unmoved, I admit, by the fact that you have sent search-parties to follow my course. Oh, and lest I forget it, may I say that I was not careless about the plug in the dinghy. I left it in the bottom of the boat. It must have washed out.

I appreciate your difficulties regarding my dispatch. I see how unfortunate it would be to hold a public execution on Kaitai, and in the absence of a jail, I do not see how it could be conducted out of the general gaze. I am especially sympathetic with the diffidence you naturally feel at undertaking the rôle of executioner.

At the same time, I am reluctant to commit a cold-blooded suicide. (And, while I have the point in mind, may I say that I have slept quite easily since my first crime.) But an alternative has occurred to me. I have spent most of the afternoon with Captain O'Reilly, the very charming pilot of the consul's seaplane. And during the last hour and a half, I have been studying the principles of aeronautics, in the fourteenth edition of the Encyclopedia Britannica. I am informed by Captain O'Reilly that his machine is specially fitted to avoid the necessity of a second or third party to swing the propeller.

It occurs to me that if I should succeed in taking Captain O'Reilly's seaplane off the water (and he was very particular in his account of the method, when I pressed him), it is extremely unlikely that I shall bring it safely down again. I propose, however, to make the attempt if I can get on board the seaplane unobserved. In the unlikely event of my safe return to the world below, you will not, I trust, bear me a grudge. I do not think, however, that you need concern yourself. A lifelong experience of my inadequacy with machinery convinces me that my flight is doomed to disaster. But, by making every effort for what, I believe, is technically known as a happy landing, I shall feel that I am not, at least, taking my life in cold-blood. (The moral point, by the way, is interesting. Should a convicted or a convinced criminal deal punishment to himself in the absence of a proper penal system?)

I fear that Captain O'Reilly may be considerably annoyed, but I have now executed a codicil to my will, and called my boys to witness it, which instructs you, as executor (I trust you will permit the liberty and do me a last service) to pay to Captain O'Reilly the full cost of his machine, as new, in the event of it being uninsured. You will perhaps inform him of this as soon as I take off, if I do take off, and so save him any unnecessary distress of mind.

I am inexpressibly grateful to you for all the courtesies and kindnesses you have shown me during my residence on Kaitai, and especially for the singular sensibility and tact with which you have handled this distressing affair.

Believe me, I am, my dear Buchanan,

Most sincerely yours,

4.

There came a sudden roar, and then the long deep hum of the propellers. She ran across the bay two hundred yards, and then she took off, like a silver gull, and flew on, on towards the wide horizons of the sea.

Buchanan looked at the neatly folded dressing gown, and the slippers. He picked up a slipper. Mr. Cooper had even remembered to empty it of sand before he took to the waters and the skies.

Ted Allbeury

THE OTHER SIDE OF SILENCE P 669, $2.84
"In the best le Carré tradition . . . an ingenious and readable book."
—*New York Times Book Review*

PALOMINO BLONDE P 670, $2.84
"Fast-moving, splendidly technocratic intercontinental espionage tale . . . you'll love it." —*The Times* (London)

SNOWBALL P 671, $2.84
"A novel of byzantine intrigue. . . ."—*New York Times Book Review*

Delano Ames

CORPSE DIPLOMATIQUE P 637, $2.84
"Sprightly and intelligent."
—*New York Herald Tribune Book Review*

FOR OLD CRIME'S SAKE P 629, $2.84

MURDER, MAESTRO, PLEASE P 630, $2.84
"If there is a more engaging couple in modern fiction than Jane and Dagobert Brown, we have not met them." —*Scotsman*

SHE SHALL HAVE MURDER P 638, $2.84
"Combines the merit of both the English and American schools in the new mystery. It's as breezy as the best of the American ones, and has the sophistication and wit of any top-notch Britisher."
—*New York Herald Tribune Book Review*

E. C. Bentley

TRENT'S LAST CASE P 440, $2.50
"One of the three best detective stories ever written."
—Agatha Christie

TRENT'S OWN CASE P 516, $2.25
"I won't waste time saying that the plot is sound and the detection satisfying. Trent has not altered a scrap and reappears with all his old humor and charm." —Dorothy L. Sayers

Andrew Bergman

THE BIG KISS-OFF OF 1944 P 673, $2.84

"It is without doubt the nearest thing to genuine Chandler I've ever come across. . . . Tough, witty—very witty—and a beautiful eye for period detail. . . ." —Jack Higgins

HOLLYWOOD AND LEVINE P 674, $2.84

"Fast-paced private-eye fiction." —*San Francisco Chronicle*

Gavin Black

A DRAGON FOR CHRISTMAS P 473, $1.95

"Potent excitement!" —*New York Herald Tribune*

THE EYES AROUND ME P 485, $1.95

"I stayed up until all hours last night reading *The Eyes Around Me,* which is something I do not do very often, but I was so intrigued by the ingeniousness of Mr. Black's plotting and the witty way in which he spins his mystery. I can only say that I enjoyed the book enormously." —F. van Wyck Mason

YOU WANT TO DIE, JOHNNY? P 472, $1.95

"Gavin Black doesn't just develop a pressure plot in suspense, he adds uninfected wit, character, charm, and sharp knowledge of the Far East to make rereading as keen as the first race-through." —*Book Week*

Nicholas Blake

THE CORPSE IN THE SNOWMAN P 427, $1.95

"If there is a distinction between the novel and the detective story (which we do not admit), then this book deserves a high place in both categories." —*New York Times*

END OF CHAPTER P 397, $1.95

". . . admirably solid . . . an adroit formal detective puzzle backed up by firm characterization and a knowing picture of London publishing." —*New York Times*

HEAD OF A TRAVELER P 398, $2.25

"Another grade A detective story of the right old jigsaw persuasion." —*New York Herald Tribune Book Review*

MINUTE FOR MURDER P 419, $1.95

"An outstanding mystery novel. Mr. Blake's writing is a delight in itself." —*New York Times*

THE MORNING AFTER DEATH P 520, $1.95

"One of Blake's best." —Rex Warner

A PENKNIFE IN MY HEART P 521, $2.25
"Style brilliant . . . and suspenseful." —*San Francisco Chronicle*

THE PRIVATE WOUND P 531, $2.25
"[Blake's] best novel in a dozen years . . . . An intensely penetrating study of sexual passion. . . . A powerful story of murder and its aftermath."
—Anthony Boucher, *New York Times*

A QUESTION OF PROOF P 494, $1.95
"The characters in this story are unusually well drawn, and the suspense is well sustained." —*New York Times*

THE SAD VARIETY P 495, $2.25
"It is a stunner. I read it instead of eating, instead of sleeping."
—Dorothy Salisbury Davis

THERE'S TROUBLE BREWING P 569, $3.37
"Nigel Strangeways is a puzzling mixture of simplicity and penetration, but all the more real for that."
—*The Times* (London) *Literary Supplement*

THOU SHELL OF DEATH P 428, $1.95
"It has all the virtues of culture, intelligence and sensibility that the most exacting connoisseur could ask of detective fiction."
—*The Times* (London) *Literary Supplement*

THE WIDOW'S CRUISE P 399, $2.25
"A stirring suspense. . . . The thrilling tale leaves nothing to be desired."
—*Springfield Republican*

Oliver Bleeck

THE BRASS GO-BETWEEN P 645, $2.84
"Fiction with a flair, well above the norm for thrillers."
—*Associated Press*

THE PROCANE CHRONICLE P 647, $2.84
"Without peer in American suspense." —*Los Angeles Times*

PROTOCOL FOR A KIDNAPPING P 646, $2.84
"The zigzags of plot are electric; the characters sharp; but it is the wit and irony and touches of plain fun which make the whole a standout."
—*Los Angeles Times*

John & Emery Bonett

A BANNER FOR PEGASUS P 554, $2.40
"A gem! Beautifully plotted and set. . . . Not only is the murder adroit and deserved, and the detection competent, but the love story is charming." —Jacques Barzun and Wendell Hertig Taylor

DEAD LION P 563, $2.40
"A clever plot, authentic background and interesting characters highly recommended this one." —*New Republic*

THE SOUND OF MURDER P 642, $2.84
The suspects are many, the clues few, but the gentle Inspector ferrets out the truth and pursues the case to its bitter and shocking end.

Christianna Brand

GREEN FOR DANGER P 551, $2.50
"You have to reach for the greatest of Great Names (Christie, Carr, Queen . . .) to find Brand's rivals in the devious subtleties of the trade." —Anthony Boucher

TOUR DE FORCE P 572, $2.40
"Complete with traps for the over-ingenious, a double-reverse surprise ending and a key clue planted so fairly and obviously that you completely overlook it. If that's your idea of perfect entertainment, then seize at once upon *Tour de Force.*" —Anthony Boucher, *New York Times*

James Byrom

OR BE HE DEAD P 585, $2.84
"A very original tale . . . Well written and steadily entertaining." —Jacques Barzun and Wendell Hertig Taylor, *A Catalogue of Crime*

Henry Calvin

IT'S DIFFERENT ABROAD P 640, $2.84
"What is remarkable and delightful, Mr. Calvin imparts a flavor of satire to what he renovates and compels us to take straight." —Jacques Barzun

Marjorie Carleton

VANISHED P 559, $2.40
"Exceptional . . . a minor triumph." —Jacques Barzun and Wendell Hertig Taylor, *A Catalogue of Crime*

George Harmon Coxe

MURDER WITH PICTURES P 527, $2.25

"[Coxe] has hit the bull's-eye with his first shot."

—*New York Times*

Edmund Crispin

BURIED FOR PLEASURE P 506, $2.50

"Absolute and unalloyed delight."

—Anthony Boucher, *New York Times*

Lionel Davidson

THE MENORAH MEN P 592, $2.84

"Of his fellow thriller writers, only John Le Carré shows the same instinct for the viscera." —*Chicago Tribune*

NIGHT OF WENCESLAS P 595, $2.84

"A most ingenious thriller, so enriched with style, wit, and a sense of serious comedy that it all but transcends its kind."

—*The New Yorker*

THE ROSE OF TIBET P 593, $2.84

"I hadn't realized how much I missed the genuine Adventure story . . . until I read *The Rose of Tibet*." —Graham Greene

D. M. Devine

MY BROTHER'S KILLER P 558, $2.40

"A most enjoyable crime story which I enjoyed reading down to the last moment." —Agatha Christie

Kenneth Fearing

THE BIG CLOCK P 500, $1.95

"It will be some time before chill-hungry clients meet again so rare a compound of irony, satire, and icy-fingered narrative. *The Big Clock* is . . . a psychothriller you won't put down." —*Weekly Book Review*

Andrew Garve

THE ASHES OF LODA P 430, $1.50

"Garve . . . embellishes a fine fast adventure story with a more credible picture of the U.S.S.R. than is offered in most thrillers."

—*New York Times Book Review*

THE CUCKOO LINE AFFAIR P 451, $1.95

". . . an agreeable and ingenious piece of work." —*The New Yorker*

A HERO FOR LEANDA P 429, $1.50
"One can trust Mr. Garve to put a fresh twist to any situation, and the ending is really a lovely surprise." —*Manchester Guardian*

MURDER THROUGH THE LOOKING GLASS P 449, $1.95
". . . refreshingly out-of-the-way and enjoyable . . . highly recommended to all comers." —*Saturday Review*

NO TEARS FOR HILDA P 441, $1.95
"It starts fine and finishes finer. I got behind on breathing watching Max get not only his man but his woman, too." —Rex Stout

THE RIDDLE OF SAMSON P 450, $1.95
"The story is an excellent one, the people are quite likable, and the writing is superior." —*Springfield Republican*

Michael Gilbert

BLOOD AND JUDGMENT P 446, $1.95
"Gilbert readers need scarcely be told that the characters all come alive at first sight, and that his surpassing talent for narration enhances any plot. . . . Don't miss." —*San Francisco Chronicle*

THE BODY OF A GIRL P 459, $1.95
"Does what a good mystery should do: open up into all kinds of ramifications, with untold menace behind the action. At the end, there is a bang-up climax, and it is a pleasure to see how skilfully Gilbert wraps everything up." —*New York Times Book Review*

FEAR TO TREAD P 458, $1.95
"Merits serious consideration as a work of art." —*New York Times*

Joe Gores

HAMMETT P 631, $2.84
"Joe Gores at his very best. Terse, powerful writing—with the master, Dashiell Hammett, as the protagonist in a novel I think he would have been proud to call his own." —Robert Ludlum

C. W. Grafton

BEYOND A REASONABLE DOUBT P 519, $1.95
"A very ingenious tale of murder . . . a brilliant and gripping narrative." —Jacques Barzun and Wendell Hertig Taylor

THE RAT BEGAN TO GNAW THE ROPE P 639, $2.84
"Fast, humorous story with flashes of brilliance."
—*The New Yorker*

Edward Grierson

THE SECOND MAN P 528, $2.25
"One of the best trial-testimony books to have come along in quite a while." —*The New Yorker*

Bruce Hamilton

TOO MUCH OF WATER P 635, $2.84
"A superb sea mystery. . . . The prose is excellent."
—Jacques Barzun and Wendell Hertig Taylor, *A Catalogue of Crime*

Cyril Hare

DEATH IS NO SPORTSMAN P 555, $2.40
"You will be thrilled because it succeeds in placing an ingenious story in a new and refreshing setting. . . . The identity of the murderer is really a surprise." —*Daily Mirror*

DEATH WALKS THE WOODS P 556, $2.40
"Here is a fine formal detective story, with a technically brilliant solution demanding the attention of all connoisseurs of construction."
—Anthony Boucher, *New York Times Book Review*

AN ENGLISH MURDER P 455, $2.50
"By a long shot, the best crime story I have read for a long time. Everything is traditional, but originality does not suffer. The setting is perfect. Full marks to Mr. Hare." —*Irish Press*

SUICIDE EXCEPTED P 636, $2.84
"Adroit in its manipulation . . . and distinguished by a plot-twister which I'll wager Christie wishes she'd thought of." —*New York Times*

TENANT FOR DEATH P 570, $2.84
"The way in which an air of probability is combined both with clear, terse narrative and with a good deal of subtle suburban atmosphere, proves the extreme skill of the writer." —*The Spectator*

TRAGEDY AT LAW P 522, $2.25
"An extremely urbane and well-written detective story."
—*New York Times*

UNTIMELY DEATH P 514, $2.25
"The English detective story at its quiet best, meticulously underplayed, rich in perceivings of the droll human animal and ready at the last with a neat surprise which has been there all the while had we but wits to see it." —*New York Herald Tribune Book Review*

THE WIND BLOWS DEATH P 589, $2.84
"A plot compounded of musical knowledge, a Dickens allusion, and a subtle point in law is related with delightfully unobtrusive wit, warmth, and style." —*New York Times*

WITH A BARE BODKIN P 523, $2.25
"One of the best detective stories published for a long time." —*The Spectator*

Robert Harling

THE ENORMOUS SHADOW P 545, $2.50
"In some ways the best spy story of the modern period. . . . The writing is terse and vivid . . . the ending full of action . . . altogether first-rate." —Jacques Barzun and Wendell Hertig Taylor, *A Catalogue of Crime*

Matthew Head

THE CABINDA AFFAIR P 541, $2.25
"An absorbing whodunit and a distinguished novel of atmosphere." —Anthony Boucher, *New York Times*

THE CONGO VENUS P 597, $2.84
"Terrific. The dialogue is just plain wonderful." —*Boston Globe*

MURDER AT THE FLEA CLUB P 542, $2.50
"The true delight is in Head's style, its limpid ease combined with humor and an awesome precision of phrase." —*San Francisco Chronicle*

M. V. Heberden

ENGAGED TO MURDER P 533, $2.25
"Smooth plotting." —*New York Times*

James Hilton

WAS IT MURDER? P 501, $1.95
"The story is well planned and well written." —*New York Times*

S. B. Hough

DEAR DAUGHTER DEAD P 661, $2.84

"A highly intelligent and sophisticated story of police detection . . . not to be missed on any account." —Francis Iles, *The Guardian*

SWEET SISTER SEDUCED P 662, $2.84

In the course of a nightlong conversation between the Inspector and the suspect, the complex emotions of a very strange marriage are revealed.

P. M. Hubbard

HIGH TIDE P 571, $2.40

"A smooth elaboration of mounting horror and danger."

—*Library Journal*

Elspeth Huxley

THE AFRICAN POISON MURDERS P 540, $2.25

"Obscure venom, manical mutilations, deadly bush fire, thrilling climax compose major opus.... Top-flight."

—*Saturday Review of Literature*

MURDER ON SAFARI P 587, $2.84

"Right now we'd call Mrs. Huxley a dangerous rival to Agatha Christie." —*Books*

Francis Iles

BEFORE THE FACT P 517, $2.50

"Not many 'serious' novelists have produced character studies to compare with Iles's internally terrifying portrait of the murderer in *Before the Fact,* his masterpiece and a work truly deserving the appellation of unique and beyond price." —Howard Haycraft

MALICE AFORETHOUGHT P 532, $1.95

"It is a long time since I have read anything so good as *Malice Aforethought,* with its cynical humour, acute criminology, plausible detail and rapid movement. It makes you hug yourself with pleasure."

—H. C. Harwood, *Saturday Review*

Michael Innes

APPLEBY ON ARARAT P 648, $2.84

"Superbly plotted and humorously written." —*The New Yorker*

APPLEBY'S END P 649, $2.84

"Most amusing." —*Boston Globe*

THE CASE OF THE JOURNEYING BOY P 632, $3.12
"I could see no faults in it. There is no one to compare with him."
—*Illustrated London News*

DEATH ON A QUIET DAY P 677, $2.84
"Delightfully witty." —*Chicago Sunday Tribune*

DEATH BY WATER P 574, $2.40
"The amount of ironic social criticism and deft characterization of scenes and people would serve another author for six books."
—Jacques Barzun and Wendell Hertig Taylor

HARE SITTING UP P 590, $2.84
"There is hardly anyone (in mysteries or mainstream) more exquisitely literate, allusive and Jamesian—and hardly anyone with a firmer sense of melodramatic plot or a more vigorous gift of storytelling."
—Anthony Boucher, *New York Times*

THE LONG FAREWELL P 575, $2.40
"A model of the deft, classic detective story, told in the most wittily diverting prose." —*New York Times*

THE MAN FROM THE SEA P 591, $2.84
"The pace is brisk, the adventures exciting and excitingly told, and above all he keeps to the very end the interesting ambiguity of the man from the sea." —*New Statesman*

ONE MAN SHOW P 672, $2.84
"Exciting, amusingly written . . . very good enjoyment it is."
—*The Spectator*

THE SECRET VANGUARD P 584, $2.84
"Innes . . . has mastered the art of swift, exciting and well-organized narrative." —*New York Times*

THE WEIGHT OF THE EVIDENCE P 633, $2.84
"First-class puzzle, deftly solved. University background interesting and amusing." —*Saturday Review of Literature*

Mary Kelly

THE SPOILT KILL P 565, $2.40
"Mary Kelly is a new Dorothy Sayers. . . . [An] exciting new novel."
—*Evening News*

Lange Lewis

THE BIRTHDAY MURDER P 518, $1.95

"Almost perfect in its playlike purity and delightful prose."
—Jacques Barzun and Wendell Hertig Taylor

Allan MacKinnon

HOUSE OF DARKNESS P 582, $2.84

"His best . . . a perfect compendium."
—Jacques Barzun and Wendell Hertig Taylor, *A Catalogue of Crime*

Frank Parrish

FIRE IN THE BARLEY P 651, $2.84

"A remarkable and brilliant first novel. . . . entrancing."
—*The Spectator*

SNARE IN THE DARK P 650, $2.84

The wily English poacher Dan Mallett is framed for murder and has to confront unknown enemies to clear himself.

STING OF THE HONEYBEE P 652, $2.84

"Terrorism and murder visit a sleepy English village in this witty, offbeat thriller." —*Chicago Sun-Times*

Austin Ripley

MINUTE MYSTERIES P 387, $2.50

More than one hundred of the world's shortest detective stories. Only one possible solution to each case!

Thomas Sterling

THE EVIL OF THE DAY P 529, $2.50

"Prose as witty and subtle as it is sharp and clear. . .characters unconventionally conceived and richly bodied forth . . . . In short, a novel to be treasured." —Anthony Boucher, *New York Times*

Julian Symons

THE BELTING INHERITANCE P 468, $1.95

"A superb whodunit in the best tradition of the detective story."
—August Derleth, *Madison Capital Times*

BOGUE'S FORTUNE P 481, $1.95

"There's a touch of the old sardonic humour, and more than a touch of style." —*The Spectator*

THE COLOR OF MURDER P 461, $1.95
"A singularly unostentatious and memorably brilliant detective story."
—*New York Herald Tribune Book Review*

Dorothy Stockbridge Tillet
(John Stephen Strange)

THE MAN WHO KILLED FORTESCUE P 536, $2.25
"Better than average." —*Saturday Review of Literature*

Simon Troy

THE ROAD TO RHUINE P 583, $2.84
"Unusual and agreeably told." —*San Francisco Chronicle*

SWIFT TO ITS CLOSE P 546, $2.40
"A nicely literate British mystery . . . the atmosphere and the plot are exceptionally well wrought, the dialogue excellent." —*Best Sellers*

Henry Wade

THE DUKE OF YORK'S STEPS P 588, $2.84
"A classic of the golden age."
—Jacques Barzun and Wendell Hertig Taylor, *A Catalogue of Crime*

A DYING FALL P 543, $2.50
"One of those expert British suspense jobs . . . it crackles with undercurrents of blackmail, violent passion and murder. Topnotch in its class."
—*Time*

THE HANGING CAPTAIN P 548, $2.50
"This is a detective story for connoisseurs, for those who value clear thinking and good writing above mere ingenuity and easy thrills."
—*The Times* (London) *Literary Supplement*

Hillary Waugh

LAST SEEN WEARING . . . P 552, $2.40
"A brilliant tour de force." —Julian Symons

THE MISSING MAN P 553, $2.40
"The quiet detailed police work of Chief Fred C. Fellows, Stockford, Conn., is at its best in *The Missing Man* . . . one of the Chief's toughest cases and one of the best handled."
—Anthony Boucher, *New York Times Book Review*

Henry Kitchell Webster

WHO IS THE NEXT? P 539, $2.25
"A double murder, private-plane piloting, a neat impersonation, and a delicate courtship are adroitly combined by a writer who knows how to use the language." —Jacques Barzun and Wendell Hertig Taylor

John Welcome

GO FOR BROKE P 663, $2.84
A rich financier chases Richard Graham half 'round Europe in a desperate attempt to prevent the truth getting out.

RUN FOR COVER P 664, $2.84
"I can think of few writers in the international intrigue game with such a gift for fast and vivid storytelling."
—*New York Times Book Review*

STOP AT NOTHING P 665, $2.84
"Mr. Welcome is lively, vivid and highly readable."
—*New York Times Book Review*

Anna Mary Wells

MURDERER'S CHOICE P 534, $2.50
"Good writing, ample action, and excellent character work."
—*Saturday Review of Literature*

A TALENT FOR MURDER P 535, $2.25
"The discovery of the villain is a decided shock." —*Books*

Charles Williams

DEAD CALM P 655, $2.84
"A brilliant tour de force of inventive plotting, fine manipulation of a small cast and breathtaking sequences of spectacular navigation."
—*New York Times Book Review*

THE SAILCLOTH SHROUD P 654, $2.84
"A fine novel of excitement, spirited, fresh and satisfying."
—*New York Times*

THE WRONG VENUS P 656, $2.84
Swindler Lawrence Colby and the lovely Martine create a story of romance, larceny, and very blunt homicide.